FROM THE
END OF
HEAVEN

THE GREAT AND TERRIBLE

VOLUME 5

FROM THE END OF HEAVEN

CHRIS STEWART

DESERET
BOOK

SALT LAKE CITY, UTAH

To Horace—in the end He heals us all

Library of Congress Cataloging-in-Publication Data

Stewart, Chris, 1960–
    From the end of heaven / Chris Stewart.
      p. cm. — (The great and terrible ; v. 5)
      ISBN 978-1-59038-858-7 (alk. paper)
    1. Terrorism—Fiction.   2. Religious fiction. I. Title.
    PS3569.T4593F73 2008
    813'.54—dc22   2008008141

Printed in the United States of America
Publishers Printing, Salt Lake City, Utah

10   9   8   7   6   5   4   3

"The eyes of God and all the holy prophets are watching us. This is the great dispensation that has been spoken of ever since the world began. We are gathered together . . . by the power and commandment of God. We are doing the work of God. . . . Let us fill our mission."

—PRESIDENT JAMES REUBEN CLARK

"Somehow, among all who have walked the earth, we have been brought forth in this unique and remarkable season. Be grateful, and above all be faithful."

—PRESIDENT GORDON B. HINCKLEY

prologue

He sat in the long grass on the mountain's top looking over the great city. The majestic peaks narrowed to sheer cliffs that fell below him on three sides, their granite faces plunging straight down to meet the foothills mounding up from the valley floor almost five thousand feet below. A gentle breeze blew across the mountain, and he smelled the salt and wildflowers and pine. Away in the distance, the great sea reflected white in the sun, a billion stars of light glittering from the tops of the waves.

He took a breath and held it, then slowly lay back and closed his eyes, his face peaceful and content.

He was happy, yes, but not completely, not quite yet, not even in this place. There were times when he still wondered about those he'd left behind. And when it came to those he loved, he spent many nights on his knees.

Sitting up, he bit his lip. There was something welling up inside him that he couldn't comprehend. He'd searched his soul, trying to get his mind around it, but it continued to escape him, a shadow he couldn't see, a fleeting moment of anxiety that broke into his thoughts just enough to jar him and then quickly fade away.

He took another breath. Feeling the breeze upon his face, he slowly bowed his head. *"Is there something I am missing? Please help me understand."*

Time passed and he remained motionless as the sun began to set.

He felt the other's presence long before he heard the soft steps across the grass. Opening his eyes, he stared out on the valley as he waited for his friend. Teancum emerged from the tree line, his dark hair blowing across his shoulders in the breeze. The first man looked up and smiled. "Good to see you, friend." He patted the ground beside him, indicating for Teancum to sit down.

Teancum waited, looking on the enormous valley, his hands over his eyes to protect them against the sun. He looked majestic, almost perfect—which, of course, he nearly was. Broad shoulders. Firm hands. Clear eyes and strong jaw. "I've been looking for you," he said as he sat down.

The father tensed, the knot inside him instantly growing tight. He turned away, wanting to hide his concern. "Why is that?" he asked carefully while bracing for the response.

Teancum stared out, his dark eyes focused on the sea. He too was troubled, for the responsibility he carried was a constant, heavy weight. Still, despite that burden, he always wore a smile, a genuine display of the joy inside his heart. *This is my work and my glory*—that was something he understood. Where there was no work, there was no glory; the two concepts were eternally intertwined. And there *was* joy in their glory. But their world was not yet perfect, and there was still much work to do.

Teancum thought a long moment before turning to his friend. "I'm worried about your children," he finally said.

The father let out a sigh. "I am worried too." His face was strained. "It scares me, what they go through. It scares me to the core."

"It scares us all. We watch them and wonder how they're going to make it. The enemy is so powerful, he fills almost every heart. But remember, my good friend, you got through it. I got through it. Hard as it was, even we managed to muddle through."

The thought of Teancum muddling through anything made the father smile.

"They really are stronger than we were," Teancum continued, his eyes shining. "They prove that almost every day. They're more worthy. More prepared and dedicated. Even in the darkest moments, they hold on to the light. The assault they face is constant and there is no relief in sight, yet each of them faces his or her special purpose with such integrity and hope. Their courage is remarkable." He paused, brushing his hand through his hair. "It makes me proud," he said.

The father nodded thoughtfully. "They've shown great courage from the beginning."

"Which is why they're where they are."

The father closed his eyes against the breeze. "Then why are we so worried?"

Teancum squeezed him on the shoulder. "Because sometimes they need our help."

"But there is nothing I can do here."

"I think you might be wrong."

The father instantly turned toward him. "What do you mean?" His voice was hopeful.

Teancum's eyes flickered as if with a secret, and then he smiled. "There will be opportunities to help them that we might not know about right now. We have to be ready to do something when the time is right."

The father fell silent, thinking.

"None of us knows exactly what the future has in store," Teancum concluded. "But there will come a time when our Father will need you to help them in his cause. Be patient, but be ready. When the time is ripe, I will meet you. Stay vigilant until then."

"And the people were divided one against another; and they did separate one from another into tribes, every man according to his family and his kindred and friends; and thus they did destroy the government of the land."

—3 Nephi 7:2

"It is best if an enemy nation comes and surrenders of its own accord."

—Du You (A.D. 735–812)

chapter one

Despite all of its grandeur, beauty, influence, and power, it took less than two weeks for the city to die.

For a hundred years it had reigned as one of the greatest cities in the world, a center of business, finance, trade, media, and law. For a hundred years it had served as one of the world's great cultural centers as well as the home of the United Nations, making it the diplomatic center of the world. One point seven million people lived on the tiny island of Manhattan, another six million within the boroughs, almost nineteen million in the surrounding metropolitan area, making it one of the most densely populated spots on the earth.

Power. Focus. Money.

For more than a hundred years, it had it all.

Pulse. Action. Demands and rewards.

The city was as animate as any living thing: breathing, growing, exerting an undeniable force, never sleeping, always moving.

For a hundred years, New York City had shone as a jewel in the crown of mortal glitter.

A hundred years to reign.

But only two weeks to die. Two weeks to transform into a quivering muddle of death.

He could see that it was dead now—or, if not dead, certainly convulsing in its final throes.

Once the ultimate symbol of wealth and power, the awesome skyscrapers that surrounded him were nothing but empty skeletons, icons of human accomplishment protruding meaninglessly into the smoky sky, old bones jutting from a decaying battlefield, awful reminders of a tragic fall. The streets below, crammed with dead cars and buses and semis and cabs, were ghostly and still, occasional blowing papers and a few ragged stragglers the only things that moved. And there were rats. Lots of rats. He was amazed at how quickly they had scurried from the sewers to reclaim the land. From where he stood, forty floors above the city, he couldn't see them, but he had been on the streets enough to know they were there.

Drexel Danbert, founding member and senior partner of Danbert, Lexel, Taylor and Driggs, the greatest and most secretive international government relations firm in the world, stared down on the empty city from his penthouse overlooking the Financial District. The windows around his apartment reached from floor to ceiling, offering a magnificent view, and he leaned his head against the pane as he looked down wistfully on the empty streets below. From where he stood, facing east, he could see all the way down the man-made canyon known as Wall Street to the East River. Left and right, William and Broad streets ran north and south, much broader and more imposing than the narrow street below the window where he stood.

Of the millions of people who used to live around him, few remained. There were a couple of homeless wretches who had chosen to die out on the street, as well as an unknown number of vagabonds each day who crossed the bridges between

Brooklyn and New Jersey, looking for food. But that was about all. Everyone else was gone.

Well, not all. There were the gangs. The filthy gangs. He'd heard the reports: the things they'd done, the things they were eating now, some of the things they would do for food.

He shivered as he thought.

This was the world they'd created?

Had they gone too far?

He shivered once again.

Time passed. He didn't move. Staring out his window at the dying world, he felt the gloomy doubt inside him growing thicker, more oppressive, more sure.

Had they torn it down too quickly? Did those who were left hate each other too much now to rebuild? Was there any hope of reconstruction, or would people accept things as they were? Tribes and bands of friends and families—was that all that existed anymore? In their determination to break them, had they simply gone too far?

Idiot King Abdullah! The old man said that he would stop him, but he wasn't restrained.

Thinking of the Saudi king, maybe the single most powerful man left in the world, Drexel Danbert shook his head. The king and the man who grew no older might have destroyed their entire plan.

The dark fear grew inside him when he thought of the old man. Who was he? Where had he come from? And why had he betrayed them so?

The Grand Plan had never called for the destruction of *his* country. Why would they want to rule over a stone-age people struggling through nothing but devastation and starvation? They had wanted to break it, not destroy it. Break the government and people down to such a point that there would be no

11

resistance to the Brothers when they moved in to institute a government of their own.

But, looking upon the dead city, he had to wonder now. Had they taken out too much of the foundation, making it impossible for the U.S. to rebuild?

His partners didn't think so.

He was certain they were wrong.

He took a weary breath and held it, listening to the silence in his ears.

His penthouse was cool and quiet. No electricity. No running water. No sound of life anywhere. Like most of the other New Yorkers, he had been drinking out of the Hudson and East Rivers, which were toxic with floating filth. Three days before, he had run out of food. A plastic bag had been his toilet, a couple of disposable wet wipes the only way to wash his hands. The elevator in his high-rise was not working, making it a major commitment to go down on the street, but nothing like the commitment it took to climb the stairs again.

He looked down on the death around him and took another breath.

Funny, he thought, why he had chosen to stay.

He could have left the city; they'd given him plenty of warning. He could have been sitting drunk and lazy somewhere in London, Casablanca . . . even Paris, although he truly hated that pompous city. But this was what he'd wanted. He had wanted to see the end.

The firm had started transitioning its operations to Europe almost a year before, then hurriedly relocated its headquarters to Paris three weeks before the EMP attack. Most of the other partners had already evacuated, except for those who were currently engaged. Some of their most productive partners still worked within the government, and everyone recognized there was important work for them to do. But, like all of the others, he could have gone. He'd stayed, though. When his partners had demanded an explanation, some in angry voices, he hadn't answered, although deep inside his empty soul he knew.

He was old now. In a few weeks, he would celebrate— okay, *observe*—his ninety-first birthday, which made him very old indeed. His life was over and he knew that and he didn't really care.

So he stood alone beside the window, thinking of his age. For a man of ninety-one, he was in remarkably good shape— his legs were a bit arthritic, but his mind was clear and everything else was going strong. Something about the partnership seemed to do that; all of the founders had lived into their nineties, a few even making it to a hundred. They used to laugh at their unnatural longevity, saying it was because they had far too much to live for. But Drexel knew it wasn't so much what they had to live for as what they feared when they were dead.

Looking down, he stared at the age marks that pocked the back of his soft hands. Despite their best efforts to hold it back, time had moved forward. One by one, the founding partners had passed away, leaving Drexel alone now in the world. He had already outlived three wives, one of whom he had actually cared about (although he couldn't remember much about how that felt). He had half a dozen children, most of whom he hadn't seen in years, an unknown number of grandchildren and great-grandchildren he didn't even know about, let alone their names or genders or where they lived. It was true that two of his sons would soon be partners in the firm, but even they were not close and he rarely saw them anymore. His other children had sensed his evil and avoided him for years.

13

So he stood alone in silence, looking back on his life without a smile.

Only blackness lay before him, only darkness left and right. And there was no reason to turn and look behind him—he knew the shadows that hid back there. Time had caught up and finally passed him, and he couldn't change what he had done. Everywhere he turned now, the feeling was the same. Whether in this life or the other, it was going to be the same.

But it didn't matter. He was ready for something new. The next stage might not be better but he doubted it could be worse. He'd been empty and dead and desperately unhappy for almost fifty years, and the will to keep on fighting simply didn't exist inside him anymore.

✳   ✳   ✳

The dark spirit stared at the old man, looking deeply into his eyes. He knew the veil of separation lying between them now was so thin that the mortal could feel him when he was near. He took a small step toward the man and snarled.

The mortal kept on staring, hunching his shoulders against his cold.

How Balaam wished that the man could see him! How he wished he was more than just a wisp of smoke, a passing hint of darkness, a thought, a voice, a feeling of despair. How he wished that he was more than just a spirit, always sensed but never seen!

He wanted substance! He wanted texture! He wanted to feel something. He wanted to be felt!

He reached out to touch Drexel Danbert, but his hand passed through the mortal like light passing through a wisp of smoke. He shivered, cursing in frustration. No warmth, no sense of touch, no comfort or consolation could be found in the passing of his hand.

He looked at the mortal, hunger and lust and envy in his

eyes. All of Lucifer's servants worshiped flesh, and the closer they came to the end days, the more they desired what they knew they would never have. Ironic, Balaam thought, how so many of the mortals were willing to give up the one thing the dark angels wanted most. Control of their bodies. The ability to choose. Yes, the weapons the dark angels had developed to control the mortal bodies could be very powerful, and once people started down that path, they almost always slipped up in the end.

Why they were so foolish, Balaam failed to understand.

But they were. They had proven that for more than seven thousand years.

Balaam knew the old man could sense that he was near, sense the cold and the hatred and the blackness of his soul. Balaam didn't have to speak loudly for the old man to hear him anymore; they had so much in common, they almost thought the same. The same desperation and sense of hopelessness controlled their calloused souls.

Balaam watched as the mortal looked down on the empty city where his fellow mortals used to live. "He doesn't even know why he hates them," the dark angel sneered as he watched. "His heart is blackened by emotion that his head can't even understand. It makes no sense and he knows that, but he is so corrupted he can't control his emotions anymore."

Leaning toward the man, Balaam leered and whispered to his slave. "You did it," he hissed proudly to his faithful son. "You taught them to hate each other. You divided them completely, tearing them apart. You did everything we asked you and now your work is done."

Moving, Balaam stood before him so he could look into his eyes. The change had already started taking place. Every pleasure the mortal had experienced, every indulgence, every sin, was poison to him now. He had no good memories to support him, no joy in looking at his life. Everything he had done, every decision he'd ever made, had brought him to this point, and now all he had was pain. Every fleeting moment of earthly pleasure only added to his suffering, the cumulative memory a bitter realization that he had damned himself to hell.

Funny how it worked out in the end. For the righteous, thinking back on their lives seemed to bring them joy again. But for the evil, the memories of their failings created nothing but renewed suffering and pain. Even when it was over, it wasn't over, and it all came back again.

To the evil, it was a haunting.

To the good, a joyful song.

* * *

Standing by the tall window, Drexel took his glass of brandy, a clear, coconut-flower Mendis (three thousand dollars a liter), tossed it back, let it burn against his throat, swallowed, poured another glass, tossed it back, then took the bottle and threw it against the marble wall. The liquid splattered like clear honey, then flowed toward the hardwood floor, mixing with the shattered glass. He sniffed the heavy smell of liquor, then walked to the front door.

Pulling it open, he hesitated and then turned. Walking back, he looked around his twelve-million-dollar apartment a final time, taking in all the things he'd spent his life collecting.

He looked at his favorite possession in this world. Underneath six inches of fireproof, bulletproof, and airproof glass, one of the four existing copies of the original *Magna Carta* was on display, the only one in private hands, the crown jewel of his collection. To the right of the display case was a set of original Shakespeare manuscripts. On the walls, multimillion-dollar paintings. Greek and Roman sculptures. Tucked away beneath one bookshelf, a collection of Asian pornography, nothing hard, always tasteful, his favorite form of art. It was like looking at a week-old newspaper. The things meant nothing to him now.

Sitting awkwardly on the single step that separated the marble entry from the main living room, he pulled on a pair of heavy boots. Standing, he looked around again. Then Drexel Danbert, one of the richest and most powerful men in the world, stepped out into the hall.

He didn't leave a note for any of the partners who might come to look for him. He didn't take any of the cash or T-bills that were stuffed in the open safe built into the corner of his den. He didn't take the jewels, watches, paintings, rare manuscripts, any of the things he owned. Leaving the penthouse door open, he started walking down the stairs.

Going down was easy. Much, much harder coming up. Two days before, it had taken him most of the day to climb the stairs.

No worries now. He would never climb these stairs again.

He paced himself, stopping every three stories to catch his breath. Fifty minutes later, he hobbled through the heavy door on the ground floor. Lots of brass and chrome and marble greeted him; the building's foyer was as beautiful as any of the apartments on the upper floors, but it had been many years since he had noticed any of the splendors. Most of the windows that faced the street had been broken, leaving shattered glass scattered on the tile floor. Every step he took crunched broken glass under his shoes.

Dressed in a pair of old slacks, a dirty denim shirt, and a battered coat he'd picked up on the street two nights before, he walked out onto the pavement. Stopping for a moment, he felt the swelling in his knees, then turned up the collar on his coat. The wind blew down the cement and glass and granite canyons that surrounded him, and hundreds of cars still lined the streets. The vents in the sidewalks were dead now, no steam, no smells, no hiss of passing subways underneath. A stray cat walked across the sidewalk and onto the road, disappearing underneath the nearest car, a yellow cab with a couple of brightly wrapped FAO Schwarz presents still inside. Breathing deeply, he smelled it, the dank and rot that drifted from the river. Cold air. The smell of rats. The stench of garbage in the streets.

Turning, he started walking.

West on Wall. North on Broad. West on Pine. Trinity Church came into view.

Keeping to the opposite side of the street, he swung around the old brick church, feeling creepy as he stared at the ancient cross.

A crowd had gathered on the far side of the church's graveyard—a group of rough, angry, filthy men. He stared at them, hesitating, rage and loathing surging through his veins. Hot sweat started dripping against the back of his neck as a lifetime of raw emotion came crashing down on him. For almost seventy years he had gorged on hate and now it burst inside him, foul and full.

And it was inescapable. Whether in this life or the other, the pain would stay the same.

Looking up, he raised his fist and cursed his loathsome god. Then he shoved his hands into his pockets, turned toward the pack of filthy people, and walked off to die.

chapter two

Sara Brighton sat on a small chrome and plastic chair in the corner of the emergency room. The place swarmed with people, all of them sick or injured or dying, and the chaos and confusion grated against her nerves. Ammon stood beside her, his hand resting gently on her shoulder. Their clothes were filthy, caked in dried mud and stained in blood, but they were dry now and warm, at least for the moment, and there was something good in that. The emergency room looked like something from a third-world country: dazed women; blood smeared across the floor; a child crying in the corner, apparently abandoned, her dark cheeks stained with tears. Four or five litters topped with bodies, some of them covered in disposable sheets, lined the walls. Another half a dozen gurneys were clustered in groups of three in the center of the room.

Sara motioned toward the motherless child, beckoning with her hands. The little girl hesitated, then ran to her, throwing her arms around her shoulders and burying her head into Sara's neck. The child cried for a few moments, wetting the back of Sara's jacket, then fell into a whimper before dropping off to sleep, her breathing interrupted with involuntary sobs. Sara stood up carefully, holding the little girl's head against her shoulder, and walked through the emergency room, questioning everyone she saw, "Is this your child? Do you know who she belongs to?" Blank stares and impatient gestures. No one knew. No one cared. She adjusted the child's weight against her weary arms and returned to the small chair.

Sara sat in silence for a long while. The chaos bustled all around her, but she didn't seem to notice anymore. As time passed, her eyes creased in worry. Ammon watched her, seeing the anxiety fall upon her face, clouding her eyes and tightening her lips. He knelt down beside her. "What is it, Mom?" he asked.

She looked up, tried to shake it off, but the cloud remained.

"What are you thinking about?" Ammon asked again. He kept his voice low, not wanting to wake the sleeping child.

Sara thought for a moment, not looking at him. "It's not right," she answered slowly. Ammon could see she was talking mostly to herself.

"What's not right, Mom?"

She continued staring off. "Your dad warned me." Her voice was quiet.

"Warned you? About what, Mom? What did Dad warn you about?"

"About him. About what's going to happen." She shook her head.

"What are you talking about, Mom? Dad knew what was going to happen to him? He knew about the bomb in Washington? About the EMP?"

"No, no. Something else. Something with the . . ." her voice trailed off again.

"What, Mom! What's going to happen?"

She looked at him, her eyes pleading. She wanted to tell him. She wanted to get it out. But she couldn't. Not yet. Maybe never. She finally looked away.

"Mom . . . ?"

She brushed him off with a lift of her hand. "I can't talk about it. It's probably nothing anyway."

Ammon sensed the inconsistency in her answer. "Mom, it can't be something you can't talk about and still be nothing. Those two options are kind of mutually exclusive." He tried to smile at her.

She looked around the crowded emergency room. "I'm thirsty."

Ammon didn't bite on her attempt to change the subject. "What did Dad warn you about?" he asked again.

"It's nothing, Ammon." She was determined now. "If it is, or if something changes and I *think* it is, then I will tell you."

"Mom . . ."

"I'll *tell* you, okay?"

Ammon looked at her, waiting, his face impatient. He wanted to press, but he knew it wouldn't do any good. She could be as stubborn as any of her children and far more stubborn than his dad. He watched her awhile, then stood and walked away, searching for a doctor or a nurse or an attendant or anyone who might be able to tell him where his brother was.

*   *   *

They waited for almost seven hours. By that time, Sara was exhausted and hungry and scared: scared of the scene around her, scared of what lay outside the brick walls of the hospital, scared of what might be ahead.

But mostly she was scared of what her husband had whispered to her on the last night they were together on this earth.

Looking around, she took a breath and thought about her son, who was lying on a bed somewhere in the bowels of the enormous hospital. Thinking of him, she felt a warmth inside her heart.

The only thing she wasn't scared about was Luke. That was the only thing she knew would be okay.

Ammon checked his watch for the thousandth time, purely out of habit, but of course it wasn't working, frozen on the moment a little more than five days before when the world had been thrown back a hundred years. Sara watched him, then held her arm out, her old windup still telling time. Ammon glanced toward it: 2:16 A.M.

Reaching out, he tapped her silver watch. "Kind of quaint."

She looked down at her wristwatch. It was dirty now and worn.

"I know you've told us before, but I can't remember. Where'd you get that old thing?"

Sara smiled wearily. "Right after we were married, your father and I went hitchhiking around Europe. He was stationed in Germany at the time. We had seven days' leave. We bummed around, staying in student hostels, bed and breakfasts, getting every mile we could out of our Eurail pass. Sometimes we'd get on the train and just ride it until we felt like getting off, not even knowing what country we were in. On the last day, he bought this for me at a tiny shop in this little village on some huge mountaintop in Switzerland." She moved her arm, holding the watch a little closer to her, fingering the silver band. "An old windup. Hardly impressive. He always apologized, thinking I'd prefer something more modern or expensive . . ." Her voice trailed off.

Ammon watched her. He didn't want to think about his dad. "Nice to have something that doesn't run on batteries or electronics," he said.

Sara pulled on the band, looked around, then stood up. "There's the doctor!" she said to Ammon.

The young doctor, his face pale with exhaustion, was walking quickly toward them, his crumpled blue cloak unbuttoned, the tails trailing behind him. Moving through the crowd, he was inundated with pleading questions. "Dr. Mortenson, what about my daughter! Doctor, can you tell me . . . ? Doctor, you've got to come and look at this *right* now! Doctor! Doctor!" Everyone had a crisis. Everyone needed his attention. Everyone had a sick or dying relative—husband, mother, daughter, son—all their needs legitimate, and all of it far more than he could do. He worked his way through the crowd, gesturing to some, offering a calming word or two to others. Ten feet from Sara and Ammon, he motioned for them to follow. They moved quickly toward him, following as he turned. Getting to the hallway, Sara stopped and turned around. What to do with the sleeping child in her arms? With no one around to offer the child to, she found an empty gurney and laid the little girl down. Patting her back, she covered her with the bedsheet, pulling it up around her neck, then kissed her cheek. It wasn't right to leave her there alone, but what else could she do? There had to be someone who knew her; a relative or friend had to be somewhere amid the chaos. She couldn't just take the child with her.

Stepping back, she patted the little girl's back again, moved a strand of dark hair from her face, and turned to follow Ammon, who was chasing after the doctor down the hall.

The doctor passed through a double doorway, pushing the heavy electric doors back manually, then turned right and moved into a patient room. Sara and Ammon followed. Four beds were crammed into a room that should have held two. Luke was sleeping atop the first bed. The doctor stopped at the foot of his bed and turned. "Tell me again what happened to your son," he said.

Sara started. "We were out in the country, what, south of here. We were stranded, like everyone else. It was night . . . last night, I guess . . . no, two nights ago . . ."

Ammon watched the exhausted doctor grow impatient. "He was shot," he interrupted, cutting to the chase.

The doctor turned and looked at him. "He was shot?" he repeated. His face was skeptical.

Ammon hunched his shoulders. "Yeah."

"Did you see it?" The doctor spoke rapidly.

"I was standing right there."

He turned to Sara. "You're the mother, right?"

She nodded but didn't speak.

"Did you witness the shooting as well?"

Again, she nodded as an answer.

The doctor looked at them both doubtfully. "Hmmmm," was all he said.

"What is it, Doctor?" Ammon asked, his voice tight and weary. He, like the doctor, had not slept in more than two days: one night of holding Luke in the backseat of the car, another day of hiking cross-country dragging his brother on an improvised litter, another night to make it through the city, and then waiting in the emergency room.

The doctor studied him, thought, then turned and lifted an oversized folder that was hanging at the foot of the bed. Every motion was quick and efficient, not wasting an ounce of energy or time. "We have emergency power, enough to run a few of our instruments, and this is what I find." He lifted a multicolored image and pointed as he talked. "A quick MRI of Frank's abdomen."

"His name is Luke," Sara started to correct him.

The doctor clearly didn't care. He pointed with the tip of his pen. "We have an entry wound, four centimeters below the lower thoracic cage." He moved the pen. "We have an exit wound, just below the costal cartilage." He moved the pen again, pointing to a lighter image on the MRI. Pausing, he stared thoughtfully. "An entry wound below the front rib cage. An exit wound near the center of the back, six centimeters from the spine." His voice trailed off again. "But nothing in between them."

The doctor rubbed his eyes. It couldn't be right. He was too tired. Too tired to think. The MRI must have malfunctioned. Poor imaging. Poor technical support. Everyone in the hospital was running on fumes, all the doctors, nurses, technicians, staff. It simply couldn't be. It had to be a mistake.

But it wasn't. It simply wasn't.

He'd done his own exam.

Ammon watched him. "Doctor?" he asked.

The young physician looked at him. "Everything is going crazy. It can't be what it seems."

The overhead loudspeaker called the doctor's name, ordering him to room three. He glanced quickly down the hallway, nodding toward a colleague, but didn't move.

Ammon stared at him. *Everything is going crazy.* Yes it was. But he still had no idea what the doctor was talking about. "Crazy. Yes, sir, it's crazy," he said. "Tell you something else that's crazy. That's my brother lying there with a hole inside his chest. Now, we need to know what you're going to do to help him—"

The doctor raised a hand to cut him off. "Are you certain?" he demanded. "You actually saw him shot?"

Ammon swallowed hard, dumbfounded at the persistence

of the question, then shot a quick look at his mother. "Yes. We both were there."

"And he was shot with what . . . what kind of gun?"

Ammon stared at the doctor, wondering what could be going through his mind. "I don't know!" he answered in exasperation. "A handgun! BANG, BANG. A regular pistol. I'm not an expert on such things."

"Look at this!" The doctor jabbed the pen again. "I've got an entry wound. I've got an exit wound. A hole here . . ." he moved the pen again . . . "a hole here. But no damage in between." He turned to face Ammon and his mother. "Nothing. You understand that? The bullet should have passed directly through his pancreas and torn it to shreds. But it didn't. The pancreas is undamaged. Clean as a whistle. Functioning perfectly. The metal should have perforated his small intestine. But it's like the bullet entered, turned into water, passed through his intestines and pancreas, and shot out the back, all without doing any internal damage. I don't know, I'm just a doctor, but that seems kind of strange to me."

Ammon stood there, his eyes wide. Sara's hands shot to her mouth and she gasped quietly. The doctor leaned against the wall, his face impatient. The loudspeaker called his name again. Half a dozen nurses and technicians moved quickly up and down the hall. Constant noise. Constant motion. Constant stress and urgency. Ammon knew that people were sick and dying all around them and the doctor had to go. He took a quick step forward, focusing on the doctor. "There's no internal damage?" he quickly questioned.

"Nothing. I've examined the patient. There's no damage except the entry and exit wounds. I've brought in a couple of colleagues. They're as dumbfounded as I am. He's got two flesh wounds, which will be painful, but they'll heal quickly, I presume, unless you guys exercise the same magic that healed the internal damage, in which case I'm sure your brother will jump up any time and go waltzing out of here."

Sara took a step back. "Are you certain, Doctor?"

"Of course I am." He almost seemed angry. It was frustrating and mystifying and it bothered him that he didn't have an explanation. Doctors were supposed to have the answers. Doctors were in charge. He was the trained physician, master of the emergency room, lord of his kingdom, speak a word and it was done.

But not now. Not with this case. He had no explanation, not a thing to offer. He was just as confused as the two people standing there with him. Turning, he dropped the medical chart in a green plastic box between the two beds.

Case closed. Time to move on.

Sara watched him, not saying anything, though her eyes conveyed every emotion in her soul. The doctor studied her, trying to read the look on her face. Surprise? He didn't see it. It was almost as if she had expected what he'd told her. Confidence? Peace and acceptance? The doctor didn't know.

She held her hand against her mouth again and stared at her sleeping son.

Ammon walked to stand beside her. "What do we do now?" he asked.

The doctor nodded to the hallway. "He doesn't need to be here anymore. A week ago we would have kept him, but that isn't an option today. We need the bed. We can't spare the nurses or any attention from the doctors or other staff.

"So take him. Keep him down. Keep the wounds clean. Change the dressings twice a day. That's about all I can tell you. You need to take him home."

Home, Sara thought, and in an instant she was transported to the old plantation home back in Virginia. The huge, tree-lined yard. Shutters. Hardwood floors. The sounds of her husband walking in his bare feet, not wanting to wake her up as he made his breakfast at 4:30 in the morning, the sounds of her three sons sleeping in their rooms, the smells of Sunday morning . . .

Home. No, she couldn't take him home. She glanced toward the doctor. "We will take him, then," she said.

Ammon moved toward the bed and took his brother's hand. Luke's eyes fluttered and he woke up.

"How you feeling, buddy?"

Luke seemed to test his body, slowly arching his back. "Pretty good," he said.

"That's good, man. That's really good. You're going to have to help me." Ammon put his hand underneath his brother's back. "We need to lift you up."

Luke slowly raised up to an elbow. "What we doing?" he asked.

"Getting out of here."

Luke looked wearily toward his mother. "We're leaving the hospital, Mom?"

Sara moved to his side. "Yes, Luke, they don't have room for us. But you're going to be okay."

Luke was confused and disoriented. "But where we going to go?"

"I don't know," Sara said.

chapter three

EAST SIDE, CHICAGO, ILLINOIS

Lieutenant Samuel Brighton stood at the apartment window. It was growing light now, the sun just barely breaking over the horizon, illuminating the dirty highrise buildings in a golden hue. It had been a long night. The sun was comforting to him now, and he almost opened his arms to embrace it as it came.

It was completely quiet, though he thought he could hear the women breathing behind the thin bedroom doors. The morning grew brighter and he stood there motionless, watching, listening, thinking, sometimes praying. He thought of the last two days: the parachute jump, the night run through the darkness, not knowing where he was going, only knowing he had to run. "Go!" the Spirit had told him. And so he had run. He thought of finding his family, his brother's stomach bleeding, his mother in tears, Ammon in shock, almost unable to move, the black woman and her daughter in whose home he was now standing. He thought of the mud, the rain, and the peace. He thought of the blessing, the miracle, the unseen hands upon his own. He brought his palms together, still feeling the others' heat. Was his father with him? He didn't know.

It didn't matter. The experience was too sacred to talk or wonder about. He thought of the day and nighttime walk across the country, through the outskirts of the city, the improvised litter holding Luke. He thought of his mother, who had stayed with her youngest son back at the hospital, an old, chaotic, brick-and-mortar complex on the other side of the city. He thought of his best friend, Bono, another brother, wondering if he had found his family. Sam shuddered, thinking of him. Was he okay?

The morning passed in silence. He didn't hear the girl's footsteps and he startled when he realized how close she was behind him. Jerking, he turned to face her, his hand instinctively moving for the holster at his side. Seeing his reaction, she pulled back and lifted her hands, palms out, face bowed, a signal of subjection. He looked at her, took a breath, and forced himself to relax. "Hi, Azadeh," he said.

"I frightened you. I am sorry."

Sam blushed. He was embarrassed. No way that would ever have happened in the field. "No, no . . . it's okay. I was just thinking."

She looked at him as if waiting. "Good morning . . ." she then stumbled, trying to think of the word . . . "officer," she finally said.

Sam laughed. "Officer! Really! You don't have to call me that."

She glanced around, embarrassed. "Lieu . . . tant Brighton . . ."

"Sam. Just Sam, okay?"

She smiled at him again.

He watched her intently, and for a fleeting moment the world seemed almost right again. Balanced. On track. Everything okay. The feeling came and left him in an instant and he almost shook his head. Where had *that* come from?

"You found me again?" she said to him. It was a question, not a comment, and there was wonder in her eyes.

"I didn't really find you," Sam weakly explained. Still, he half smiled. It was an amazing circumstance, one that had befuddled him. "It does seem that fate has cast us here together."

"You found me on the mountain. You saved me from the camp at Khorramshahr. No, more, you saved me from the man who came to take me. I know what he was doing." She looked off, thinking of the slave traders, her eyes half open, her voice so low Sam had to strain to hear. "I was here, alone again, when you appear again."

A shaft of sun finally broke over the tallest building, sending a thin beam of pale light through the small kitchen window. The two were silent for a moment. Looking at her, Sam couldn't help but think about the first time that he had seen her on the burning hill above her village in Iran, a terrified and lonely girl, young—sixteen, maybe seventeen, it was hard to tell—in some ways almost childlike, in others, beyond her years. She was too scared to talk, watching from the edge of the ditch, reaching for her father, who had been brutally murdered for no more reason than that he had tried to protect a young prince. Sam remembered seeing her, catching the feeling in his soul. Combat had a way of humbling the hardest man, and he was susceptible to its influence because of the things that he'd been through. So he sensed it, almost hearing the words inside his mind: *You know her. She is a sister. You were sent to help her.*

It seemed so long ago now. Years. Another life. Another world. So little of it even seemed relevant to him anymore.

Watching Azadeh, he realized that she was older now, much older than she should have been, and no longer just a girl. She had always been beautiful, but there was something more about her, something wiser, softer, maybe more determined, certainly more aware. He watched her intently, almost happily. Just being there in the friendly stranger's kitchen, a warm sun shining through, was enough to make him . . . he didn't know . . . not happy, exactly. Maybe *satisfied*.

Azadeh looked up at him, her dark eyes reflecting her deep thoughts. She had her own memories, powerful to the point of overwhelming, and for a moment she was also lost in the past. Together they stood in silence, the pale morning light beginning to fill the room. Sam shifted his weight, comfortable with the silence, but finally he shook his head. "Azadeh?"

She focused on him.

"Are you all right?"

She nodded, unsure of what to say.

He continued looking at her. Her dark hair was held behind a white and silver scarf, but several strands had escaped the shiny material and were hanging at the side of her face. Reaching up, she brushed them back. She wore a thin robe, worn but beautiful Persian silk; long cotton pants, something like pajamas; and white fabric sandals. "Are you all right?" he repeated.

She nodded. "I am fine."

"You miss your country?"

She didn't answer.

"Do you have any family?"

Her eyes half closed and she barely moved her head, the light scarf shimmering, another strand of dark hair escaping. Sam watched the ringlet bounce gently at the side of her ear.

"Do you have friends? People back in Iran you are keeping in contact with?"

"I have friends . . ." She thought again, a mental picture of Omar, her father's only true ally, flashing into her mind. She envisioned the huge man whisking the young princeling into his enormous arms, turning and heading up the mountain trail, rain and smoke and fog around him. She hadn't seen him since the day her father had been killed. Then she thought of her fellow villagers rummaging through the remains of her burned-out house, leaving nothing behind but broken pots and garbage. "I *had* friends," she concluded, talking mostly to herself.

Sam could see she didn't want to talk about it and diverted his eyes, looking around the tiny apartment. "Are you hungry?" He reached for his pack.

"I have food." She nodded toward the fridge.

Sam hesitated. He knew how little food was there.

"You need some water?" His camel pack was almost empty now, but he would share what he had.

"No. I am fine." She motioned to the half-full plastic container with the melted ice from the freezer.

Sam pulled a cell phone out of his pocket and played with it, flipping the cover open and closed absently. Azadeh eyed the black and silver case. "Why do you have that?" she asked.

Sam tossed it from one hand to the other. "A relic of the past."

"Does it operate?"

He laughed. "Yeah. Kind of. I mean, the phone itself would still work. I was underground in a subway—do you know what that is?" She shook her head no. "An underground train." She nodded quickly. "Being underground, my equipment was protected from the giant magnetic surge. That's why I have a flashlight, a watch, this phone that still works. The problem is, none of the cell towers are operating . . ." His voice trailed off. He had lost her, he could see that from the look on her face. "No cell phone. Not right now. Sometime they'll rebuild the towers. Then it will work again."

She stared at him and nodded. He cleared his throat awkwardly, then moved to the kitchen table and sat down.

Azadeh hesitated, then followed. "How long have you been here?" he asked.

She thought for a moment before holding up almost all her fingers.

He counted. "Nine weeks?" That didn't seem right.

She shook her head. "No. Sunsets . . . days."

Nine days. "Not very long," Sam said. He pressed his lips, almost smiling at the irony. She had barely made it to America before it had all come crashing down. Was that a good thing, being here after the EMP attack? He didn't know. Truth was, there were lots of places he would rather be than in the United States right now. For the first time in modern history, this was the last place in the world anyone might want to be. "Your timing is ironic, isn't it, Azadeh?"

She pulled the top of her robe. She probably had no idea what *ironic* meant, but still she seemed to sense his meaning. "I am glad I am here," she said. "I have nothing here, that is true, but," she nodded east, "I had less over there. It is bad in your country now, but it can be as bad over there. Or it will be. Soon. But all that does not matter." She stopped talking as she thought. "I am a person here," she concluded.

Sam stared at his hands, his fingers moving anxiously. "I have to go," he said.

Azadeh looked suddenly terrified. "Going?"

"Yes. I have to check on my mom and brother. Then we've got to form a plan."

"A plan?" Azadeh wondered.

"Yes. You know, decide what we're going to do."

She bit her lower lip. "What *will* you do?" Her eyes were wide now, fear showing through.

Sam reached across to touch her fingers. "Don't worry about it, Azadeh. We're going to work it out."

She kept staring, finally whispering, "You will be going?"

Sam looked around, his eyes resting on the window. He knew the scene that lay outside. "I don't think we can stay here."

"You will take your brothers? Your mother? You will go?"

"Yes. Probably soon."

She stared again, not saying anything, then looked around as if searching for something before bringing her eyes back to him. "I cannot go out there. A Muslim woman. An Iranian. It is not safe."

Sam nodded, understanding.

"Please." She motioned toward the back bedroom with her hand. "Mary? Kelly Beth? Me? Please. Can we go with you? If not, I do not know what we will do."

Sam hesitated, looking at her in surprise. "Azadeh, did you think that I was going to leave you?"

She only stared at him.

"We're not going to leave you. We are together now, kind of like a family."

She looked down, too frightened to believe him.

He leaned forward across the old table. "I promise you, Azadeh, we're going to stay together. It's going to be okay." He stood up and grabbed his jacket. "I've got to go and find my family now," he said.

Northwestern University Medical Center
Chicago, Illinois

The hospital was in utter chaos. There were no gurneys or wheelchairs available, so Sara and Ammon wrapped Luke in a blanket and propped him up, one of them under each arm. He stepped gingerly and winced a time or two, but Ammon was surprised at the strength with which he moved; his legs didn't wobble and he seemed to hold his own weight. They walked slowly down the hallway toward the main entrance. Pushing the heavy door back, they found themselves in the covered horseshoe parkway jammed with half a dozen ambulances and other cars, all of them dead. Stepping into the light, Ammon felt grateful to be out of the hospital, which seemed like nothing but a black pit of despair.

He looked around, squinting at the sun. "Where do you think Sam is?" he asked his mom.

Sara looked up and down the crowded streets. There were many more people out now than there had been the night before. They gathered in the streets, on the corners, near the hospital door. They seemed more angry, and more desperate. A nervous knot grew in her stomach. She searched the crowd for Sam, hoping his tall shoulders would stand above the growing mass of people. "He said he'd come back after he got Mary and her little girl back to their apartment," she said.

Luke nodded toward the nearest bench. Sara and Luke sat down. Luke immediately bent over, resting his head on Sara's lap. Ammon paced, looking up and down the street. "We need Sam," he mouthed to his mother so that Luke couldn't hear.

"He'll be along," she said.

"I don't know what to do or where to go."

"He hasn't forgotten us."

After about twenty minutes, Luke opened his eyes and sat up slowly. Ammon looked down at his brother. "Luke, buddy, you okay?" he asked.

His younger twin smiled. "Doing pretty good."

"Do you think that you can make it?"

"What do you mean by *make it?*"

"We need to do some walking."

"Yeah. I can walk." Luke started pushing up.

Sara suddenly squealed and pointed toward the crowded intersection. "Look!" She stood up beside Luke. "There's Sam. You can see his uniform."

Ammon turned and looked. There, almost lost in the line

of dead cars and the mass of people, a young man, taller than the others and dressed in a tan camouflage army uniform, was walking quickly toward the hospital entrance. Sara called his name, and he started moving toward them. "Okay. Very cool," Ammon said as he turned to Luke. "Sam will be able to help me hold you. He'll know what to do."

Sam approached them, almost at a run. Seeing Luke, he stopped suddenly and stared. A long moment passed. "What are you doing here?" he asked in disbelief. "You should be in the hospital!" He broke into a smile. "You know, with a bed-pan and good-looking nurses all around."

Luke laughed and caught himself, his hands shooting to his side. "Been there, done that, the whole bedpan thing."

Sara threw a knowing look to Ammon before she said, "They kicked us out of the hospital. They don't have room for him."

Sam's face turned angry. "Are you kidding me!" He motioned toward Luke. "Sit down there. Save your strength." He turned toward the entrance and started walking. "Come with me, Ammon. We're going to talk to them."

Sara ran beside him, reaching for his hand. "Sam, Sam, it's okay." She tried to pull him back. "He's going to be all right."

Sam stopped, staring at her. "What do you mean? He's clearly not okay."

She looked into his eyes. "He's okay," she said.

"He isn't okay. He's been shot. They just don't want to have to keep him. They want to—"

"No, Sam, he's *okay*." She emphasized the word. "He's hurt, yes, and he'll have to be careful, but he's going to be all right." Glancing around her, she motioned to the burgeoning mob of people on the street. "There isn't enough time to explain everything right now. We've got to get him off the streets. We've got to figure out where we're going, how we're going to get there, and what we're going to do."

chapter four

Drexel Danbert was dead. A new leader of the firm had been selected and put in place.

As the sun set, the lights about the city began to shine, a million dots beneath a haloed prism that had formed around the moon. The sky was clear of clouds but tinted with blood-red dust from the strong currents that stirred in the upper atmosphere. A faint smell of smoke and acid still drifted in the air.

The penthouse stood atop a glass high-rise building in the *2ème*, the primary business district just north of central Paris. Across the street and down one block, the Bourse, the French stock market, was still abuzz. The Bibliothèque Nationale was to the right, the Louvre directly ahead.

The recently elected senior partner of Danbert, Lexel, Taylor and Driggs closed his eyes. He smiled, thinking of his old boss. Drexel Danbert had simply disappeared, leaving his apartment and walking off into the night, a fitting end to a life that was as storied as it was mysterious, as convoluted as it was dirty. The problem was (and they had all known this would be a problem), the old man had retained some sort of conscience,

38

and it had driven him insane. Too bad. He had been a great talent. The good news was, they didn't need his kind of talents anymore.

With the old man's disappearance, Edward Kelly was the senior partner now. Thin, with white hair, bushy eyebrows, and a mean downturn in his lips, he stared in silence, sniffing the breeze that blew in from the partially open window. The air was warm but far below him, in the floodlights, the foliage around the Jardin du Palais Royal had turned prematurely red. No one could remember a fall that had come so early or so fast. It seemed that overnight every tree within the city—and there were many—had burst out in red and deep orange. Now, just a few days later, the leaves were falling, turning brown and lifeless just as quickly as they had ruptured into flame. The grass was also prematurely turning brown. And there was no reason for the sudden change: It hadn't been cold, it hadn't frozen, there'd been plenty of rain. It wasn't just the dormant sleep of coming fall, nature getting ready for the freezing snows and colder temperatures that December would bring. This was something different. Something none of them could explain.

The grass wasn't hibernating, it was *dying,* turning brittle as strands of dry confetti.

Earlier in the afternoon, Kelly had walked along the rock-lined pathways that ran around the Palais Royal, pulling occasional tufts of dead grass and examining the roots beneath, all so dry he could blow them away with his breath. Wondering, he had stared. It was happening all over the city. All over Western Europe. Crops dying in the fields. Fruit shriveling on the limb. Vegetables decaying on the vine before they could be picked. Most suspected it was some kind of unforeseen effect from the nuclear attacks in the Middle East, United States, and

Iran, but anyone who knew anything about the effects of radiation and nature knew that wasn't true.

There was no correlation.

This was something else.

It was as if nature were completely disregarding the rules that had governed it before.

They would eventually understand it, Kelly was certain. There was no need for real worry. Still, it was curious and caused him just a hint of alarm.

He stared through the deeply tinted windows of the high-rise building. Below him, business carried on as usual, thousands of people going on about their lives, working late, putting in their time for the system they adored. Money. Always money. War, nuclear explosions, massive death and rage, whatever else, it didn't matter as long as there was money to be made. And since the partners had been warned to move their headquarters from Manhattan to their building here in Paris, they were in a great position to make more of it. A lot more. More than they could count. More than they could ever comprehend.

He stared as the moon rose, casting a yellow shadow across the great city. Normally he loved this view, but with the city so brown and lifeless, it offered no beauty to him now. He breathed and stared another moment, then turned to his partner. "Drexel thought we went too far," he stated matter-of-factly. "He told me that. He thought we pushed them beyond their ability to rebuild their country."

The other man smoked, a blue haze drifting toward the wood-paneled ceiling twelve feet over his head. He pretended to think, but he wasn't really doing so—he had already made up his mind. "I think they will," he answered slowly. "Some will try to stop them, and of course there will be many who won't help, but most will buy our vision. When we step in with the answers, how could they possibly tell us no?"

The first man grunted, unconvinced. There was a tension between the two partners, subtle but pervasive in everything they did or said. They were no longer friends but contenders in an always deadly game, especially since Kelly had been named managing partner of the firm. Theirs was a game for money, a race for power, for supremacy in the order. There were no friends. All of the partners walked around with targets on their backs. Still, he didn't worry about it. He was prepared.

The smoking man, a former U.S. senator, lifted his heavy body from the Chippendale mahogany camelback sofa (circa 1770, $464,800 U.S. dollars) and moved to stand beside the window. For a moment the two of them were silent, looking out. The smoker finally spoke. "They will rebuild." His voice was tight with impatience, as if he were speaking to a foolish child. "I don't think that is the question. The question is, will they rebuild on *our* terms? I am certain that they will. They are pliable and open now. Vulnerable and defeated, beat down to their knees. It is hard, once the top dog, to get knocked off the pile. No, they'll do *anything* to get it back, believe me, they will.

"And we have laid the foundation. Three generations of work have come to fruit. A constant dripping can hollow out the hardest rock, and we've been dripping on them a long time now. All around the world, their values and ideas are despised. Most of the Americans hate their own country as much as the world hates them now. Former government leaders even one of their former *presidents*—academics, entertainers, educators, trusted officials, all of them have been our allies, helping to spread the word.

"We've actually convinced them that their country was the problem, not the answer; the cancer, not the cure. They think their nation was too powerful, too greedy, too racist and full of war. The time is right. It's almost perfect. We have our man. We have a plan. They'll listen to us now."

The senior member of Danbert, Lexel, Taylor and Driggs grunted again, then sipped his wine. He was not young, and the sense of history was not lost on him.

He thought a moment, letting the words *they* and *them* turn over in his mind. Then he thought about his home. Born and raised in Massachusetts, he traced his family roots back to Plymouth Rock, almost four hundred years before. Yet he and the partners always spoke of the Americans as *them* and *they*.

There were the Americans and there were the *others*, and the members of the firm were part of the *others* now. Their society had no borders, no love for country, no love for people or culture, and certainly no love for home. They were above that—no, *beyond* that—and happy that they were. America was not the enemy, just an obstacle that had to be overcome. Very simple. No emotion. Just another part of their job.

Still, Kelly understood the United States more than most. And yes, its people had the tenacity to rebuild their nation. If the partners didn't think they would run into opposition, they were painfully wrong.

Sensing his thoughts, the fat partner glanced toward him, hiding his contempt, then took a final drag before snuffing the half-smoked cigarette onto the palm of his hand without feeling any pain. "The Great Experiment failed, and you know it," he almost sneered. "We knew it would. You and that idiot Drexel might not have believed it, but the rest of us knew. They tried to share it, they tried to force this thing they call *democracy*," his voice slipped into a sneer, "but the Middle East wasn't ready and their timing couldn't have been worse. Democracy doesn't mean anything if you're worried about getting shot out on the street. Democracy doesn't mean anything if you don't have anything to eat. They pushed too hard and failed. Just as they were at the apex of their rotting, they tried exporting their philosophy throughout the world. Now it has failed, or it is failing, in every quarter of the globe. Iraq. Iran. South America. Central and Eastern Europe. Tiny convulsions of democracy sprouted here and there, but none of them were self-sustaining. Some of them survived a generation, some more or less than that, but it's over for these countries. Everything is crashing down."

Kelly stared down at the glistening city as he listened. Sipping his wine, he wished that he were drunk.

The other man lit another smoke. "Little wonder it fell upon them. The truth is—and even you recognize this—most people no longer want to bother with actually governing themselves. They want a nanny more than freedom, someone to feed and bathe them and take care of the details, someone to make decisions, to make life easy if not satisfying or complete. They don't want to really understand and analyze all their problems—those are far too complex. Free will is such a bother when there are so many other things to think about. Morality is such a distraction when there are parties and food and sports and drugs and sex and computers and corruption and . . . well, you get the point."

Kelly didn't answer.

"Life in the States was so easy and undemanding, the Americans would have given up anything to preserve it," the junior partner continued, smoke escaping from his nose. "And in the end, they did. They gave up everything. Now they are the cotton candy of world cultures, soft and sweet, entirely without substance." Another whiff of smoke drifted from his nose. "So," he concluded, "there will be no rebuilding, not without our help. We'll be able to fashion the government. Shape it and mold it. And we will hold the power."

Kelly shook his head. It might have proven true in Asia, mostly true in Europe, and certainly true in former Russia and dozens of other countries throughout the world, but the

United States was different. It had always been different. And it was different now.

Still, he held his tongue as he stared at the dead trees that lined the streets below. It was too late to convince his partners, and he just didn't care that much about it anymore.

The partner watched him out of the corner of his eye, shifting his massive weight, and started in again: "The United States is the most hated nation in the world. Is there a better indication of the magnificent job we have done! *The United States is the monster*—not Cuba or North Korea, who have institutionalized starvation and poverty for generations now. Not Middle Eastern monarchies who beat little girls who learn to read and behead their older sisters who have the misfortune of being raped. Not China with their forced abortions—where are the civil libertarians on that?" He stopped and laughed, the irony forcing his fat belly to roll. "Evil is good and good is evil. We have crested that plateau. As long as they believe that, as long as they really hate each other as much as they love themselves, as long as they think their own nation is the evil one, they will comply with our demands.

"We can take the Constitution and shred it, then mold a new society into what we think is right. The Society we all belong to. It is clear our time has come."

Kelly sniffed again. A long silence followed. "You are aware, I am certain, who the president of the United States is now?"

"Of course," the fat man grunted.

Kelly turned, looking directly into his eyes. "She is not a part of us."

The fat man lit yet another cigarette. "I know that. *They* know that." He gestured vaguely in some direction toward the east.

"So, then—how do they propose we get past that?"

The fat man shook his head. "Of course they're going to kill her. What did you think they'd do, my friend?"

chapter five

T here was no reason to lie to her. She was with them
or she wasn't. Either way, she wouldn't leave the
command post without making a decision. Nor was
there any reason to soften the impact of what they wanted her
to do. And there certainly wasn't any reason to speak to her as
if she really was in charge. She was a custodian of the presidency, but she hadn't been elected. She didn't speak with the
voice of the people, nor did she carry the support of the military or the cabinet or—more important—the men who were
in charge. She was a happenstance of the Constitution and that
was all.

The blast over D.C. had already killed the president and
vice president. The Speaker of the House of Representatives,
third in line to the presidency, lay in a hospital somewhere in
western Virginia, but she hadn't regained consciousness since
the explosion. If she ever did (and the two men were
absolutely certain that she wouldn't), it was extremely unlikely
that she would regain even a fraction of her faculties.

Which meant the poor woman propped up before them,

the former president pro tempore of the Senate, was now in charge.

A fractured leg and third-degree burns, hardly worse than a sunburn from a too-long nap on the beach, were the disappointing total of her injuries. Which meant that, one way or another, they had to deal with her before they could move on.

The new president of the United States sat at the head of a huge wooden conference table, her casted leg hidden under a full skirt, a pair of chrome crutches leaning against the side of her chair. Her hair was full and straight, with fashionable strands of gray. Her face was red but weary, her eyes full of energy, her mouth puckered in determination. She looked off as she thought, breathing in the purified underground air.

Her name was Bethany Rosen. Fifty-six, a Californian, three terms within the Congress, she had been selected as a Senate leader for her congeniality and middle-of-the-road politics—that, plus the fact that her husband had made a billion dollars producing movies and could raise more money for the party than any other person on the West Coast.

The new president put the red binder aside, took a frightened breath, then reached down and moved her leg, feeling the heavy cast against the chair. A shot of pain moved up her spine and, for a moment, she thought of the day the injury had been sustained. She remembered the emergency alert, her cell phone going off, scrambling down the front porch of her townhouse east of the Capitol, the wailing sirens, the sound of an approaching chopper sent to take her away, the white-hot light, the blazing heat against her face and arms, the falling steps and crashing metal, the sound of splintered wood, the pain against her knee. She remembered passing time, blurred visions and urgent voices, an ambulance ride and then a chopper, the softness of white sheets and the peacefulness of sleep as someone poked a needle in her arm. Then she remembered slowly waking and finding out that she was in charge.

If the rush of power was good for recovery, then she would recover very soon, for the office of the president was something she had coveted for almost thirty years. And she intended to make a difference while enjoying every moment of her command.

Which might be a long time or a little, depending on the decisions she now made.

*　　*　　*

The meeting had begun at exactly ten o'clock. The two men had entered the room and sat down, one on her left, one on her right, and slid a four-page, red-bound document across the table. "Read this," the first man had commanded, then sat back in silence as she read.

The conference table inside the presidential office suite at Raven Rock was huge, easily accommodating twenty-five or thirty people, and the three individuals seemed small, their chairs tucked up against the edge of the thick oak table. The room was very quiet as the president read. Ten minutes later, her heart racing, she lifted her eyes, pushed the red binder away, and adjusted her leg. "You want me to *what?*" she whispered at the men in disbelief.

The first man, a former president himself, leaned forward, his voice patronizing and sickeningly friendly. A bitter old man beneath the soft tone, he'd been voted out of office almost thirty years before and his eyelids were heavy now with age, the pupils dull and empty underneath the drooping lids. The anger of his rejection had grown more acidic through all the empty years, and most everything he said or did now revealed the poison in his soul. "Bethany," he insisted as he reached out for her hand, "this really is important. You have to listen to us now."

She stared into his face, spiderwebs of tiny purple veins running up and down his cheeks. "You want me to hold back," she hissed. "You don't want me to retaliate. You've got to be kidding me!"

The former president shook his head. "It's the best thing for us now."

"It's outrageous," she answered simply. "Outrageous and impossible! And that is not all." She tapped the red binder. "Everything you've suggested here will weaken us to the point—"

"What we've suggested, Madame President, will ensure the survival of our nation."

She openly scoffed. "No. It wouldn't be the same nation, not after you were through."

The other man, the current National Security Advisor, cleared his throat. Young. Extraordinarily good-looking. Lots of family money. Supremely confident. "It's too late for all that, Bethany," he answered in an impatient voice. "We already are not the same nation. The old days have passed us. It's a new world now." He turned away to keep from glaring. He and the newly sworn-in president had a history of conflict that went back several years, and their philosophies of government relations couldn't have been more opposed. The ugly truth was, he considered any one of his current girlfriends far more capable of being the president than the woman who sat across the table from him now, and it was all he could do to hold back his disdain.

Her black eyes flickered and her mouth hung open. She thought for far too long. "So, while we leave our enemies untouched, you want me to . . ." She glanced down at the binder, reading from the list. "Suspend habeas corpus. No more evidentiary hearings. Arrest them and hold them as long as it takes. Months. Years. A lifetime. No evidence. No trials. Keep 'em all locked up forever." She glanced down again. "Declare martial law—now, maybe I could go along with that but for the fact that giving military members law-enforcement authority would break the Posse Comitatus act; you both know that. We have always forbidden the military from exercising police duties within our own borders." She paused and took a breath. "This isn't the Third Reich, my friends. I don't care how difficult things are right now, we can get through this without—"

"Without what!" the former president sneered. "Without exercising a few understandable precautions?"

She turned to face him, adjusting herself painfully in her seat. "Listen to yourself, Mr. President. Listen to what you just said. Understandable precautions!" She angrily tapped the binder. "It seems to me that shutting down the court system is a bit more than just an understandable precaution."

"We don't have time for trials right now. Don't you see that, Bethany? The nation is hanging by a thread! It's nothing but chaos out there, worse than anything you could imagine. In very short order, you're going to have food riots in the streets. You're going to see murder and mayhem over a single loaf of bread. Do you think, in your naivete, that the courts can begin to handle that? You can't have sympathetic judges releasing prisoners because the prison food isn't warm and there aren't enough beds! More important, half the federal judges will interfere with what you have to do right now. And what is that, Madame President? The answer is perfectly clear. You've got one priority, and that's security. You've got to buy yourself some time to put this thing back together. Until then, you've got to keep a firm grip on the situation or it will spin completely out of control. You keep a tight grip, and we *might*—probably not, but we might—keep this nation together. But if you go soft, if you go all civil rights and sympathy and ACLU on us, then believe me, we're *through*. Do that and it won't matter—you won't have anything left that is worth fighting over anyway!"

The president looked down in pain, uncertain. Nervously, she flipped the pages. "Detention centers. Expanded powers. Look at this!" She slapped the binder closed. "You want me to nationalize industry, the media, all means of transportation . . ."

The National Security Advisor sat back and scoffed. "You really don't understand the situation, do you, Beth? You don't understand it at all! You think nationalizing industry and transportation is going to matter? You think taking control of the media will make a difference? *There is nothing up there,* Beth. Nothing left at all, not since the EMP—no MTV, no television, no radio. A few old-fashioned printing presses have shown up, but believe me, Madame President," he seemed to choke, "no one is concerned with editorializing right now. The only things that *are* working, the government owns and controls anyway. Military transportation, computers, Command and Control. The Emergency Broadcasting System. That's about all there is. A few other things here and there, but not much, you have to know. So believe me, Madame President, taking control of industry and transportation is the very least of your worries. No one's going to give a whit who owns what if you can't get things going anyway."

He paused and leaned toward her, his eyes simmering, traces of red around the lids. "Lay the foundation for rebuilding," he concluded forcefully, "and no one's going to complain about the niceties of ownership. No one's going to ask the driver of the rescue wagon if he's a member of the government!"

She looked up, her face growing pale. Something desperate and dark had settled over the room. She felt a cold shiver run through her and fought a sudden urge to move away from these men, to remove herself from the feeling. Still, she summoned her strength and held the binder up, shaking it at the former president. "Disband the Congress. Send them home. You can't seriously be advising me to—"

"Federalize power within the presidency? Absolutely we are!"

She turned away, too stunned to react, her breathing shallow, her heart throbbing in her ears. "I don't believe it. I simply *can't* believe it. You *can't* be serious."

"Of course we're serious, *darling*." The National Security Advisor leaned toward her ear. She looked at him and almost recoiled from the anger in his eyes. There was no respect within their burning and certainly no fear. *You are a pretender,* they seemed to scream at her, *an unfortunate happenstance of history, but that is all. You are not the president, at least not really! You have no power. You have no judgment. You will do what we tell you to do.*

It stunned her, the burning hatred, and she had to look away. "I don't think you would have called the previous president *darling*," she barely whispered, trying to hide her rage and fear.

The NSA snorted, letting the insult hang like a bad smell in the air, then wiped his brow. "You'll forgive me, I'm sure, Madame President."

His apology was only more demeaning, and she looked away again.

The NSA fell silent. He was much smarter and more experienced and certainly more capable of managing this crisis than she was. It galled him to even talk to this woman who was called Madame President just because she was next in line.

51

The president glanced down at the paper, stabbing the first item on the list. "You don't want me to retaliate for the EMP attack?"

The former president edged toward her, leaning on his arms against the table. "Beth, who are you going to retaliate against? Do you even know who launched the missiles? How are you going to prove it?"

"Prove it! We all know who did this. The missiles were Iranian variants of the Al Abbas Scuds! Soon we'll know where the warhead nuclear material was refined, but even now we all can guess . . ."

"Guess, Bethany? I don't think we should be *guessing*."

"We won't be guessing," she shot back, feeling hostile now. "We'll take our time, we'll analyze it carefully, but when we have our answers, I swear to you, we will retaliate."

The former president sadly shook his head. If he didn't believe what he was saying, it was impossible to tell, for lying was such second nature to him that he hardly knew himself. He was so comfortable in his many skins that he didn't notice when one shed. *What do I need to believe in order to convince them? Close my eyes, think a moment . . . poof! that's what I believe now.* "It won't make any difference," he countered sincerely. "Bethany, we have known each other now for what, twelve . . . fourteen years? I have watched you and admired you. I'm comfortable, and I mean this—no, I'm grateful that you are in this position now. The nation will be well served by your considerable judgment and intellect, but you *must* listen to what I tell you. Forget retaliation. It solves nothing. Certainly, you could order the deaths of a couple million Arabs. But what will that do to improve things for the United States? And the Persians you would kill are innocent! You understand me! They are innocent, every one. Sure, you might kill some of those who are responsible, you might take out a few of the mullahs, but remember, all of them are buried now in blast-proof bunkers in the desert that we can't identify or target. Even if you get lucky and kill a handful of the leaders, what about the millions of innocent civilians who are collateral damage to your cause?"

The president shook her head. "I know King Abdullah is responsible. So far, he's been behind every—"

The former president interrupted. This was the main reason he was here. "King Abdullah is innocent of this attack," he shot back. "I have known King Abdullah for many, many years and there is no way, *no way* he had anything to do with these EMP attacks. To even suggest that the Saudi royal family had anything to do with this is patently absurd."

The former president stopped and held his breath, glancing angrily toward the NSA. "I'm begging you, Bethany," he said again, this time more softly, "do not retaliate. It doesn't help us. All you'll do is cement a hundred generations of Muslim hatred against us. Do this and there won't be peace in your lifetime, the lifetime of your children, or of your great-great-great-grandchildren after that."

The National Security Advisor leaned impatiently back in his chair. "Worse, you'll be wasting time and resources—resources that we need in order to rebuild. And that's the only thing you should be concentrating on right now: rebuilding our nation, our military, our security services, our infrastructure, all of the things we need to survive."

The new president lowered her eyes uncertainly. She didn't know . . . she didn't know. For the first time she considered that they might be right.

But the other suggestions on their list, she was certain of them. She slid the red binder across the table, nudging it up against the NSA's arm. "These other things you're recommending are patently unconstitutional. Not a single thing you have presented here is within my authority. The courts will never allow it, the Supreme Court will—"

"Will what? Roll over in their graves? There is only *one* surviving member of the entire Court! Does his one vote control our world? Does one man decide our fate! No! It cannot be. We have no courts or Constitution. We have no laws now, no organization, no state borders, no state militias; we've got no working infrastructure, modern equipment, machines, food, sanitation, and no, we have no courts. All we've got is a hundred million people out there who are a few weeks from starving to death!"

"The nation will not allow me—"

"*You don't have a freaking nation! Don't you see that?* You've got absolutely nothing now! Nothing but what little you can scrape together and somehow manage to rebuild. And that is the entire point. That's the only reason we are here. Yes, we are going to rebuild our nation, but it won't be like the nation we had before. It will be stronger, more defensible, more perfect and intent. It will be different, we all realize that, but it will be better."

The president shook her head, her cheeks growing pale. She looked down. Her hands were shaking. She slipped them under the table and bit her lip.

She was scared now. No, she was more than scared, she was almost terrified. She had a feeling—a terrible, dark, hopeless feeling—and it was coming from these men. They reeked of desperation and despair. They reeked of lies and deception and power and lust; she knew that, she could feel it. And there was something more, something . . . evil, something loathsome. The only thing she wanted now was to get away from them.

Taking a quick breath, she pushed back against her chair. "I thank you for your input." She struggled to move her fractured leg. "You are well regarded, and I will certainly consider the advice you have provided." She started to stand.

The NSA pushed back and stood beside her. "Consider carefully, Madame President." His cold eyes narrowed on her now. "There is danger all around us. None of us are safe."

The former president took a short step forward and placed his hand upon her arm. Lowering his voice, he whispered to her: "We must work together on this, Bethany. That is so important now. If we combine our talents and our powers, we can salvage what we need to in order to raise this nation once again. But we must work quickly and in combination. And yes, it might be necessary to work in private, at least until we have a better understanding of the situation. But working in secret, our combination," he suddenly paused and cleared his throat as if he had said something wrong. "Our combination of talents and abilities will be enough to see us through," he finished.

"Think about it," the NSA mumbled roughly. "I think you'll see that we are right."

*　　*　　*

The president pushed a button underneath the table and an aide appeared to escort the two men out. They left the large conference room and walked down the hallway in the Command Center, away from the presidential office suite, then paused and turned to face each other.

The former president shook his head. "She's not going to do it, is she?"

"I told you she wouldn't," the younger man said.

The two men stood in the crowded corridor, half a dozen military officers and civilians hurrying by them. They waited, letting them pass. "I do think we convinced her not to retaliate

55

against our brother," the former president whispered when the two men were alone again.

The NSA considered, then slowly nodded. "Yes, I think so too. If not, I would have killed her before we left the room."

A moment of silence followed, the sound of the ceiling fans and air purifiers humming overhead.

"Regarding the other items, she isn't going to move," the NSA hissed.

The former president hunched his shoulders and thought. "Let's do it, then," he said.

The NSA turned and started walking. "It's already done."

The older man followed, his steps short and weak. "You have ordered it already?"

"Yes, I did."

"You weren't going to give her a chance to think about it, to come around?"

The NSA kept on walking.

The former president rushed to catch up. "You didn't give us much time to convince her." He didn't sound disappointed.

The NSA turned to him. "I wasn't as optimistic about her as you were, I guess."

chapter six

The servant slipped into the room late at night. Moving silently across the leather-covered floor, the lambskin supple and warm from the heated coils under his feet, he walked toward Edward Kelly's side. The red moon cast dim shadows through the fifteen-foot-high arched window, and he could see that Kelly was awake, the whites of his eyes shining in the dim light. "Sir," he whispered carefully.

The senior partner didn't move.

"Sir," the servant whispered once again.

The man's eyes fluttered, moving wildly left and right. Then they opened wider in panic, and his face contorted as if in pain. He breathed heavily, as if he had been running and was suddenly out of breath.

The servant waited, scared, watching his master's eyes as they fluttered and moved in fear. Realizing the man was dreaming, he reached out and touched his shoulder. "Sir," he said more loudly.

Kelly sat up quickly, instantly awake. "What . . . what . . . what is it?"

"Sir, you have a call."

"A call? Call who . . . ? " He stopped and held his tongue, fighting the lingering fear and disorientation, then moved his feet to the side of the bed and placed them on the floor, forcing himself to calm down.

The nightmare had left him breathless and it took him a few seconds to collect himself.

Late-night calls were the norm in his business. The truth was, he hardly ever slept. Like a father of a fussy newborn, he couldn't remember the last time he'd slept through an entire night. At any given moment, about half of his clients were awake, stretched across the globe as they were. And at any given time, about a third of them were dealing with some crisis or another for which they needed the firm's help. None of them gave a second thought to jarring him awake—for the money they paid him, they would have called him at his own funeral and been furious if he was a little slow to respond from the other side of the grave. Still, as he sat at the edge of his bed, something about this phone call seemed to cause a sense of worry. It was a sixth sense he had developed. He knew when to tighten up before the punch. "Who is it?" he asked as he stared at the mobile phone.

"General Lafferty, sir."

General Lehman Lafferty, the new chairman of the United States Joint Chiefs of Staff.

Kelly cleared his throat, took a breath, and reached out for the phone. "General, what can I do for you?" he said.

"Edward, we've got a little problem," the chairman answered.

"The world is full of problems, General Lafferty."

"You think?" The general wasn't happy. Clearly not in the mood to laugh. "We've got a personnel issue we've got to deal with."

Kelly checked the luminescent clock atop his ancient

Roman nightstand. "They told me the president would be taken care of within the day."

"She will be. That isn't why I called."

"Unless you believe in instantaneous resurrection, I can't imagine what you're so worried about."

The general snorted. The phone hummed a moment, the military STU-IV secure voice encryption creating a quarter-second delay. "You remember my old friend General Brighton?" he asked.

Kelly had to think. "I'm starting to remember."

"He worked for President—"

"Yes, yes, I know who you mean."

Another half a moment of silence. "It appears he might have known more than we thought he did. It appears he might have talked."

Kelly didn't move, his white legs hanging over the side of the pillow bed. He studied a few strands of hair protruding from his shins. "Okay, that could be a problem, but hardly, I have to believe, one that would be impossible to overcome."

"That depends on who he talked to, doesn't it, Edward."

Kelly brushed a hand across his face. His mouth was parched and tart from the nightly shot of whiskey and he wanted to spit the dryness out. "Maybe. But anyone he might have talked to is certainly dead."

"To use your word, maybe. If we're lucky. But there might be one we didn't think about."

"*We didn't think about.* You know, Lafferty, I thought that was what we paid your group for. The people over here would be a little disappointed . . ."

"No, no, you can't pin this one on me. It was never part of my contract to—"

Edward instantly shot back. "Listen, you snot-nosed little whit. Before we made you an offer, you were, what, some

nameless three-star general counting tanks and training soldiers
while looking forward to selling Amway when you retired to
pay for some brat's tuition there at Harvard. I hardly think,
General Lafferty," he spat out the general's name, "you need
remind me of responsibilities or any sort of financial arrange-
ment that might be in place."

The STU-IV hummed. The other man cleared his throat, a
soft muffle through the line.

Kelly arched his back, feeling angry and impatient. "Look,
okay, so Brighton might have suspected . . ."

"He way more than suspected. He was *very* close."

"Okay. It doesn't matter. Say he knew. Say he talked. Whoever it was he talked to, it couldn't be that hard to take care of
them. We killed General Brighton. We've killed others. Surely
we can kill anyone else he might have talked to."

The general hesitated before he responded, "What about
his wife?"

Kelly didn't move. "The blonde witch. The goody-two-
shoes."

"Yeah. That's the one."

"No freaking way Brighton confided in his wife. He
wouldn't have trusted her."

"Apparently he did."

"He wouldn't do that to her, put her in such danger."

"He might have if there was no one else to turn to."

Kelly swished a wad of spit around his mouth. "Is she
alive?" he prodded.

"We think so."

"Have you looked for her?"

"Of course we have."

"And . . . ?"

"Is it possible you've missed the newspapers, Edward?"
The general's voice dripped with deep sarcasm. "Maybe you've

been busy with French wine and the lovely ladies down in Cannes, but things have been going kind of poorly over here. It's proving a bit difficult to find her, under the circumstances, don't you see? We can't find Washing-freakin-ton D.C., let alone a missing person from the city. So no, we haven't found her. If we had, she would be dead."

"Don't you know *anything* about her?" Kelly was incredulous now.

"We know she left the city."

"Alone?"

"No, with her kids."

Edward's mind was spinning now. He had an incredible memory, more than photographic, he remembered nearly everything he saw, heard, or read. He wouldn't have been worth a hundred thousand dollars an hour without extraordinary mental capabilities—and his brain was spinning now, sorting through his cerebral files. "She's got a son who's in the Special Forces."

"He set out to find her. He might be with her too."

Edward Kelly swore. Rubbing his feet against the leather floor, he thought. "Okay, let's say that Brighton told her. Assuming you are right and that he knew . . ."

"Let me say it again, Mr. Kelly. He knew. That's why we killed him."

"Okay, whatever, let's say he knew. I'll even give you that he told her. Who's she going to tell? Who would possibly believe her? I'm sorry, general, I still don't see what's got your shorts in such a wad."

The general snorted angrily. "What if I told you that, over the past couple of months, General Brighton had developed a very close and personal relationship with that idiot Brucius Marino."

"The Secretary of Defense!"

"Yeah. That's the one."

"We've been watching him! No way they could have been together and we not know."

"But we *do* know. Which makes us a little anxious. Why were they meeting? Why were they keeping it a secret? And where is Brucius now?"

Edward Kelly stood up from the bed, his heart racing. He walked toward the window, looking out. The sun was four hours from rising, but he wasn't going back to bed. He thought, pacing, his body casting a dim shadow across the soft floor from the moon. "We'll take care of Brucius Marino," he finally said.

"You've been saying that, Edward . . ."

"Shut up! You hear me, General Lafferty. Shut up and listen to me now. We *will* take care of Brucius. Now you go find that woman. We can't have her out there talking around, not until we've taken care of Marino. How many historic corners have been turned because of some meddling, wenchy *wife*? We're not going to let her turn this corner because she's messing with things out there.

"So take care of her, okay? We've got other problems, much more urgent and demanding. Smash this little fly so the group can concentrate on more important things."

chapter seven

RAVEN ROCK (SITE R), UNDERGROUND MILITARY COMPLEX
SOUTHERN PENNSYLVANIA

President Bethany Rosen sat uncomfortably at her large office desk, her broken leg stretched out before her. She was tired and irritable and, worst of all, terrified—for her country, her countrymen, her staff around her, herself. She felt the crushing responsibility of the presidency and wondered, deep inside, if she was up to the task. Leading the country, even at the best of times and under the best of circumstances, was a nearly impossible task. Leading them out of the darkness that enveloped them now . . . well, she simply didn't know. Could she do it? Could anyone do it? She took a breath and sat back, looking at the crowded desk around her. She had a pile of security papers on her left, another pile on her right, two piles right before her, another stacked against the wall behind her chair. She popped an antacid in her mouth and glanced down at her watch. It was impossible to keep track of time inside the artificial environment of Raven Rock and she was shocked to see that it was 2:05 A.M.

She moved her back painfully. She had no feeling in her broken leg. She'd been working for almost twenty hours straight and she desperately needed rest. So did her staff. She'd been driving them very hard. For every hour she worked, they worked two, and some of them had been without sleep now for almost three days.

Leaning back, she rubbed her eyes, feeling the strain against her forehead and down her neck. She stood and reached for her crutches, then looked over as her chief of staff, a former campaign manager and close friend, entered the private office. "How are the fallout readings in D.C.?" was the first thing she asked.

The chief of staff glanced at his notes and then looked up. "I'm not sure, Madame President. I could find out very quickly."

The president frowned. It was the answer he had given her this morning when she had asked the same question. "What about the results of the EMP? Is there any residual fallout or other health considerations?"

The COS glanced down at his clipboard once again. "Ma'am, from what I understand there are not now, nor will there ever be, fallout considerations from the warheads that were exploded over the United States. The detonations took place too high to settle through the upper atmosphere. But Bethany, you've got to remember, we are treading on virgin ground here. I'm not convinced anyone really understands . . ."

"I'm leaving Raven Rock first thing in the morning, then. I won't hide down here any longer. We'll stay away from D.C. for the moment—heaven knows there's nothing there to go home to anyway, not with the White House and Congressional complex and office buildings completely destroyed. We'll move the nation's capital to . . . where, Tom? I don't care, you and the staff pick a place. Richmond might be as good a spot as any; we'd be close enough to the remains of the government in D.C. that we could have access to whatever we have left.

But if you want to go to New York or Philadelphia, I'm okay with that, too. Either way, I won't stay down here any longer. I want to be up there and see for myself what's going on. I want to be up there with my people. I want them to see me and hear me and know that something, someone is still there, that the government hasn't completely folded and we are going to move on."

The COS dropped his clipboard to his side, his face concerned. "I'll check it through the Secret Service. They'll have to clear it first."

"Fine. Talk to them. Get it cleared. But tell them I will not take no for an answer. I'm not going to hole up here in Raven Rock forever. Three days have passed now since the EMP attack. I want to get up there and it's critical that I do."

More scribbling on the clipboard, the chief of staff's brow creasing as he wrote.

"And I want to address the nation as soon as possible," the president said. "Have the Emergency Communications Center set it up. I want to stand before our people and assure them that we are still here."

The COS looked around, almost laughing with sarcasm, but managed to hold it back. *We are here!* Yeah, there was a little truth in that, but it was pretty hard to sugarcoat the fact that the government had pretty much been destroyed. The nation was about to hear from their new president, a woman 95 percent of them didn't know and fewer of them could have even identified. And what was she going to tell them? *Hope you all got some food and water stuffed away because it's looking pretty grim.*

Hard to be optimistic when things had already crashed down on their heads.

Still, he kept his face straight, holding the sarcasm in. "I'll talk to the communications coordinator," was all he said.

"How many stations . . . what kind of coverage across the nation can we get?"

"I'm not sure, Madame President. I would think, based on the afternoon briefing, we can cover almost everywhere. A few remote pockets out west might be out of range, but it's my understanding you'll have pretty much coast-to-coast coverage, at least on the AM frequencies. The larger consideration is, how many people have access to working radios? Not too many, I am thinking, and even fewer will have working television sets. We're going to have to provide them. It's going to take some time."

The president nodded, then rubbed her eyes again. The chief of staff waited, his own knees feeling weak.

Through the silence, he reflected on the highly classified report sitting in the secure safe back in his office. The National Intelligence Brief was short and terrifyingly clear. And it was hot. Boiling hot. He felt his safe would explode. The picture that it painted of the country was as depressing as anything he'd ever seen. Many Americans had not eaten since the day of the attack. Most of them didn't have any drinking water. Perhaps half a million had died already from lack of emergency medical care. And the devastation was just beginning. It was going to go downhill. The United States didn't have a stockpile of food, not nearly enough to feed them all, and no way to distribute it anyway. They didn't have medical supplies, not to speak of, beyond the few days of inventory stockpiled on pharmacy and hospital shelves. They had no electricity, no sanitation or clean water; the list was so long and overwhelming it was crushing even to think about.

Worst of all, of the three hundred some-odd million Americans, two hundred and ninety-seven million of them were completely unprepared, expecting the government to take care of them. Not a highly accurate expectation, it turned out.

He cleared his throat and looked around, thinking of the president's request to get out of Raven Rock. Yes, they might be able to leave the underground command post for a few days, a few weeks even, but they wouldn't be up-ground for long. Conditions on the surface were deteriorating so quickly, they would soon be driven back to the safety of the secret command post. Within a few weeks, mass starvation was going to sweep across the nation. There would be food riots and chaos unlike anything ever seen before. Once that started—and his estimate of it being a few weeks away might be an overly optimistic one—they would need the security of Raven Rock once again, the food supplies and clean water and medications, everything the underground complex could provide.

It killed him to have to face it, but the truth was, they would end up back inside the Rock.

He looked around at the heavily paneled walls, thinking of the cold stone and thick cement that surrounded him two hundred feet beneath the surface. Putting the image aside, he turned to the president. "We'll set up the broadcast to the nation as soon as possible, but I have to ask you, Madame President, what are you going to say? What will you tell the people? How can you give them any hope?"

The former Californian senator closed her eyes and thought, almost wincing at the weight of the pressure on her shoulders. *What can I tell them?* she wondered to herself. *What can I tell them that they don't already know? They're not stupid; I can't fool them. But I can't just give up and lead them down a road of death and despair.*

She considered a moment, exhausted, her leg in real pain. Breathing slowly, she almost slipped into micro-sleep before the sound of the COS's body movements brought her back to the room. She opened her eyes and looked around, then turned to him. "All I can do is tell them the truth. It is ugly now. It will get worse. But we have to keep our faith and go on. Most of all, I want to remind them that we are not alone. God has guided our nation in the past and He will guide us even now. This greatest of all nations is still His magnificent cause, and the only thing we can do now is put our faith and trust in Him."

The COS stared, his mouth open. It wasn't what he expected, not from a woman who, outside of weddings and funerals, hadn't been inside a church in many years. Funny, he thought, how the situation had a tendency to refocus one's heart. Still, he understood it. Truth was, he was feeling a bit of religion himself.

"I will tell them that help is on the way," the president continued. "We have allies and friends across the globe. None of them were impacted by the EMP attack. They will stand by us now as we stood by them in the past."

No, the COS wanted to counter, *we are friendless and alone and we must recognize that now.* But he held his tongue, keeping his eyes on the floor.

"We have indescribable challenges," the president concluded. "We all know that. But we'll work together. We'll stand together. And yes, we will rise again." She hesitated, thinking. "The one thing I won't do," she concluded, nodding toward a red binder on her desk, "is shred the Constitution as we begin to rebuild."

* * *

The president slept inside a small apartment off the main command post. Twenty minutes later, as she lay atop her bed, her eyes closed, the stillness of the night around her, she was amazed at the almost perfect silence. Rock walls. Cement floors. Thick, blast-proof steel doors. All of it combined to stifle every sound and vibration, leaving the air unnaturally soundless and dull.

The night passed and, though she was exhausted, sleep was slow to come. Too many thoughts. Too many worries. Her chest was tight and every time she thought about the next day her heart raced again. Rolling to her back, she breathed deeply and, starting with her lower body, stretched her muscles to relax. Her toes. Her feet. Her legs. Her abdomen and arms. Everything was limp and soft now . . . her breathing was growing heavy . . . the tightness in her chest was gone . . . she was falling into darkness as she drifted off to sleep.

A final thought ran through her mind just before she fell asleep: Her husband and son were still out in Sacramento. She'd already made arrangements to send out a military jet. Soon they would be with her. Things would be a little better then.

With that thought, the president smiled lightly, then drifted off to sleep.

Twenty minutes later, she was dead.

*　　*　　*

The potassium chloride had been administered in the herbal tea she had swallowed just before slipping into bed. As expected, it was a perfect hit, leaving no trace of foul play behind.

Because both potassium and chloride are naturally found within the human body, the forensic pathologist had no evidence that an assassination had taken place. Later, during the autopsy, when examining the dead woman's heart, the pathologist noted all the classical indications of a massive heart attack: discoloration and swelling in the aorta, pockets of clear liquid throughout one chamber. His notes were textbook clear:

Unstable angina. Fatal outcome. Dynamic coronary thrombosis leading to infarction and sudden death. Possible peripheral embolization culminating in total vascular occlusion.

The only other medical discovery of any significance was the slightly elevated $CaCl$ levels within the blood—hardly interesting and certainly not suspicious.

Ventricular fibrillation leading to heart failure was the final conclusion of the forensic pathologist.

✳   ✳   ✳

Upon being told of the president's sudden death, the National Security Advisor turned away and sadly shook his head. "It was simply too much for her," he whispered to the general who had brought him the shocking news. "Truth is, the burden of the presidency might be too much to ask of anyone right now."

chapter eight

EAST SIDE, CHICAGO, ILLINOIS

They helped Luke up the bare cement stairway. Ammon held his brother's weight, his right arm around his waist, Sara on the other side. Luke was getting heavier as they climbed. Sam felt a mushy wetness against his hand and knew the dressing on Luke's back was saturated. His brother was growing weak now, but they all were. They were all exhausted, barely hanging by a thread, the last couple of days, the last week, the last month stripping them bare of any emotional reserves, leaving them physically and mentally worn down to the bone. As they worked their way up to Mary's apartment, Sam sucked a shallow breath. The stairwell stank, graffiti covered most of the walls, and just a hint of light bled in from the small, wire-mesh windows on each landing. Rounding the second corner, Sam heard a woman gasp and looked up. Mary Dupree was waiting for them on the third floor, Azadeh at her side.

Mary stared, her dark eyes wide in disbelief, her mouth wide. Stepping down, she glanced at Azadeh, then ran down the flight of stairs. Nudging Sara aside, she draped Luke's arm across her own shoulders. Azadeh followed, her face clouded with concern. Reaching out to Sam, she spoke in Farsi, but he didn't catch her hurried words and didn't understand.

Mary moved carefully, matching Luke's slow steps. "Why isn't he in the hospital?" she whispered to Sara as they climbed.

Sara patted her arm reassuringly. "It's okay," she said.

"They should have kept him in the hospital!" Mary's voice was angry.

"It's okay. Don't be upset. We'll explain everything."

Something in Sara's words settled Mary down and she turned her attention now to Luke. "Come on, baby!" she said as she helped him up the last flight of stairs, whispering encouragingly in his ear, like a mother to a child. "Almost there, baby. You can do it. Almost there." Her voice was soft, her accent musical.

Luke turned to her and smiled weakly. "I'm not dying here, Miss Dupree. You know that, right?"

"Shhh, child. You save your strength now. Mary's going to take care of you."

Sara listened, a weak smile crossing her weary face. So good. So strong. Mary was her family now.

* * *

They sat around the small kitchen table: Mary holding Kelly Beth, who was asleep now in her arms; Sara next to her, her hands resting on the table; Azadeh against the back wall, her eyes moving constantly, unsure of her status among the group; Ammon in the last chair, leaning heavily upon the table. Sam was sitting on the counter. Luke was in the back bedroom. He had a bit of fever but was sleeping now.

Ammon looked at all the others. "It's amazing," was all he said.

They sat in silence, thinking, wondering, trying to put the miracles they had witnessed into perspective. Mary held her little girl ever tighter, rocking her in her arms, holding her as if she'd never let her go. "It's not amazing," she countered, resting her chin on Kelly Beth's head. The child's eyes remained closed. "It's the hand of God, Ammon. Pure and true. The hand of God, just like in the Holy Book. The virgin birth. The rise of Lazarus. The healing of the leper. Mercy of the Father." She choked, her voice falling as she glanced down at the floor, then lifted her eyes up to Sara. "These sons of yours. This priesthood. Angels. Blessings. I don't understand any of it. I don't understand it at all. I don't know how it happened. All I know is what I know: My little girl was dying, dying right before my very eyes. I've watched others passing; I know what happens to them just before they slip away. They lose interest in the world, folding into themselves. They become smaller, shallow, the darkness drawing near. That was happening to my baby. She was just a day away . . ." Her voice trailed off again and she swallowed hard. "I had taken on her suffering as if it were my own. Her pain was my pain, her suffering was my suffering, her despair my own. How many nights had I begged Him for my daughter? Lord, I believe. Forgive me for my weakness. Help my unbelief. Lord, will you have mercy? Will you help my little girl? Help us, Lord, I begged him." She glanced again at Sam, who had given Kelly Beth the priesthood blessing, then shook her head. "I don't know how it happened. All I know is that it's true."

No one spoke. A sweet, peaceful feeling settled over the room as the sounds from the crowded streets drifted through the window. Azadeh kept her head down, trying to understand. So many new words, so many new ideas. Still, she understood the general feeling and somehow she knew that what Mary said was true.

Sara reached across the table and took Mary's hand.

"You're a good person, Mary, and God has heard your prayers."

"I know lots of good people who don't get answers to their prayers. At least that's the way it seems. So why me? Why my daughter? I feel so unworthy." Her lower lip trembled and her cheeks were stained with tears, but she didn't look away or waver, staring into Sara's eyes.

Sara tightened her grip on Mary's hand. "No one can answer that, Mary. You'll probably never know. But I do think that we were meant to be together. I think we were sent to find you, to help you and Kelly Beth. I think you were sent to help us, too."

"Me! I can't do anything for you."

"You don't know that, Mary. You don't know what the future has in store."

Mary's face was clearly skeptical. Sara patted her hand a final time and sat back. "Everything that has happened has to have happened for a reason. Everything we've been through, it is all part of the plan."

"The plan?" Mary wondered. "Do you really think God planned for this to happen?" She nodded to the small apartment window, indicating the death and chaos taking place down on the street. "Is all this really what He wanted?" She wasn't doubting. She wasn't faithless. She just really didn't know.

Sara looked down at the table, her mind flooding with memories of her husband, the strength of his arms, the smell of his hair, his patience, his faith, his determination to do the right thing, regardless of the cost. The life that he had chosen was full but as demanding as any she could imagine, hard and short. She thought of the endless nights she had waited for him to come home—days, weeks, months when he didn't come home at all. And now she would have to wait for years.

Such a long time. But she accepted that. It wasn't over, and she knew that she would see him again, maybe before she was even ready. She sighed, then turned to Mary. "*Everything* that happens is a part of His plan. No matter what happens to us, to our children, to either you or me, there is a purpose and reason for it."

Mary didn't answer as she clung to her child.

Ammon looked up at his mother. "How serious are Luke's wounds?" he asked.

Sara twirled her fingers nervously. She had wiped the blood away with a towel, but without any water she couldn't wash them and they were tinted crimson now. "I don't know. The wounds are deep, or at least they look deep to me. I changed the dressings. They bled awhile, but I don't know if . . ."

"They're fine," Sam broke in. He had examined Luke's injuries as well. "Two small entry and exit wounds. Believe me, I've seen way worse. They have perforated the skin and muscle and a little of the fat and tissue underneath, but they're not into the organs, certainly not as deep as bone. He seems kind of weak, but frankly, we all are. I'm sure the wounds will heal nicely and it won't take too long."

Mary stared at Sara, her eyes still wide in wonder. "An entry wound . . . an exit wound . . ."

No one said anything.

"My little girl here was dying . . ."

A deep and sacred silence.

Mary looked up at the heavens and lifted both of her arms. "Thank you, God," she prayed.

✴   ✴   ✴

They had dinner. It wasn't much, but it was enough to fill them: canned beans, Spam, a handful of crackers. They sipped the water carefully—it was the most precious thing they had, and they had much less of it than of food. After eating, Sam shot a wary eye toward the closet where they had hidden the three packs of supplies they had brought with them. Underneath the backpacks were two camel packs of water as well as a few other emergency items they had taken from the trunk before hiding the car in the stand of trees along the road. He thought of the other things left in the car: the gold coins, the rest of the food, the clothes, the sleeping bags, more emergency supplies. They had taken everything that they could carry with them, but they had also had to find a way to carry Luke, and so they hadn't been able to bring as much as Sam would have liked. Many items had been left behind, buried in the muddy earth not far from the abandoned car.

"All right, what are we going to do now?" Sara said.

No one answered. No one knew. Sara thought she heard a clock tick and looked around suddenly, the sound already foreign and out of place. No electricity. No clock. Of course, she had been wrong.

Sam slid off the counter and walked to the kitchen window. Something from outside had caught his attention, and he leaned across the old sink, standing on his toes to peer down on the street. "I don't know what to do," he said. "It seems there aren't any good options. But I will tell you this, we can't stay here."

Azadeh looked around anxiously. Up to this point she'd been quiet, but her eyes were expressive now and full of fear. Sara saw the look on her face but didn't understand it. Mary, who knew her better, leaned across the table. "We're trying to figure out what we're going to do now," she said to Azadeh to assure her. "Where we're going to go, how to get there, you know, all that kind of thing."

Azadeh concentrated, then turned to Sara. "When you say 'we,' you mean you and your sons . . ."

"All of us," Sara assured her. "We're going to stay together. We *need* to stay together. It's better for us all."

Azadeh's eyes remained wary. She didn't believe them, not yet, not completely. She wanted to. She desperately wanted to believe they wouldn't leave her, but little in her life experience indicated that that would be true. It seemed much likelier that they were going to dump her, abandon her at the earliest possible moment. She was a liability, not an asset, and she had been around long enough to understand how it worked. So, though she tried, she remained on guard, searching for advantage as they talked.

Sara turned to Sam. "You say we can't stay here," she said. "Are you certain that's true? This might be the best place we could be. It's safe, at least, and certainly better than being out there on the street."

Sam shook his head. "Maybe, but I don't think so. It's a rough neighborhood. We stand out. We're a minority and not a welcome one." He glanced at Azadeh. "Some even less than others. Hard as it will be for us, it will be much worse for her. She can't blend in. Everyone will know where she came from. And let's face it, no one's too thrilled about Muslims or Middle Eastern people right now, especially out there on the street."

"But she's going to be the minority anywhere we go."

"That's true, but it's a lot more than that, Mom. We need to get out of the city. From the looks of it, most people have decided to stay here. I'm guessing, like us, they don't have anywhere else to go. But it's going to get harder and harder to exist here. No food. No clean water. It can't hold up for very long. And when it falls, I like our chances much more out in the country than here."

Sara glanced at Ammon, who slowly nodded in agreement.

"I don't know if I should leave my home," Mary said, looking around the apartment she had lived in for so many years.

"We can't tell you what to do," Sara answered. "We'll do everything we can to help you, but the truth is, there's little we can do if you decide to stay here." She glanced down at Kelly Beth, who was still sleeping in Mary's arms, then nodded toward Azadeh. "You've also got to consider what is best for Kelly Beth and Azadeh. Are you going to be able to take care of them?"

Mary fell quiet. "I don't know how I'll even take care of myself."

Another cold moment of silence.

"We need to get to some other members," Ammon said.

Sara pressed her lips together. Her blonde hair was hanging limp now, dirty and lifeless, but she was still beautiful, and her face creased while she thought. "I've been thinking the same thing."

"If we could get to a church house, I think they would help us. They'll be organized. They'll have a plan. And it seems to me they'll have some instructions on what the Saints should do. They'll have food, maybe some other supplies . . ."

"Food?" Mary asked. "Why would they have food?"

Sara shrugged. Her mind shot back to the many times she and her family had been forced to move during her husband's military career. She thought of the moving agent walking through their house to estimate the total weight of their household goods, then going into the basement and seeing cans of wheat stacked up to the ceiling. She could almost hear his voice as he called out to his companion, "Hey, Ronnie, looks like we've got a bunch of Mormons here," swearing at the thought of hauling a thousand pounds of wheat and rice up the stairs. She smiled as she remembered, and Mary waited while she thought. "It's a little hard to explain," Sara finally said, "but members of our church have been encouraged to have a year's worth of food storage for themselves and members of their families. Some don't, but many do."

Mary's eyes grew wide. "You have a year's worth of food stashed away somewhere?"

Sara laughed. "I don't know if 'stashed away' is such a good description. Anyway, all of our storage, like everything else we own, we had to leave back in D.C."

"But all the other Mormons have an *entire* year's worth of food?" Mary sounded stunned.

"No, Mary, most don't have that much, I don't suppose, though I really don't know."

Mary thought, always rocking gently to keep the little girl from waking in her arms. "Does that mean the hard times are going to last a year?"

"I don't know, Mary. No one knows, though I kind of doubt that we can mark a calendar and start counting down a year. It's never that simple, is it? And it seems to me that God might have guessed there would be some people like us, members who have been cut off somehow, some people who couldn't get their own food storage—"

"Or didn't," Ammon cut in.

Sara pressed her lips. "Yes, or didn't choose to follow the counsel we were given. But either way, maybe God told people to have a year's worth of food not because He knew they'd need that much but because He knew that most people wouldn't do it and those who were faithful were going to have to share. Now, that's just my own opinion and maybe it's completely wrong, but I can't imagine some of our fellow members won't be willing to help us once they know the situation we're in."

Sam, who had been listening quietly to the exchange, finally spoke. "I don't have much time," he said.

Sara turned to him, her face falling.

"This war isn't over. I only have two weeks."

She stood and moved toward him and rested her head on his shoulder. "I'm just so thankful you were able to come to us even for just a few days. Imagine where we'd be if you hadn't come." The soldier held his mother. "How I wish you could stay," she whispered to him.

"Mom, you know I can't."

She pulled away and put the palm of her hand across his mouth. "I know. I understand. And I'm not angry. I've been married to a soldier for more than twenty years. Believe me, I understand. What it means is that we've got to move more quickly. We've got to figure out where we're going and what we're going to do."

Ammon stood and moved toward the telephone. Mary watched him. "It's not working," she said.

The phone was sitting on the edge of the kitchen counter. He didn't even pick it up. "You have a phone book?" he asked her.

Mary stood, walked to the cupboard, opened it, and dropped a thick black-and-yellow book into his arms. Ammon took it, thumbed through the back, referred to a couple of the maps in the front of the phone book, then motioned to his mother and Sam. They talked together. Wards. Stake centers. Bishops and presidents. Lots of things Mary didn't understand.

Ten minutes later, they had a plan.

chapter nine

The lieutenant sat alone on a cracked vinyl crew seat in the front cargo compartment of the air force transport, his army pack at his feet, his handgun strapped in a camouflage canvas holster at his side. Sometimes he dozed. Sometimes he stared, his head back, his vacant eyes looking straight ahead. Inside the cabin, it was noisy enough to make it difficult to communicate, and the crew members who passed up and down the cargo compartment seemed more than happy to ignore him as they went about their work. For two hours he hardly moved, though sometimes he would glance down at his watch. The interior of the military transport aircraft was illuminated only by a line of small, recessed bulbs that ran along the sides of the floor and a few red lights spaced out on the cabin ceiling overhead. The vibration of the four enormous engines hummed throughout the aluminum frame and the air smelled like ozone, dry and clean but a little too sterile to be comfortable. There weren't any windows in the cargo compartment but the cockpit door was open; if the lieutenant leaned over, he could look forward to the cockpit and through the front windscreen to see the utter darkness that had settled outside. It was shocking, how little starlight or even moonlight penetrated the clouds of dust that were blowing through the upper atmosphere—and there was not a single ground light anywhere.

Bono watched for a long moment, shook his head, then leaned back against his seat again.

The cargo master, an air force sergeant, walked past him to check his load, cursing the loose straps in overly colorful language and pulling them tight again. Walking back toward the cockpit, the sergeant—himself a little weary from having worked for more than thirty hours now—couldn't help but notice the strain in his passenger's face. The lieutenant was young and his hair and skin were so dark that he looked almost like a foreigner—Mediterranean, maybe Greek, maybe even Arab. It didn't matter, the sergeant figured anything but straight-up American was a real unpopular look right now. And the lieutenant acted tired. Dirt tired. Combat tired—the bone-crushing, muscle-sapping, eye-drooping weariness that comes only with war. The young man had seen a lot of combat; the master sergeant could see that in his face.

The loadmaster stopped and nudged him. "Hey, lieutenant, remember, you can sleep when you're dead."

Bono opened his eyes and looked up. The sergeant offered him a bottled water, which he took gratefully and almost emptied in a single gulp. The sergeant leaned toward him, talking loudly enough to be heard above the noise from the jet engines and hissing high-pressure environmental systems. "How come your watch is still working?" he asked, nodding toward Bono's wrist.

Bono didn't seem to hear him but looked down. "I was underground when it hit," he said. The sergeant tilted his head questioningly. "The Metro in D.C.," Bono explained.

The sergeant nodded. "You know how much a working

watch is going for down on the street? I know a guy who was over in Germany when the EMP hit. Just got back a couple days ago, so his watch was still working. Sold it for two thousand dollars yesterday. At least that's what he claimed. But he was an army guy so, you know, who knows if it was true." The air force sergeant smiled. Yeah, the world was falling apart, but things weren't so bad he couldn't still get in a little army dig.

Bono lifted his eyes but not his head. "Believe me, dude, I know what you're saying. Can't trust an army guy any farther than you could throw 'im."

The sergeant smiled again.

"Really, two thousand dollars?" Bono asked.

"That's what he said."

"Know what?" Bono answered. "I'd have kept the watch."

The enlisted man leaned forward, bracing himself as the aircraft bumped through a pocket of turbulence.

"U.S. bills, Monopoly money, it's all the same now," Bono said.

"No," the loadmaster shook his head, "it won't always be like that. Remember, the rest of the world is still out there, pretty much unfazed. They'll step in to help us. Things will soon get back to normal."

Bono thought of the nuclear bombs over Gaza, D.C., other cities in the world. He thought of the EMP attacks and the utter devastation they had swept across the country. "You really think so?" he asked. He wasn't smiling anymore; his eyes were sincere.

"Promise you, lieutenant." The sergeant patted Bono's shoulder. "Keep the faith, sir, keep the faith."

"Hope you're right." Bono closed his eyes and lowered his chin to his chest.

The master sergeant watched, then prodded him again. "Where you headed?"

Bono lifted the collapsed water bottle and sucked the last few drops. "Trying to get to Memphis. My wife and daughter are there."

The sergeant nodded toward the Special Forces emblem on Bono's lapel. "Special Forces, eh?"

Bono looked down at the pin. "I only wear it so I don't have to remind air force guys that I'm better than they are."

The sergeant faked a laugh. "Hey, good one. Never heard that one before."

Bono smiled and winked at him.

"You've been away a long time?" The sergeant was serious now.

"Way too long."

"Your family, they're okay, though?"

"Far as I know. They went to stay with my in-laws before the EMP hit. It should be pretty safe there, out in the country."

The sergeant nodded, then turned and walked toward the cockpit. Half a minute later he returned with a couple more bottles of water and handed them to Bono. The lieutenant took them, thanked the enlisted man, and stuffed them in his pack. The sergeant watched, then handed him his own half-empty bottle. "You need this more than I do."

Bono hesitated. "No, I'm cool. Thanks."

The sergeant shoved the bottle to him. "Take it."

Bono took the bottle and gulped the water down, a single drop escaping to his chin. "Thank you," he said.

The sergeant leaned toward him. "I hope you find your family," he shouted above the sounds of the cargo compartment.

Bono didn't answer.

"You got a ways to go to get from Little Rock to Memphis."

"Yeah. About a hundred miles."

"You got a way to get there?"

Bono looked away before he answered, "Not yet."

"That's going to be a problem."

Bono thought of his trek across Washington, D.C., just the day before: the forming gangs, the murdered husband and stranded wife, the fires, the unending lines of stalled vehicles, thousands of them, civilians hanging on him, begging him for water, food, or information. Yeah, it was going to be a problem. That much he knew.

The sergeant looked at Bono for a long minute, then slapped his shoulder. Standing, he made his way toward the back of the aircraft to check the cargo for their final approach and landing.

Bono's heart raced, a tinge of adrenaline rushing through him as he felt the aircraft begin to descend. Little Rock Air Force Base was straight ahead. A highway map was folded across his lap, and he spread it out and held it up against the dim light to study it. The base was twelve miles northeast of the city limits. He pressed the map with his finger, tracing a path toward the outer edge. He'd seen enough back in D.C. to know it would be better to avoid the major highways, so he planned to head cross-country for eight miles toward I-40, cross the Interstate, and continue southeast until he hit State Road 70, which ran toward Memphis. It would be far less crowded. Once he hit the state road, it was just a little more than a hundred miles to his in-laws' home.

A hundred miles. Less than a two-hour drive back in the old days. At least a four- or five-day hike in the brave new world.

Five days just to get there. *If* he didn't have any problems or run into trouble, which he knew he would.

He glanced at the empty seat beside him, wishing that

Samuel Brighton were there. He missed him. He missed his friend's company and sense of humor, but mostly he missed having someone he trusted at his side. He felt safe now, in this aircraft, but that was soon going to change. He was about to set off on a cross-country hike in a strange and uncertain world, and it would have been nice to have a buddy with him for the trek. Thinking of Sam, his mind drifted back to the last time he had seen his friend at Langley, when the two men had said good-bye. "I'm going to Chicago," had been Sam's last, frightful words. The decision made no sense, and at first it had left Bono completely speechless. But he knew now, though he wasn't certain why, that it had been the right choice. For whatever reason, Sam was on the right path.

The aircraft lurched through a bubble of cold air as it descended through a layer of clouds, then began a slow turn to the right. Bono felt the gentle pull of the turn pressing him down against his seat, and he leaned back. As his mind drifted, a twinge of excitement ran through him, a warm, fuzzy feeling that had sustained him through months of separation, loneliness, and fear.

Closing his eyes, he thought about his wife.

*　　*　　*

Bono would always remember the first time he had seen her, the entire scene forever imprinted on his mind. He could hear the sounds of the wind through the trees, smell the wet, fresh-cut grass, see the color of the sky, feel the lurch inside his stomach as she walked toward him, the sunlight on her face, the afternoon breeze playing with her hair. A senior at UCLA, he spent a lot more time hanging out at the ROTC building than he did with his fellow economics majors, most of whom were preparing for law school or MBAs. Truth was, he was dying to graduate, get through infantry school and into battle.

The last thing on his mind was getting married. After dating what he felt like was every single LDS girl in southern California, he'd pretty much given up on the whole marriage thing.

He was sitting on the steps of the Wooden Building (all of the campus buildings seemed to be named after someone famous), waiting for his ROTC squad to take to the intramural field, when she suddenly came around the corner of the building with a couple of her friends. Being drill day, he was wearing his cadet khakis and leather boots and, as she walked by, he felt suddenly self-conscious and unsure. Though she looked in his direction, she seemed to pay him no attention. He watched her approach, unable to pull his eyes away. She was tall and athletic (attending on a tennis scholarship, he would later learn) and the most beautiful girl . . . no, the most beautiful *thing* he'd ever seen. She was out of his league, he knew that, but he really didn't care. He'd never seen her before and chances were, large as the university was, he might never see her again. He had to talk to her, he simply had to, and he had to make his move *now.*

But he didn't. He just sat there, his mouth open, his eyes wide.

She passed by him, the cadet staring at her like a puppy. Ten feet down the sidewalk she unexpectedly stopped and turned around.

Taking a deep breath, he gathered all his courage, stood up, and walked toward her.

She waited. Her two friends kept on walking. Out of the three, she was the only one who had turned around.

"Hey there," he said as he drew close.

She looked past him, lifting on her toes as if she were looking for someone else. He shot a quick look behind him but there was no one there.

"Hey there," he said again.

She lowered off her toes and looked at him. Tan face. Killer eyes. His stomach flipped again. "Hi," she finally answered.

He stared, suddenly unable to think of anything to say, his mind empty as an arctic landscape. He felt stupid, his mouth dry, his mind completely blank. Through the awkward silence he started praying that she wouldn't ask him something complicated like, "What's your name?"

"What's your name?" she asked.

He almost panicked, his mouth open.

She watched, waited, then smiled, her eyes teasing. Tall as she was, she still had to look up at him. "Okay, we'll get that later." She nodded toward the cadet rank on his shoulders. "Are you a general?"

He shook his head. "Ahhh . . . yeah." He corrected himself. "I mean no. No. I'm not a general."

She moved her head again, tilting it to the right. "You're not?"

Bono completely missed the teasing in her voice. "No. Not yet. But I will be one day."

She couldn't help but laugh. "I was, you know, kind of kidding."

Bono realized how foolish he had sounded and looked down. She glanced toward her friends, who were waiting for her now, then nodded for them to go on. Bono stared down the sidewalk but hardly saw them. All he saw was her.

He swallowed painfully. "Whoa, that sounded kind of . . . you know, kind of . . ."

"Dumb," she answered for him.

Panic settled in again, his mind fading. She reached up and toyed with the lapels on his cadet shirt. "These are pretty cute."

Cute. Yeah, that was it. Cute. That was why he was going

into the army. "I've always thought the army had the cutest uniforms," he said in a very serious voice. "No reason you can't look good when you're out there killing people."

She looked at him, taken aback, then they both began to laugh. Extending his hand, he introduced himself.

"My name's Caelyn," she answered after learning his.

He watched and waited. "I don't get to know your last name?"

She eyed him without blinking. "No, not yet. You have to earn that." Another shot of sunlight cut through her hair. That killer smile once again.

He nodded to the steps but she didn't move to sit down. "Does anyone ever learn your last name?" he asked carefully, more than happy to stand if that was what it took to keep her there.

"A few. Not too many. As an army guy, I'm sure you understand. Got to make the enemy earn every inch he gets."

"Is that what we are, the enemy?"

"Believe me, if you'd dated some of the buffoons I've been out with, you'd know exactly what I mean." She always seemed to smile, but he could see that part of her was serious.

She glanced down at the book he'd been reading. Black leather. Lots of pages. Reaching down, she turned it over, her smile shifting just a bit. "The Book of Mormon?" she asked in surprise.

He fingered the scriptures nervously.

"You're a Mormon?" She almost seemed to laugh.

Was there disappointment in her voice? He wasn't sure. Still, for the first time since he had met her he didn't hesitate. "Yes, I'm LDS." He moved the scriptures to hold them in both hands. "I joined the Church my senior year in high school. It's been pretty much amazing since then."

She looked away, seeming to think. "That's going to be a problem," she answered slowly.

"How's that?"

"Well, let's say that one day I take you home to meet my parents. Now, not only would I have to tell them that you're going into the army, but you're a Mormon too. My mom's not going to like that. I don't know what she'll do."

Go home to meet her parents. He was ready right now. Meet the family. Set a wedding date. He was ready for it all. But all he did was nod slowly, unsure of what to say. Her sense of humor was unpredictable, like trying to stay ahead of a swirl of leaves in the wind. Then she nudged him on the shoulder. "Hey, general, don't worry too much. I'm sure we'll figure something out."

He pressed his lips together with concern. "It gets worse," he admitted, his voice low and tense.

"Really?"

"Afraid so."

"How's that?"

"Well for one thing, I'm Jewish. And I always vote Republican. On Wednesdays, I go door-to-door with a couple of friends who are Jehovah's Witnesses. On weekends I sell flowers on the street corner for the Moonies. I make my living telemarketing. And I just got out of jail."

She stared at him with a straight face. "Pretty much everything they could ask for in a potential son-in-law."

"Pretty much."

She stared off again, thinking deeply. "I don't know if they're going to be able to handle the whole Republican thing," she muttered sadly.

He matched her far-off stare. "My dad voted for Kennedy." His voice was hopeful.

"So you're open to negotiation."

He shrugged. "On a couple of things, I guess."

She reached out for his hand and shook it. "I think maybe we can reach a deal, then," she said.

*　　*　　*

They sat on the cement steps of the Wooden Building and talked for three hours. He missed his ROTC drills. She missed a lab. Neither of them noticed. Neither of them cared. Sometime after sunset, he walked her home. Sitting on the front steps of her apartment building, they kept on talking until sometime after twelve.

Early the next morning, he called her on her cell. She picked up as if she'd been waiting. What was the point in pretending? A ball had started rolling that neither of them could control. They didn't *want* to control it. They wanted it to roll.

"Have I earned an inch?" he asked before she could even say hello.

She didn't answer, puzzled.

"*You got to make the enemy earn every inch,*" he reminded her.

She laughed and answered, "Yeah, I guess you've earned an inch."

"Then I get to know your last name?"

"All right, general, my last name is Mckenny."

"Well, Miss Mckenny, are you doing anything tonight?"

"I'm sorry, but I'm afraid that I have plans."

The line was silent.

"I've got a date with a guy I'm really smitten with," she went on.

She could hear him deflate, his breath exhaling in her ear.

"He's intelligent and good-looking, but it seems like there's . . . I don't know, something more. I can't explain . . ."

He was silent; then he got it. He sat there stunned. Everything that he was thinking, she was thinking too.

"What time's good for you?" he asked urgently.

"Soon as you can get here, general."

"I'm on my way," he said.

Six weeks later she was baptized.

Two weeks after that, they decided on the wedding date.

✳   ✳   ✳

That was the way it was for them. They met, fell in love, and never once looked back. They didn't second-guess. They didn't wonder. They didn't have to. They knew they were lucky; only one in ten thousand relationships worked out like theirs did. And they were smart enough to appreciate it and be grateful every day.

As time passed and Bono got consumed with his military career, the months of separation, months of longing and waiting and dreaming of each other, only made the times they spent together seem that much more important and intense. Together or apart, when everything was said and done, when the frustrations and joys and disappointments were considered, they simply loved each other.

Some people said it was a fairy tale, but they knew it was more than that. This wasn't a fairy tale, this was real, and it was as eternal as it got.

Sitting inside the large cabin of the military aircraft, his face illuminated only by the dull red bulbs overhead, Bono smiled.

A hundred miles was all that separated them. A hundred miles. He would crawl to Memphis if he had to. He was going to see her soon. He was going to see his wife. He was going to hold his little girl.

His stomach fluttered just like on that first day that he had seen her. Life was good. He was happy. He was almost home again.

chapter ten

Something told her. She didn't know what it was or where it came from but something told her and she knew. *He's thinking about me right now.*

Caelyn stared up at the darkness. Okay, her husband, Bono, was still alive. That was good. But where *was* he? Iraq? Iran? Syria? Would he ever come home? Would she ever see him? Would she ever cling to him, press her cheek against his neck, and hear him whisper in her ear?

She wanted to cry, thinking of going through these dark days by herself. But she didn't. There were no tears now, just resolve and determination as strong as the family oak that was swaying in the night wind out in the yard.

As an army wife, especially the wife of an army Special Forces soldier, Caelyn was used to being on her own. She had known she would spend a lot of time alone before she'd decided to marry him. Still, the decision had been a no-brainer—better to have him briefly when she could than not to have him at all. And she'd never once regretted her decision, even on the loneliest of nights, even when she worried for his life.

93

Still, there were too many nights now spent down on her knees, pleading with God to bring him back to her. "*You promised me,*" she would whisper to the heavens in the dark. "*You promised. I believe you! Please don't let me down.*"

Moving slowly, she rolled toward her daughter, who was sleeping with her in the bed. A heart-wrenching sense of dread was building up inside her. She shook it off and sat up, placing her feet on the cold floor. Time to be strong, time to hold her fear in, time to brace herself for whatever it was that God had in store.

She looked at the dark window, then bowed her head and said another silent prayer. "*He's thinking of me right now. I know that. Will you please tell him that I'm thinking of him, too?*"

Opening her eyes, she stood up. Morning was coming soon, and there was a lot of work to do.

* * *

Later that day, Caelyn and her mother were working in the basement of the old farmhouse. The blonde-haired army wife turned toward the older woman and forced herself to smile. "It's going to be okay, Mom. We'll figure something out."

The other woman frowned as she turned back toward the shelves. Her hair was salt-and-pepper gray, her shoulders tired and smaller than they used to be, but her face was animated, her eyes defiant.

Looking at her mother, it was difficult for Caelyn to imagine how such a small woman could carry such a big stick. But it was true. Her mother was a fighter; she'd proven that all her life. Trouble was, sometimes she didn't know what she was fighting for. As the years had passed, Caelyn had sensed the frustration building up inside her mom. The woman had suffered a lifetime of battles, sacrifice, and unselfishness, most of it unspoken, and never known what it all was for.

If you'd only listen to me, Mother, I could help you. If you'd swallow your pride for just a moment, I could help you understand.

As Caelyn watched, her mother's eyes faded just a little. Caelyn realized the real change that was taking place inside: The confidence was fading, the fire inside her mom was growing cold, leaving just a flicker where there used to be flame.

Sometimes, when she was younger, Caelyn had wondered what it would take to bring her mother down.

Now she knew the answer.

It would take something like this.

Caelyn stepped back, felt the wooden stool behind her, and leaned against it, watching her mother count the bottles of peaches, beets, beans, and corn. Her mother had canned all the time when Caelyn was a little girl, but it was a lost art now and she hadn't done it in years. Why go through all the work and hassle? It didn't save any money. In fact, by the time they paid for the bottles, food, and supplies, it ended up costing more than store-bought food, not to mention all the work.

Caelyn looked around the basement storage room. Some of the bottles were so dust-covered she had to wonder if the food inside them was even safe to eat, knowing botulism was just as deadly as starvation. She thought back, trying to figure out how long it had been since she'd seen her mother in the kitchen bottling vegetables or fruit. Sometime back in college—probably her sophomore year, she decided, maybe five or six years before.

The air inside the storage room was cool and musty, the cement walls damp to the touch, and she almost shivered, pulling her arms tightly around herself as she watched her mother counting the bottles of food that were probably spoiled anyway.

Her mother finished counting, stood quiet for a moment, her eyes searching as if for more, then turned around. "Forty-two," she announced.

Caelyn forced another smile. "Okay, Mom."

"I counted them twice."

The younger woman stood up from the stool. "Good, Mom. Every little bit is going to help."

The older woman hesitated, disappointed. "I thought there was more. There *should* have been more. I was thinking last fall, Gretta, don't be so lazy. I know how much your father likes bottled peaches but it seemed like there was always something more pressing to do."

Caelyn heard footsteps on the kitchen floor above her and turned her head to listen. "Come on, Mom, let's go up and check on Dad."

Her mother moved toward the cellar stairs. As she walked by, Caelyn noticed that the soft skin around her cheeks was patchy white. Her mother had already lost a lot of weight and she was growing frail. Caelyn tried not to think about it, but she was worried about her mom.

"I should have been more prepared," her mother said as she started climbing the stairs.

Caelyn reached out and placed a hand on the small of her mother's back to brace her as she climbed. "No one saw this coming, Mom. There was no way you could have known."

Her mother shrugged, walked to the top of the cellar stairs, then turned. Caelyn looked up from two steps below her, blonde hair falling in front of her eyes. Her mother frowned uneasily, staring at her only child. "Your people knew," she answered. "We used to call you crazy." She turned and walked into the kitchen, heading for the sink. "Guess we're not laughing anymore."

Caelyn followed. Hearing squeals of laughter drifting from the backyard, she walked to the kitchen window to look outside, where her daughter was playing with the dog.

It had been several years since she'd been home. Looking out, she noticed that the oak tree was fuller now, the pines a good ten feet taller than when she was a little girl, the grass a little thinner beside the path, the honeysuckle that lined the ditch as high as the detached garage. She inhaled deeply, taking in the smells of the old house: pine cleaner, fresh dirt from the fields, the air heavy with lilac and hay, a bit of musty odor drifting up from the basement. The house creaked with a sudden gust of wind, the floor joists creating the familiar sound of old wood under strain.

She had been born and raised in this house. In fact, she'd never slept under another roof until she'd gone away to college, never called anywhere else home until she had gotten married and started following her husband around the globe. Every sound, every corner, every smell was as familiar to her as the back of her hand.

She stood there thinking of the old house as she watched her daughter playing in the yard. Her mother moved beside her and for a moment they watched together.

"She looks so much like you," her mother whispered, looking out on the blonde-headed child.

Caelyn smiled softly and answered proudly, "I think she looks like her dad."

"Either way, she's lucky." Caelyn's mother lifted onto her toes and kissed her daughter's cheek.

The little girl was playing with the old bloodhound, Miller (named after her father's favorite beer, though Caelyn would never tell her daughter that). The dog lay almost lifeless on the grass, the six-year-old draped over him like a blanket. The little girl rested her chin on his head and lifted his enormous ears against the sides of her head. The old dog endured the humiliation, lifting his eyes to the back of his head; then he rolled over, knocking the child onto the grass. He licked her face, his pink tongue covering her entire cheek, until the little girl giggled and squirmed away.

For one fleeting moment Caelyn was transported back in time, back to the day before the world had been turned on its head. She had awakened early that morning, what was it, a week ago now. Walking outside to watch the sunrise, she had felt the morning dew between her toes. It had been a peaceful, easy morning and she remembered feeling good. But as she had watched the eastern sky turn from purple to pink and then to gray, she had almost heard a voice. "*All of this is going to go away.*"

She had shuddered, not understanding.

"*What* is going away?" she asked.

But the voice had not answered.

Of course, now she understood.

The old dog got up and lumbered toward the shade at the side of the house. The little girl, Ellie, laughed and followed. The screen door to the kitchen opened and Caelyn's father plodded into the room, empty beer can in hand, the smell of smoke and pepper drifting in. Seventy-two. Gray hair. Small face. Her father was still a handsome man even if a little thin. Staring at him, she saw the simple innocence that seemed to keep him young. But she could also tell from his awkward walk that he was hurting with arthritis and it worried her, knowing he had less than two weeks' worth of medicine to treat the painful disease. A couple of days before, she'd walked four miles into town to see the pharmacist, but it was too late, they'd already sold out of everything. It was shocking to see how bare the grocery store shelves had been just three days after the attack. No food. No medicines. None of the most basic supplies.

Turning to her dad, she asked, "How's the jerky coming?"

Her dad coughed. "Pretty good. You're going to love it. I've got some Cajun jerky. Some pepper. A little jalapeño and salt."

Like most ranchers, Caelyn's parents had a freezer full of beef, but without electricity to keep it frozen they'd had to do something to preserve it before it rotted. So her father had improvised a smoker, spent a full day cutting the meat into thin slices, marinated it overnight, and was smoking it now, creating long strips of beef jerky that would keep for months.

"Be sure to get it dried all the way through," Caelyn reminded him as he walked through the kitchen. "We don't want any of it to rot."

Her father didn't answer, and she realized he hadn't heard her. "Dad," she said again, taking a couple of steps toward him, "are you drying it all the way through?"

He sat on a plastic-covered chair and looked up. "I don't know. You want to check it?"

Caelyn knelt down in front of him. "No, Dad, I don't have to check it. I'm just asking. We don't want to waste any of the meat."

Her dad wiped a sheen of sweat from off his temple. "I want you to check it for me, okay? I can't tell for certain. I don't want to mess it up."

Caelyn's mom walked over and patted him on the shoulder. "It's okay, Len. I'll check it for you. I'm sure you're doing a great job."

He reached up and touched her hand as she rested it on his shoulder. "A drink of water?" he asked.

Caelyn went to the container sitting beside the kitchen sink. Droplets had condensed on the metal can and she wiped them with her finger before pouring her dad a glass. Holding it up, she examined it against the sunlight. The water had been pulled from the small fishing pond down near the hay field, and though it had been strained and boiled over an open fire, there was no way to remove the tint of green from all the moss and vegetation in the pond. It tasted bad, even after being boiled, but she figured it was safe. Green or not, she knew what a huge blessing it was to have anything to drink. How many people out there had nothing now?

Turning, she took the glass of water to her dad.

"No beer?" he asked with disappointment. He'd been a two-beer-a-day guy for almost forty years. One in the morning, one at night. Never more. Never less. It was one of the peculiar habits he'd picked up after the accident.

"Nope, Dad, no more beer. Isn't that great! I've been trying to get you to quit that nasty stuff for how long now?" She patted him on the shoulder. "Looks like I get the last word."

Her dad took the glass of water and drank half down. "I'm not sure it's worth it anymore," he said sincerely. "Life without beer. No TV to watch the Yankees. Might as well be dead."

Caelyn smiled, hoping he was kidding, but not really sure. It was another peculiar habit of her father's—he was brutally honest, the connection between his brain and his tongue as straight and sure as any truth machine.

Her mother watched them, then turned toward the screen door. "I'll check the jerky," she said.

Caelyn gently rubbed her father's shoulders, feeling his thin muscles and tired bones.

*　　*　　*

Everyone who met her parents thought they were an extremely unlikely couple. And it was true, although Caelyn knew that hadn't always been the case.

100

Her father was from Buffalo, New York, and held a master's degree in chemical engineering from NYU. Graduating magna cum laude, he was on his way to a very successful career when he met the young woman who would become his wife. Her mother was a southern belle, her family roots going back to the gentlemen's South of Charlestown and the Civil War. Her mother's parents, the grandparents she'd never known, were the last of the old southern heritage. Solid, frugal, and pampered by old money until the Great Depression came and took it, her grandparents had been left with nothing. Without financing for proper upkeep, the old family farm, plantation house, and outbuildings fell into decay, forcing her grandparents to sell. They moved to Memphis, where her grandfather bought a much smaller farm and eked out a humble living while raising nine kids, Caelyn's mother being the youngest one.

Part of a song-and-dance troupe during her freshman year in college, her mother had met her father on a weekend trip to New York City, where the group had performed for a local talent show. Three months later, to the dismay of both families, they were married. Scandalous to marry a Yankee, a man who had never even *visited* the South; her mother's family had nearly gone into shock. Wanting a fresh start, the young couple had moved to California, where Caelyn's father took a job with an up-and-coming pharmaceutical firm. Big money was on the horizon. Soon there would be children, one day a big house with a pool. Life was good and getting better and there was no reason to expect that anything would ever change.

Eight months after they had moved to L.A., her father's car was struck head-on by a drunk driver coming at him on the exit ramp of the 101 freeway. Two cars, each traveling forty miles an hour. Eighty miles an hour between them. Metal on metal. Engine on engine. Glass on glass. The drunk driver was killed, the steering wheel of his Plymouth compressing his chest against the back of his spine. Her father wasn't wearing a seatbelt—no one wore seatbelts in those days—and the collision sent him crashing through the glass. The police found both men in the front seat of the drunk driver's automobile.

At first the doctors told her mother that her husband had been killed. Then, even with the sheets pulled up over the patient's head, an intern had found a pulse, weak and erratic. Frantic work from a brilliant team of doctors seemed to bring her father back to life.

Three months of coma followed, each day full of fear and dread. Then one Sunday morning he opened his eyes, told his wife he loved her, stared at the ceiling for a moment, then rolled over and fell asleep again.

But it was a sleep, not a coma. He snored. He moved. He even mumbled once or twice. That night, Gretta stood beside his bed, desperately holding his hand. In the morning, he woke up and rolled over. This time he tried to smile.

Five months after the accident, he went home from the hospital and started another journey, learning to walk and talk and feed himself again.

Two years later, he proudly struggled through a first-grade book of *Dick and Jane*. Gretta smiled at him broadly as he read, but inside, she was weeping like a child, knowing he would never work as a chemical engineer again.

The years came and went with very little to note their passing. They sold the new house down in Huntington Beach and moved up to Ontario, not as nice, but much cheaper. Her mother worked as a receptionist while attending night school, then started teaching first grade. Her father took care of the neighbors' yards. Five years of teaching came and went. Her father learned to ride a bike. Her mother turned thirty, then thirty-five, and still no children. Her father got a job as a custodian at the school. Forty came. Not much changed. Her father worked weekends in the yard.

Then something happened to stir things up a bit.

Back in Memphis, Caelyn's grandparents fell sick and died within five days of each other. None of the other children wanted the family farm so, after almost twenty years in southern California, her parents decided it was time to make a change. Caelyn's mother packed up their belongings, sold the house, gave up the California sunshine, and moved back to the family farm twenty-one miles outside of Memphis, where they settled in to grow old. She got another job teaching school. To her great delight, her husband seemed to thrive taking care of the old farm.

Caelyn's mother accepted things for what they were, thinking this was as good as her life was going to get.

Then she received another piece of astounding news. For weeks she lay awake at night, smiling at the darkness, far too happy and excited to sleep.

Seven months later, on her mother's birthday (surely a sign from God, her mother always said), and with a rare Memphis snow outside, Caelyn was born into this world.

After twenty years of feeling as if she was more or less alone, like a sudden gift from heaven, Gretta held a little baby in her arms.

*   *   *

Caelyn Mckenny Calton watched through the kitchen window as her mother poked at the fire underneath the homemade smoker. Watching her mother was like looking into a crystal ball; a time machine couldn't have shown her any better what she would look like when she was sixty-nine. And they had much more in common than just their looks. Both had quick hands and quick emotions, quick to joy, quick to anger, quick to cry. Both were fiercely independent, opinionated, and strong.

Southern women. Southern pride. It shone in both of their eyes.

Yet as much as they were the same, there was a vast difference in their outlooks now. And the differences between them had grown larger with the passing of each year.

Caelyn had a softer side. A gentler side. A certain trust in God. Her mother was not like that. She was less feeling underneath. She'd lost her religion out in California and wasn't particularly interested in looking for it anymore. She wasn't hardhearted, really, just less willing to feel, the experience with her husband having left her cautious and on guard. Like a drying limb on a gnarled cedar tree, she was strong and unbending, but tight and knotted up inside. Making her caution worse, the only good thing that had ever happened to her had been her little girl, and the years they'd spent together had proven far too short. Before she knew it, Caelyn had gone off to college and fallen in love with some army guy.

It had proven very hard for her mother to let go.

Which made their relationship difficult at times.

chapter eleven

The man was exhausted. His muscles ached, his head hurt, his arms were sore from driving, and it was getting late. He was hungry and thirsty and more than ready to head home. He and the boys had been up since way before dawn. The sun was close to setting, and he knew how utterly dark it would be once it went down. And there weren't any headlights on the old tractor that he was driving, which meant that if he didn't turn around, it would be a long, stressful drive back home. He glanced up at the setting sun, thinking of the moon. Yes, it would be up there, but he almost feared it now. Bloody red. Evil looking. Like the devil glaring down.

He shifted in the old seat and almost swore. He didn't understand it at all. They'd completed their assignment. It was time to go home. On the old tractor it was an hour's drive, at least, back to his home.

Yet he kept driving in the other direction, steering the tractor down the road. "*Keep on going. There are others,*" the voice inside him seemed to say.

But there *were* no others. Whatever foolish prompting he was having, his mind told him it was wrong. He knew everyone who lived within their ward boundaries—he knew them very well. And no one else was out there. He had seen them all.

He slowed the tractor. It was time to head on home. He didn't want to be out here after dark. He could feel the evil growing close.

Still, the voice persisted in his heart. *"Keep on going. There's one more."*

The driver shook his head. He was a simple man. He wasn't ever going to make a million dollars or watch himself on TV; he'd never be famous or elected to some big-time public office. But this much he knew: The Spirit was talking to him now. He recognized the feeling. *"Keep on going. Keep on going. Yes, there is one more."*

He mentally reviewed the list of ward members for the third or fourth time. No. There were no more. He had visited them all.

If it was the Spirit that he was hearing, then the Spirit had it wrong. No matter what it told him, he knew there were no more members down this road.

Still, he kept on driving, fighting the terrifying urge to turn around.

The Spirit wasn't the only voice inside his soul.

"I own the night!" the evil taunted him. *"Stay out here and I'll kill you. I'll send a mortal out to find you—there are dozens of them around here who are under my control. Fear the darkness. It's my kingdom. Don't be a fool. You've got the two boys. I could kill them too."*

The man hesitated, glancing fearfully over his shoulder.

"Stop," the evil hissed again. *"Stop and turn around!"*

"No," the Spirit whispered, *"there is another out there, someone the Father cares about. She's been praying for you, brother. You cannot let her down. Don't fear the darkness, it is empty. They cannot hurt you if you keep your faith strong. You are on the Master's errand. He'll protect you. Now please, don't turn around."*

chapter twelve

Caelyn gave her dad a final pat on the shoulder, then moved toward the kitchen door. It creaked on its hinges, but the spring that pulled it closed behind her was firm and strong. Like everything else on the farm, the house was well maintained. She stepped onto the back porch. The clapboard home, two stories, white with dark green shutters, faced west and the sun was setting now, providing cool shade on the back porch. Her mother had moved around to the south lawn where the smoker had been set up at the edge of the grass. Caelyn walked to the side of the house and rested against the corner, taking in the view. Green pasture in the back, a heavy tree line on the far side, a strangely shadowed sky overhead. It was quiet, so quiet she could hear her heart pulsing in her ears. The road out front was completely deserted. No birds. No wind. No movement of the trees. To her left, a golden field of wheat had been cut down to the nubs, leaving only straw, the grain having been harvested back in July. What would they give to have the wheat back now? A lot. A real lot. But it didn't matter, it was gone, sold to the granary on the edge of town, augured up into the silver tower, then dropped

107

into waiting railroad cars and hauled off to General Mills or Betty Crocker or some other mill somewhere. Caelyn swallowed, wishing desperately that her father had held onto even a little of the grain, but he didn't have anywhere to store it. Truth was, no farmers raised food for themselves anymore. They grew the crops and sold them, then, same as everyone, bought the finished products at the store. Turning her head, she looked north. Barns. An old milk parlor. A cement and metal manger where they used to feed the cows. Her father ran a simple operation. A little wheat. Corn. Soybeans. He had a herd of forty heifers but the yearlings had all been sold. Most of the mother cows were pregnant now and would calf again during the coming winter.

As a precaution, they had moved all the cattle into the back pasture, where they couldn't be seen from the road. Was it necessary? She didn't know. So far, they'd been left alone. A couple of the neighbors had come by a time or two, but those were the only people they'd seen since the EMP attack. Still, they'd heard rumors of things that were happening in the city and the suburbs: mean things, scary things, desperate stories. People were getting hungry now. Could parents watch their children begin to starve without doing something to help them? Not for long. So, thinking it might help avoid a conflict, Caelyn and her parents had moved the cows into the south pasture. Having the cattle out of sight would probably help, at least for a while, but eventually they were going to run out of hay to feed the animals. As it was, they had enough to last through December, but that was about all. And it would be impossible to buy any more; her father had checked. No one was selling. Without extra hay, come December, their mother cows would start going hungry. Caelyn knew it wouldn't matter anyway; the herd would be slaughtered and eaten long before then. She didn't know how or by whom, but it would happen. The cows were food. Food was scarce and getting scarcer. Eventually someone was going to come and take their herd.

The wind suddenly picked up and shifted from the south and the smoky smell of mesquite blew toward the house. She sniffed, her stomach growling, an empty pit between her ribs. She hadn't eaten much over the past four or five days—partly out of nerves, mostly out of a sudden, deep-seated drive to conserve whatever food they had—and her mouth started watering as she smelled the drying meat.

She walked toward her mom. "How's it going?" she asked as she approached the silver smoker.

Her mother lifted the lid from the metal garbage can, and a puff of white smoke billowed out. Picking up some old hot pads, she carefully removed the meat-covered grates fitted inside the can, dropped a handful of water-soaked mesquite chips into the fire box, replaced the grates, and put the lid back in place. "You know, this smoker your dad made is working really well."

Caelyn studied the homemade smoker: an old metal garbage can, a metal chip box, a couple of metal grills. Her father had cut a six-inch hole in the bottom of the garbage can, dug a pit to allow for venting, then built a small fire and put the lid in place. He'd even installed a small thermometer, an engine temperature gauge he had taken from an old tractor, which read 224 degrees, right where they wanted it to be. "It's amazing he could come up with this so quickly," Caelyn said, glancing back toward the house. Her father had followed her out and was now sitting in the wicker rocking chair on the porch.

There was no greater evidence of the intellect that remained inside him than his uncanny ability to build or fix almost anything on the farm, working on machinery as if he'd designed it himself. He couldn't tell you who the president of the United States was, balance a checkbook, or add up a simple column of three-digit numbers. He couldn't follow a story from a newspaper or tell you anything about the war, yet he could quote the batting records of his beloved Yankees for every year since 1970 as well as every Super Bowl final score. Most times it was like he was in a deep fog. But sometimes the stupor lifted. Muttering, he would scribble on hastily arranged pieces of paper as old designs and formulas popped into his head. It was as if he knew, somewhere deep inside him, that his brain used to work on a different level than it now did, as if a part of him remembered the statistical formulas and chemical theorems he'd spent so many years coming to understand. Sometimes she could see the frustration that was bottled up inside. *"It's still there,"* his eyes would plead. *"Can you see it? Do you believe me? The intellect is still inside me! But it's just so jumbled up!"*

It was as if, after the accident, part of his brain had been sent back to when he was a small child, making him almost impossible to predict or understand. But from time to time there were powerful reminders that the man trapped inside the wounded mind was still there.

Her father saw that she was staring at him and he smiled happily, the youngster inside him always friendly. She smiled and waved back, then turned toward the smoker. The jerky was almost done, a full side of beef, enough to keep them in meat for at least a couple of months.

If they were careful and didn't waste it.

And if other people left them alone.

Her mother adjusted the garbage can lid, making certain it was tight, then brushed a smoky strand of hair away from her eye. "Where's Ellie?" she asked.

Caelyn nodded over her back. "Last I saw she was chasing Miller around the other side of the house."

Gretta turned and shaded her eyes to the dropping sun. "She's doing okay, I think. Don't you?"

Caelyn pressed her lips before she answered. "She doesn't really understand what's going on."

Gretta frowned a little, her eyes moving constantly up and down the road. "I don't know," she answered carefully. "Sometimes I think little kids know more than we give them credit for. She hears us talking. She hears the tone of our voices. But it's more than that. Children have a sense for these things. Ellie certainly does. She's a smart girl. She knows something's going on."

Caelyn folded her arms across her chest. "I hope not. I really hope not. She's far too young . . ."

"She's a strong girl, honey."

"Yeah, but she is a *little* girl. Hardly more than a baby. I don't want to steal her childhood. She deserves more than that. I absolutely want to keep things on an even keel for her for as long as we can."

Gretta hunched her shoulders, thinking. "Maybe that's not the right thing to do."

"How's that, Mom?"

"Maybe you should tell her. I don't mean tell her everything, but you know, give her some idea why things have changed. You can't hide it from her forever. She's eventually going to know. We've got no car. No electricity. No running water. We're scared to go into town. You don't think she's noticed any of this already? No, she's noticed, and she wonders. I think you need to tell her enough so she won't worry even more. If you don't, trust me, Caelyn, her imagination is going to kick into gear. And a six-year-old's imagination can come up with some pretty scary things all by itself."

Caelyn thought before she answered. "I don't know, Mom. I don't want to worry her. There's no reason to make things any worse."

"Caelyn, she already knows that something's *very* wrong. You need to give her some information, even if just a little. Assure her, yes, we all need to do that, but you've got to explain to her that the world has changed."

Caelyn put her hand out toward the garbage can, exposing her palm to its heat, letting her fingers drift through the smoke that was seeping from under the heavy lid. "She'll be okay, Mom."

"She'll be okay! Caelyn, are you kidding? What is there about this situation that makes you think any of us are going to be okay?"

Caelyn dropped her eyes, feeling the burden of responsibility once again. "It'll be okay, Mom. You'll see. There's help out there. We aren't in this alone."

Gretta stared at her daughter. "I love you, honey, you know I do. I love you more than anything I have left in this world. But you've got to understand something. I've been alone for almost my entire life. Yes, I've had your father, but you know the situation there. He's loyal and dear and I love him through and through. If there is any justice in this world—and maybe in the end there isn't—but if there is, he will die and go to heaven without having to stop at Peter's Gate. He'll be saved with all you Mormons, he's that good of a man. But that aside, I've been alive long enough to know you've got to take care of yourself. And that's truer now than it's ever been. We can't count on anyone to help us. We are alone now, you and I."

Caelyn nodded slowly but didn't say anything.

Gretta checked the temperature on the garbage can,

started to say something more, then cocked her head and listened. "You hear that?" she asked.

Caelyn turned toward the road, catching an occasional sound drifting and fading with the wind.

"Something's coming," her mother said anxiously, turning toward the house. Walking across the grass and onto the porch, she told her husband, "Come inside with me, okay?"

Caelyn faced the road and squinted. Her back to the house, she heard the screen door behind her open and then shut. She stepped toward the road. A large, green farm tractor, the raised exhaust pipe belching black smoke, pulled a small wagon down the road. Two young men steadied themselves near the front end of the wagon. The tractor driver was hidden inside the tinted cab.

Caelyn lifted her hand to protect her eyes against the sun. The tractor lumbered closer. The hair on the back of her neck stood on end.

chapter thirteen

It was a worn-out John Deere, old, layered with dust and tinted with rust spots on the metal fenders that wobbled over the back tires. The glass cab reflected the slanting rays of the late afternoon sun as the tractor turned into the driveway that led toward the detached garage on the back side of the house. Caelyn glanced toward the wagon. Two young men balanced themselves beside old cardboard boxes stacked three high. She tensed as they approached. She didn't know these men. Somewhere behind her, she heard her mother calling, "Ellie, come on in here." The urgency in her mother's voice left no room for the little girl to argue, and almost immediately Caelyn heard the sound of light footsteps across the porch. Caelyn kept her eyes on the strangers, her shoulders square. The tractor moved toward her and stopped. The driver cut the engine, the cab door popped open, and a white-haired man dropped from the tractor to the ground.

"How you doing?" he called out. He stood beside his tractor, pulling leather gloves from his hands. Caelyn studied him quickly. Weathered face. Dark, drooping eyes. Old Wranglers. A checkered shirt. Obviously a man who'd spent his whole life on the farm. She answered cautiously, "Doing good. How are you?"

The old man shrugged, then nodded around him. "Been better, I guess. Figure we all have."

The two young men—she could see now that they were no more than teenagers—moved to the front of the wagon and seated themselves, their legs hanging over the edge. They didn't say anything. She quickly took them in. Short hair. Clean faces. Old work clothes. Neighbor farmers? Probably. She started to relax.

The older man took a step toward her and frowned. "You alone?" he asked, glancing over her shoulder to the old farmhouse behind.

She immediately grew tense again. "My mom and dad are in the house," she answered quickly, her voice hard.

He stared toward the house. "Are you sure?" he pressed.

Caelyn's eyes grew angry. "Of course I'm sure."

"You're Caelyn, right?"

She hesitated. "Maybe. Who are you?"

The old man turned away from the house and focused on her.

She knew she had to be careful but, as she looked into his soft face and friendly eyes, she relaxed again. She had a sensitive spirit. It was one of her gifts—she could sense a person's goodness before that person said anything—and looking at him, she knew instantly that she need not fear this man.

The stranger took a step toward her. "I'm Brother Simpson." He extended his hand. "You probably don't remember me. You and your husband were out here a couple summers ago. I used to be the bishop. We met once or twice at church."

Caelyn froze, too stunned to move. "Really?" she said, her voice cracking. "Really. Yes, I remember, Bishop Simpson. Of course." She moved toward him and they shook hands. She stood back, her face radiating relief, then started bouncing up and down. "Of course! Of course! I remember you. I am so glad to see you. Thank you, thank you, for coming by." She bounced again, embraced him, then quickly pulled back again. "I'm sorry, I'm sorry, it's just that I'm *so* glad to see you!" She embraced him one more time.

Simpson smiled at the happy greeting, then wiped a leathery hand across his brow. "These are a couple of my grandkids, Josh and Boyd." The teenagers waved and muttered "hey" but didn't get up from the trailer. In fact, they hardly seemed to move. She studied them. Taking in the weary shoulders and hanging heads, she realized they weren't being rude or disinterested—they were just exhausted. And maybe a little scared.

"They're good kids," Simpson said, seeming to read her mind. "Usually they're more outgoing, but we've been up since nearly four o'clock this morning and I've run 'em pretty hard. But they're young, right men," he looked back over his shoulder, speaking to his grandsons now, "and tough as nails. A hard day's work isn't going to kill 'em."

"Sure, Grandpa," the oldest one said, though the tone of his voice made it pretty clear he wasn't sure.

Simpson turned back to Caelyn and studied her. Blonde hair down to the top of her collar. Deep blue eyes. Small frame. Long neck and slender fingers. He frowned and looked around, thinking of the neighbors and others who lived along this road. Dangerous to be so pretty in this unpredictable new world.

She bounced again, not seeing the concern on his face. "What are you doing here!" she asked, her smile so radiant he finally couldn't help but smile back.

Simpson adjusted his worn-out White Sox baseball cap. "We've been going around some of the ward, checking on a couple of folks. Thought I'd . . . you know . . ." He hesitated, looking off at the horizon.

"You knew that I was out here?"

"Not really. I just . . ." Again, his voice trailed off.

Caelyn watched him, waiting for more explanation. Simpson was quiet, seeming lost in thought. Caelyn smiled faintly, then nodded to the house. "My mom and dad are inside."

Simpson glanced across the grass. "I don't know your parents very well. Met your mom a couple times. She can be a real rascal." He laughed. "She's probably got a deer rifle aimed at my chest right now."

Caelyn's eyes sparkled. "I don't think so. A potato shooter, maybe. Far as I know, my parents have never owned a gun. They came here from California, remember. Not much of a gun culture out there."

Caelyn's mother stepped out onto the porch.

"Do you know my dad?" Caelyn asked.

"No, not really. I live five or six miles down the road, then up toward the highway, so our paths have crossed from time to time, but that's about all. Your parents haven't ever visited church though, am I right? You're the only member of your family who is LDS?"

"My husband is as well. He joined the Church in high school. I was baptized a couple of weeks after we met. We visit the ward whenever we come home to see my parents, but I'm afraid that isn't very often and they never come with us to church. Not much interest, I'm afraid. Maybe someday. We keep on trying."

"Understand. We keep on trying. Sometimes that's all we can do." Simpson stepped to his side and waved to Caelyn's mom. Gretta hesitated a moment, then stepped off the porch and walked toward them.

"Hey there," he said when she approached. "Walter

Simpson." He extended his hand. "We've met a couple times, but it's been a long time."

Her mother stopped in front of him and shook his hand. "Sure, Walter, I remember. What brings you out here?" Caelyn sensed the edge in her mother's voice.

"Just out checking up on people, you know, seeing if everything's okay."

"You live . . . ?"

"On the other side of Edmondson."

"Kind of a long way from home, aren't you?"

"Oh, I don't know, not too far, I guess. Of course, we're not checking on everyone between here and my place, just a few members of our ward. I used to be the bishop of the local LDS congregation. I was about finished and ready to head back home when . . ." he paused. "It occurred to me that Caelyn might be out here visiting her parents. Thought I'd come out and see if everything's okay."

Caelyn watched her mother closely. Gretta didn't relax at all. Always too suspicious. Not unfriendly, just overly careful. It was the way she'd always been.

Simpson saw the reservation on her face. "So, you're doing okay?" he asked. "Do you need anything?"

Gretta squared her shoulders a bit too proudly.

Simpson saw it and grinned again. "No, Gretta, we're not out inviting people to come to church and get saved, although," he nodded toward the small town of Edmondson off to his right, "there's plenty of that going on at some of the town churches, from what I understand. But anyway, like I said, we're just out checking up on everyone."

Gretta shook her head. "We're doing fine. Thanks for asking, Walter, but there's nothing we need here."

There was the sound of footsteps crossing the wooden porch and Caelyn turned around. Her father had walked out of the kitchen and was standing near the screen door, holding it open. Ellie ran out of the kitchen, jumped off the porch, and fell onto the soft grass, then pushed herself up and ran toward her mom, grabbing her by the knees. Simpson knelt down to look at her. "Holy cow, what a little cutie!" He looked up at her mom. "The spitting image of you. People must tell you that all the time."

Caelyn smiled proudly, patting her daughter gently on the head. "Thank you," she said, pulling Ellie close.

Simpson glanced back toward his grandsons.

"How'd you get your tractor working?" Gretta asked.

"Mostly because it's so old. Not much as far as electrical wiring and fancy stuff for the EMP to burn out. All the new tractors, heck, they've got more wiring and computers than the space shuttle, I think. But these old things, they're pretty simple. Easier to keep them chugging along."

Gretta nodded toward the road. "I haven't seen any tractors or other farm machinery up or down the road. None of ours is working, and we've got some old stuff too."

Simpson shrugged. "I don't know . . . it's kind of a long story." He glanced at Caelyn as if somehow he expected her to help him explain.

"A long story?" Gretta said. "I think we've got time to hear it, Walter."

The older man shifted from one leather boot to the other. "It's kind of hard to explain."

Caelyn's mom kept her eyes on him, waiting.

"Okay, I guess it's not so hard to accept if you've a mind to. A couple weeks ago I was into the Farm Supply in Edmondson getting some sheer bolts for the plow when," he paused, reached down, pulled a long blade of grass from the ground, and put it in his mouth, holding it between his teeth, "when I heard a voice," he continued. "'*Pick up parts to rebuild the wiring on the old John Deere tractor,*'" it said.

"At first, I tried to ignore it, but it seemed to come back again. '*Pick up parts to rebuild the wiring on the old John Deere tractor.*'

"Kind of weird, huh, hearing voices when I'm out shopping for farm parts. But there it was. I figure, who am I to argue? So I bought some electrical parts. Turns out I got everything I needed to get Bertha running after the EMP attack. None of the secondary electronics on the tractor work—the wiring for the lights and stuff has been fried and I had to wire the battery directly to the starter—but, as you can see, I got the old girl running."

Caelyn watched him, a new understanding in her eyes.

Gretta's face was disbelieving. "You heard a voice?" she asked.

"Kind of," Simpson answered sheepishly.

"Really? It helped you with your shopping list?"

Simpson kept his eyes on her, a friendly smile pasted on his face. "God works in mysterious ways, doesn't he, Gretta."

She started to answer but Caelyn quickly interrupted. "Bishop Simpson, are you telling us that even when something's been destroyed by the EMP, it can be fixed?"

"Certainly. If you have the parts. But that's the problem, of course, no one has the parts. Not near enough to go around. How much of our farm equipment will we have replacement parts to fix? I don't know. Not too much, I guess. Maybe a dozen or two tractors in the county. Two dozen out of two or three hundred. That's not enough to make much of a difference, I suspect."

"But if we can get the parts, we can rebuild things? And replacement parts can be made, is that right?"

Simpson sucked the piece of grass. "Yeah, but think of this.

All the factories are down. No electricity anywhere. Most of these kinds of things are made overseas anyway. Now, that might be good news or bad news, depending on how this works out, I guess. Will the Chinese or whoever sell us the things we need right now? How will we get it shipped here? How long will it take? Can we ever get enough? We're left without any transportation systems. No computers. No banking systems. No communications to coordinate the effort." He spit out the chewed piece of grass, a tiny speck of green sticking to his lower lip. "So yeah, Caelyn, I think we're going to be able to rebuild, it's not like the entire country has been destroyed by a nuclear bomb, but it's going to take some time. A couple months to get started. Half a year to make a difference. Maybe a full year, maybe more."

Gretta shook her head and muttered, then stared toward the quickly setting sun. Shadows had grown long now, stretching dark and thin across the deep green grass, and the house cast a dark outline almost to the fence along the backyard. "A month is too long," she whispered in desperation. "A couple months is hopeless. A whole year! Don't make me laugh. None of us are going to make it, not if we have to get by on our own for that long." She turned to Walter. "Don't you think the government is going to step in and . . . I don't know, *do something!*"

The old farmer hunched his shoulders. "I don't know, Gretta. I'm no prophet and no civil servant, so take everything I tell you with a great big ol' grain of salt, but I think the government is pretty much like you and me, completely overwhelmed. I just hope they can keep control of the people, keep some sense of law and order . . ." his voice trailed off. "Do you have a radio?" he asked.

"No. At least not one that's working."

"You hear about things out in California? L.A. and San Francisco?"

"We haven't heard anything," Caelyn answered, brushing her hand through Ellie's thin blonde hair.

Simpson glanced down at the little girl, who was looking up at him, her eyes wide, listening to every word. "Maybe we can talk about that later. Just know it's kind of a mess out there. Like I was saying, I only hope the government can keep a lid on things. Keep things a little bit under control."

"Surely they've got some plan, some kind of program for such a time as this?" Gretta's voice was angry now.

"Are you aware of any government programs that could take care of everyone within the U.S., or even part of us? I wish there were. Water, of course, is a huge problem and the most urgent need for most people, and it's going to take every resource the government has just to provide the most basic water service. Even with that, I think pretty much everyone's going to eventually end up drinking from the rivers and the lakes. After that, I just don't know, but it's my opinion that the government isn't going to step in and help us. They just aren't prepared. It's too big a job."

Gretta kept her eyes on the dropping sun. The sky was turning red now, a deep, fierce, unnatural glow. "So you're telling me we've got to make it for a year on our own."

"Who knows? Maybe it won't be that long. It's too late in the fall now to plant anything, but we can plant again in the spring. Everyone can grow a garden—"

"But that's *next year.* We're not even talking spring, you're talking about harvesting in fall!"

Simpson shrugged, his face pained.

"I don't have a year's supply of food, that's for sure."

Simpson and Caelyn glanced at each other, a knowing look between them. A moment of silence followed. The little girl hanging on her mother's knees looked up with blue eyes, then motioned toward the tree swing. "Can I, Mom?" she said. Caelyn nodded toward it and the little girl ran off, her cotton skirt rippling behind her in the breeze. Caelyn watched her go, then turned back to Simpson.

"What happened out in San Francisco?" she asked quickly.

Simpson bent for another blade of grass. "There was an earthquake. A real beauty. Lots of damage throughout the city, but the worst thing was the fires. Once they got started, no one could stop them. Sounds like the entire city is in flames. The whole thing might be burned. Same down in L.A. It's an unbelievable thing, from what I heard."

Gretta turned to him, a sick look across her face. She had spent much of her adult life in California and had many friends out there. "How do you know that?" she demanded as if the whole thing were Simpson's fault.

"A lot of wards have coordinated some training with members who own shortwave radios. Enough of them are still working that we get some word."

Gretta hesitated, not understanding but too tired and discouraged to press. "The entire city of San Francisco . . . L.A., such a beautiful city . . . so many, many good people . . ." she whispered.

Caelyn put her hand on her mother's shoulder. "It's okay, Mom. Maybe it's not as bad as you think."

Simpson waited a moment, then kicked his boots through the long grass at his feet. *It's worse,* his face seemed to say.

"There are a couple other news items you might want to know about," he went on after a moment of silence. "Things are kind of tough all over. Other cities are in shambles. New York is completely deserted, they're saying. Chicago's got some fires, though not like out in L.A., but I've heard they've got a dysentery epidemic, too. St. Louis has been torn apart by a week of race riots. South, the borders have burst open. Millions of Mexicans are making their way across the Rio Grande. The government simply doesn't have the people or equipment to stop them from pouring into our country. They said two or three million illegals have come across the borders already. Some of them are led by Mexican drug lords with their private armies. They're coming up in old trucks and cars. I guess a lot of the vehicles and equipment in Mexico were far enough away from the EMP that they weren't damaged in the attack. There's lots of looting, lots of violence." He stopped and cleared his throat. "Some of the border towns have been destroyed."

A sudden, violent picture flashed in Caelyn's mind. Men. Guns. A dark sky. A feeling of cold dread. She almost couldn't stand to listen anymore. Glancing away, she looked for Ellie, then stared at the ground and thought. There was a scripture, she didn't know it well, but it seemed to return to her now and she was surprised at the clarity with which it came. She didn't know it all, but she could paraphrase: *If the Gentiles don't repent after they have scattered my people, then the remnant of the house of Jacob will go among them as a lion* among the flocks of sheep, tearing them in pieces.

As the scripture ran through her mind, she shivered with fear. Out of all the things there were to worry her, why did *this* scare her so? Out of all the scriptures she could think of, why did this one come to mind? She thought on it a moment, but didn't know.

"Listen, we've got to be heading on," Simpson said, nodding to the wagon. "We've got some emergency supplies. Canned goods, spaghetti, things like that." He waved to the boys, who stood and lifted a couple of boxes. "Tell me what you need," he said.

Caelyn glanced anxiously toward her mother, who shot her

a glaring look. "I think we'll be okay for a week or two, but I don't know what we're going to do after that," she said, ignoring her mother's angry stare. "Back home, my husband and I have some food storage, enough to see us through, but that's five hundred miles away from here. I don't have any way to go and get it and bring it back here, and even if I could, I couldn't leave my mom and dad."

Simpson nodded to the boys, who climbed down from the wagon with their boxes and looked at him. "Put them on the back porch," he said.

"Where'd that come from?" Gretta demanded.

"We have what we call a bishop's storehouse."

"Whatever, we don't need that," she protested, but the two boys ignored her, moving with the boxes toward the house. "Look," she continued, her voice angry now, "I don't know what you all expect from us in return for your favors, but I don't think you should expect me to be showing up at your meetings in a baptism dress anytime real soon."

Simpson laughed, not at all offended. "Gretta, we don't expect anything from you. It's not like we're going around trading food when people agree to set up appointments with our missionaries. We just thought we might be able to help. And remember, Miss Gretta, Caelyn is a member of our church. We have an obligation to help her. So yes, we're going to help."

Gretta stared coldly, still suspicious. "I still won't be visiting your church this week."

Simpson laughed. "That's a relief." His voice was teasing.

She scowled, then turned toward the young men on the porch. "I'll take care of those," she called out, marching after them.

The old farmer watched her walk away, then quickly glanced to Caelyn. "Your mom's a real handful."

Caelyn was dying with embarrassment. "I'm so, so sorry," she said.

"Don't worry, I can handle her. And I think I understand her a lot better than you might think. She's a proud woman, a woman who's made a go of it on her own for a long time. She's been responsible for your father since they were first married, from what I understand, and she takes great pride in the fact that she can take care of herself. Nothing wrong with that, nothing wrong at all." He watched as Gretta walked onto the porch and took one of the boxes from the nearest boy. "Listen, Caelyn," he said, turning back to her, "there's a couple things you need to know. First, we're having a meeting at the ward house next Saturday afternoon. The bishop wants to take an evaluation of where we stand. We'll be setting up a communications tree, taking an inventory of everyone's supplies, making a list of the number of people in every household and their needs. Basically, we'll be setting up a community resource of available food, reserves, medical supplies, tools, generators, working vehicles, everything. We can't have someone out here trying to scrape by on their own, not if they don't want to, not if there are others who are willing to help. It's all strictly voluntary. It's not like we're going to go around confiscating people's food or anything like that, but we recognize that some people are going to have resources that others won't, and they're willing to share. I think you're a pretty good example. From what I understand, you and your husband have done everything you could to take care of yourselves. Now your husband is off somewhere." He paused. "Where is your husband, Caelyn?"

The young woman suddenly choked. "I don't know," she said.

"He's not, you know . . . he's okay, though?"

"As far as I know. Last I heard he was being pulled out of

Iraq. All the American forces were being pulled back. He called once, a few days after the nuclear attack on D.C., saying he'd be back in the country within a short time. I haven't heard from him since."

Simpson watched, his face soft and sympathetic. "I'm glad to know that he's okay."

"Yes. I count that blessing every day."

"Still, like I was saying, you did everything you could to prepare, but now you find yourself in a difficult situation. We need to help take care of you; we *want* to help take care of you. Sure, my family has a pretty good supply, we've tried to listen to the prophet, but do you think I could live with myself if I wasn't willing to reach out to those good people who need my help?"

Caelyn listened, her eyes misting. "What do I do, though? I could come to the meeting, but I don't have anything to offer. I'm a liability; I have no assets. And I'm a stranger in your midst."

Simpson shook his head. "I think you underestimate both yourself and your own people. And we *are* your people. You're not a stranger. I mean that, Caelyn."

She nodded, her head dropping.

"Okay, then. Now, I'm trying to think. Maybe I've got this wrong, but it seems to me that you're a nurse?"

She nodded slowly.

"Don't you think someone's going to have a need of your expertise? That's the way it works. You give what you can. You help others. Others give what they can. They help you. We take care of each other and put the rest to God. We lay what we have upon the altar, then turn around, go to work, and hope for the best."

Caelyn lowered her head again. "What time is the meeting?"

"One o'clock. It will take you a couple hours to walk there, but that's okay, lots of people will be walking, that's why we're starting early. We want to get in, take care of as much business as we can, and give people enough time to walk home before it gets dark."

Caelyn was quiet as she thought. Gretta's voice drifted toward them from the kitchen, and the two young men emerged through the screen door.

Simpson glanced anxiously around the empty landscape. "You've got to travel careful," he said.

Caelyn didn't understand.

"There some rumors going round. Started in some of the other churches. Some of the more . . . hmm, how's a good way to say this . . . some of the more believing Christians aren't a big fan of us Mormons right now. They blame us for the last election. Say they lost because of us. Some of 'em are sayin' we're part of some conspiracy . . ."

Caelyn laughed sarcastically. "Good heavens, are you kidding? With all the bad around us, they think that *we're* the problem?"

"Kinda weird, I know, but you know how it is. We've always been outside the mainstream, and that's only going to get worse. Our Golden Age, such as it was, is over now, I figure."

Caelyn pressed her lips, pulling a strand of hair away from her mouth.

"I want to see you at the meeting," Simpson ordered as he watched her. "If not, I'm going to come and get you. I mean it, Caelyn, no way we're going to leave you out here on your own."

Caelyn looked up, her eyes wet with tears now, a clear drop clinging to her cheek. "Brother Simpson . . ."

"*Walt* is okay with me."

"Walt, did you know that I've been praying for someone to come here? I've been praying that for days. I needed you so desperately. How did you know to come?"

He looked at her, his face firm but kind. "The Spirit brought me here," he told her.

She looked up, again not understanding.

"I was going to turn around. I wanted to get home before it got dark. But I couldn't. I knew that someone else was out here. It wasn't until I saw your parents' house that I remembered meeting you a couple years ago in church."

He cleared his throat. "I think you prayed me to you, Caelyn. Your faith is strong enough that God was able to use even an old fool such as me. And let me tell you, that's amazing. My wife is going to be impressed. She's been praying for me for almost forty years, so far as she can tell to no result."

Caelyn laughed with gratitude, then fell into his arms, giving him a hug. "Thank you. Thank you for listening to the Spirit. Thank you for being the kind of person who would come out here to find someone like me. Thank you for not giving up. And yes, I'll be there Saturday."

The two boys walked past them. "Come on, Grandpa," one of them said.

Simpson glanced to the porch where Gretta was standing now and waved. "See you in church next week," he called to her. "Don't forget, wear something white for the baptism."

She waved him off and walked back into the kitchen.

Simpson laughed and climbed back onto his tractor. The engine turned, then churned, black smoke rising from the exhaust pipe. He waved, used both hands to turn the heavy steering wheel, and drove away.

Caelyn watched the tractor disappear down the road. She knew her mother was watching from the kitchen window, but she didn't turn around.

Standing there, she felt a sudden sense of loneliness falling on her like a blanket from the sky. She shivered from a heavy heart while staring at the completely lifeless road.

Turning slowly, she looked east. The sun had set now and the sky was turning dark. It would be a few minutes more before the first star or the moon would appear. Overhead, a pair of swallows flew by, searching for the first of the nightly mosquitoes. Standing at the edge of the grass, alone, looking east, Caelyn was consumed by a longing for her husband. She reached out, lifting her arms sadly to the sky. "Are you out there, babe?" she whispered. "Are you out there? Are you alive?"

She stood and waited for an answer, but nothing came.

"I miss you so much. We both miss you. Will you find us? Will you come home? How long will it be until you hold us both again?"

Again she waited. Then, taking a long breath, she turned and walked into the darkening house.

chapter fourteen

East Side, Chicago, Illinois

They ate together, what little they had, sitting around the kitchen table, some of them on the floor. Sara watched Luke carefully out of the corner of her eye. It was the first time he had joined them to eat, and he was looking better. She'd changed his dressing just an hour before and the wounds were clean and healing, the broken skin pink, the tissue bonding. He was stronger now; she could tell that from how much he ate.

Luke realized the others were watching him and suddenly flushed. "I'm okay," he said, embarrassed. "Y'all don't have to stare at me like that."

Mary reached out to pat his hair, almost reverently, as if she were touching the Pope. She treated him like a saint, some kind of earthly manifestation of the power of heaven. Kelly Beth sat on her mother's lap, playing with a pair of animal crackers they had found in the back of the cupboard. Sara watched and smiled.

Sam looked at his watch. "I'm going to do a little recon in the morning to figure out what's going on out there."

Ammon was staring at a road map. "You know, if we went

down a different highway, we would pass our car. Think about the food and gold and things we left there. It'd be really good to . . ."

Sam thought of the men on the road, the bandits who'd commandeered the bridge the night that Ammon had been shot. "All that stuff will be there later," he said. "It isn't our priority right now." He nodded to the women on the other side of the table. "I want to gather it up same as you do, but I don't want everyone with us when we do. There might be trouble. You and I and maybe Luke can go get it later."

Ammon pressed his lips together, then nodded.

Ten minutes later, it grew dark. The sun was setting quickly now, with winter coming on. There was nothing to do. It was dark. It was growing cold. They got out the bedding and sleeping bags and started getting ready for bed.

*　　*　　*

Sara slipped into the bedroom to check on Luke. He was lying on a mattress on the floor, his feet hanging over the worn edge, and though his eyes were closed, she knew he was awake. She watched him a moment, then walked quietly across the matted carpet and sat down in an old wooden rocking chair. Rocking gently, she closed her eyes and started softly singing an old song her father used to sing to her when she was just a child. The melody was slow and haunting but comforting to her now.

> *Oh, don't you remember,*
> *A long time ago.*
> *There were two little babes,*
> *Their names I don't know.*
> *They strayed far away,*
> *One bright summer's day,*

And got lost in the woods,
I've heard people say.
And when it grew night,
So sad was their plight.
The bright sun, it went down,
And the moon gave no light.
They sobbed, and they sighed,
And they bitterly cried.
Then those two little babes
Just lay down and died.

She stopped singing, drifting away, almost asleep, her mind lost in other thoughts. Then she heard Luke moving on the mattress and she looked down at him.

"*And when they were dead,*" he started singing, and Sara softly joined in.

The robins so red
Gathered strawberry leaves,
And over them spread.
And all the night long,
They sang this sweet song,
Poor babes in the woods.
Poor babes in the woods.

Luke smiled at her. "Out of all the songs you used to sing us, that was always my favorite one."

"Are you kidding?" Sara laughed. "Talk about a song that just kind of makes you want to go out and slit your wrists or something." Her face scrunched in the dark.

"A little depression can be a good thing for a kid, you know: 'song sung blue' and all that kind of thing."

"Oh yeah, we need a bunch of that right now."

They both laughed again.

"It's a good song," Luke finished, thinking of his childhood.

Sara nodded slowly. "A good song."

Luke stared up at her from the dirty mattress.

"You're feeling better," she said. It was a statement, not a question. She could see that he was stronger now.

"Yeah, I'm feeling pretty good."

Sara leaned forward on the old rocking chair and the spindled legs creaked under her weight. "We're going to be leaving soon."

"Good. Everyone is ready to get out of here." He rolled to his side and rested his hand on his arm. "Do you think God talks to us in dreams?" he asked unexpectedly.

She resumed rocking, the creaking chair soft and comforting in the growing darkness. "Maybe not to everyone, but to some people, I think he does."

"Has he ever talked to you in a dream, Mom?"

She thought a moment. "No, I guess that's not my gift. But I know that other people have it. Your dad did. He had warnings in dreams more than once. My mother used to talk about her dreams all the time, but hey, she used to talk to angels." Sara paused and laughed. "She was such a character, especially in her older years."

Luke watched his mom. "Do you miss her?"

"My mom?"

"Yeah."

"Sure I do. I miss her all the time. It doesn't matter how long it's been. I suppose that when I'm ninety-five, assuming I live that long, I'll still miss her. It's supposed to be that way."

Luke rubbed his hand through his short hair. "I had a dream last night." He cleared his throat.

"Yeah?" Sara said so that he would go on.

"I was walking with some of the handcart pioneers. Kinda

weird, huh? None of our ancestors walked across the plains. Heck, most of what we know about our ancestors could be written on the back of a three-by-five card, yet there I was, walking up a steep and snowy mountain trail, pushing an old handcart. There were hundreds of pioneers around me, families without their dads, without their moms—almost all of them were missing children. They talked all the time about the loved ones they had lost. I was walking, sometimes crying, my feet were frozen. I was so hungry, so tired. I didn't know if I could make it."

Luke hesitated, his eyes turning to stare at nothing, his face thoughtful, his head slightly cocked. Sara waited, listening, not wanting to interrupt. "It grew dark and a pack of wolves came, dozens of them, thick hair bristling on their necks and shoulders, their teeth flashing in hungry growls. I was alone now. They prowled so close. You could see them in the shadows. They weren't afraid of my fire anymore. And it didn't matter what I did, I couldn't scare them off. They wanted me so badly. Thin as bone, I could see that they were starving, but there was something more. You could see it in their yellow eyes, hear it in their growls, feel it in the air. It was like they didn't want to just kill me, they wanted something more. And no matter what I did, they didn't go away. All night long, I could see their yellow eyes glinting in the firelight, never blinking, getting closer, always closer." Luke fell silent and lay back on the mattress.

They sat a long time in the quiet darkness.

"Do you think it means anything?" he finally asked.

Sara brought her hands together in a fist before her face and gently bit her finger. "I don't know, son. I really don't. It might mean something, but I don't know what it'd be. If I were to think about it, maybe pray about it, maybe I would know."

Luke took a deep breath and held it before he sighed. "I've thought about it, Mom." He looked away. "They're out there, the wolves. Yeah, we've got to worry about food and water and the cold and where we're going to go and all that kind of thing, but that's not the thing that's going to kill us. It's going to be the wolves. They're not afraid anymore. No matter what we do, they're not going to go away. And they hate us. They want to kill us, to destroy us. All the other stuff, I think it'll be okay. But not the wolves. They're the thing we've really got to worry about."

* * *

Sam was staring out the kitchen window when Sara came up behind him and stood close. "I need to talk to you," she whispered.

Sam turned around. "Yeah, Mom."

She put a finger to his lips. "Alone." She nodded to the door.

They slipped out of the apartment and stood in the hall. "Azadeh told me you have a cell phone that is working."

Sam reached into a thigh pocket and pulled it out. "I was in the Metro subway in D.C. when the EMP struck."

"It's working, then?" She sounded so hopeful, he thought she was going to cry.

"No, Mom. I mean, the cell phone is working, yes." He flipped it open and held the green switch to turn it on. The screen glowed red and blue and he showed it to her. "But there's no coverage. All the cell towers are down."

"What about the military stations on the lake? I know there's some navy and coast guard stations along Lake Michigan."

"I've tried them, Mom. Nothing."

"When was the last time you tried? How long has it been?"

Sam thought. "I don't know. When we first got here."

Sara took his hand, pulling him toward the stairs. "Let's go try again."

Four minutes later, they were standing on the roof. Sam watched his mother carefully. "Mom, it's time you told me what's going on."

Sara ignored him, reaching for his phone. The soft light from the small screen bathed her face in a ghostly silver. "I know the military has all kinds of communication facilities," she said. "They contract with local carriers for their service, even for the military stuff. It's not like the coast guard or air force own their own phone lines, cell phone towers, that kind of thing. They're going to push to get that stuff up so they can use it."

Sam continued watching, not saying anything.

"Where's the nearest military station?" Sara asked.

Sam hesitated, thinking, then waved vaguely off to his right. "I don't know, Mom. I think there's a coast guard training facility somewhere east of here."

She pointed the cell phone in that direction and lifted it over her head. "They would have hardened some of their facilities. They would have the equipment to rebuild." She gasped suddenly. "Look at this," she whispered.

Sam took three steps toward her and looked at the phone. A single bar. Sometimes two. "Whoa," he said. "No kidding . . ."

Sara gasped again. "Good, good, good. Okay," she dropped the phone as she thought, suddenly flustered and unsure of what to do. "Okay, okay, who, who, who do I talk to?" She acted as if Sam wasn't even there. "I can't call the Pentagon. No one there. No, no, not no one, *nothing* there. Okay, okay, who? How do I get a hold of them? What am I going to say—"

"Mom!" Sam grabbed his mother by her shoulders. "What is going on?"

"I've got to call and warn him."

"Warn *who*? About what?"

She picked up the phone. "I'll call the Strategic Command Post in Nebraska. How do I get the number?"

She held the phone up and dialed 911. "It's ringing, Sam, it's ringing!" She waited and waited. No answer. Nothing but a constant ring. "All right." She disconnected. "I'll try the number for the emergency switchboard at the White House. They might have, they *must* have transferred that number to a working phone." She punched the cell phone as she talked, excited once again. She listened, holding her hand up by her face in anxious expectation. "Ringing . . . ringing," she whispered. "It sounds like . . ." she turned her head suddenly and talked into the phone. "Yes, yes, can you hear me?" She took a step toward the edge of the roof. "Can you hear me? Yes, I can barely hear you. My name is Sara Brighton. My husband was General Neil Brighton, Special Assistant to the President. This is an emergency. I need you to connect me to the Secretary of Defense. Yes, Secretary Marino's office." She paused and listened. "No, no, I can't wait. What! Are you certain he is dead? Then who is his replacement? No, this is an emergency . . ." Another short pause. "I already told you, my name is Sara Brighton . . . hello . . . hello?" The phone was dead.

She lowered the cell and looked at Sam. "He hung up on me," she said.

Sam checked the cell phone. The low battery indicator was now on.

"He hung up. Or maybe the line was disconnected."

"Mom." Sam took a step toward her. Taking her by her shoulders, he looked into her eyes. The moon was barely rising now and the sky was black. "Mom?"

Sara hesitated. "But if I tell you . . ."

"It's time to tell us, Mom."

Sara looked at him. Her eyes were big and teary, round and glistening in the dim light. She was suddenly young and vulnerable and frightened as a child.

Sam heard her sniffle, felt her shoulders shuddering; then she fell into his arms.

When she was finished with her story, Sam sat for a long time without speaking. Then he looked down at his cell phone. "This was a huge mistake," he said.

* * *

MISSILE AND SPACE INTELLIGENCE CENTER (MSIC)
HUNTSVILLE, ALABAMA

Electronic transmissions were intercepted, identified, and flagged by a series of enormous antennas stationed throughout the country, but concentrated primarily along the East Coast and in a few locations along the western mountain ranges. Some of the radio intercept devices were the normally anticipated satellite dishes pointing upward, although these were mounted on bearings and hydraulic cylinders to move them to appropriate pieces of the sky. Others were tall and slender trestles that reached several hundred feet above the ground. Some had been built in clusters and were situated on remote, stripped-down pieces of federal land with extremely limited access, including strictly enforced no-fly zones. Others of the listening devices were positioned within the cities, hidden behind nearly translucent material alongside civilian buildings, the occupants clueless about the immensely powerful radio intercept equipment that was operating next door. A great many listening devices were disguised as cell phone towers, radio antennas, or television broadcast dishes, whatever was required to minimize the speculation as to what the devices were used for, how many there really were, and how deeply they could reach.

On a normal day, before the EMP attack, the United States government was capable of intercepting and monitoring hundreds of millions of cell and telephone conversations, emails, Internet access, and instant messages every day, the sheer volume making it possible, even likely, that this particular conversation might have been missed.

But since the EMP attack, the use of such electronic communications had dropped off dramatically.

So they listened and they noted and they passed the information on.

chapter fifteen

HEADQUARTERS, NATIONAL SECURITY AGENCY
FORT GEORGE G. MEADE, MARYLAND
TEN MILES NORTHEAST OF WASHINGTON, D.C.

There were two enormous buildings, side by side, one a little longer and lower than the other, both of them black metal and glass cubes that reflected the sun, passing clouds, radar sensors, laser intelligence listening beams, heat, cold, conventional listening devices, everything and anything that might connect the occupants of the two buildings to the outside world. The buildings housed one of the most secret and secretive agencies within the intelligence community; for many years the federal government denied that NSA (No-Such-Agency) even existed. Once it had been revealed, extensive precautions had been put in place to isolate it, including the construction of its own exit of the Baltimore-Washington Parkway, labeled "NSA Employees Only." Hidden behind a wall of trees (most of northern Virginia and southern Maryland was covered in dense forest), the NSA complex housed more mathematicians and supercomputers than any other organization in the world. It also drew more electricity off the grid than any other private or public entity within the entire state of Maryland, including the largest steel manufacturers and shipbuilders along the coast. (In 2006, the *Baltimore Sun* reported that the entire

NSA complex was susceptible to severe electrical overload because of insufficient infrastructure to support the geometrically growing demand.) The agency had its own hardware, software, and semiconductor production facilities, as well as its own cryptology research center. No one knew how many people worked for the NSA, although sometime early in the century some overly ambitious counterculture guy had Google-earthed the parking lot, counted the number of parking spaces (18,000), driven northeast of Washington, D.C., pulled off the nearby highway and counted the average number of occupants in every car that passed, then announced across the Internet that the agency employed 39,000 people, which was surprisingly close. Aircraft over-flight of the area was strictly forbidden, the nearby streams and trees were scattered with hidden motion sensors and listening devices, and there wasn't an inch of the security fence and surrounding buffer zone that wasn't covered with redundant surveillance cameras.

Because Executive Order 12333 directed the agency to limit its resources toward the collection of information regarding "foreign intelligence or counterintelligence" and not "acquiring information concerning the domestic activities of United States persons," the NSA's eavesdropping mission concentrated on overseas diplomatic and military sources. With a few controversial and well-published exceptions, the NSA had complied with this directive. But it surely didn't now. The world had tipped, almost fallen. Nuclear explosions had taken place over Israel, Iran, and other portions of central Asia, not to mention Washington, D.C. The nation had been incapacitated with an EMP attack. No one cared a whit about Executive Order 12333 anymore. The NSA was listening to *everything*. The agency's footprint was huge, stretching across every continent, including North America, and the sheer volume of information that passed through its system simply boggled the mind. And though the agency had a few branches scattered around the country (the Texas Cryptology Center in San Antonio, Texas, being the most well-known), the vast majority of the dirty work was done at the headquarters building at Fort Meade.

And because the buildings were sealed, stocked, and secured, neither the EMP nor the previous nuclear attack against Washington had had any impact on the work that took place there.

*　　*　　*

The man was short, a civilian with a thin mustache and black, slippery hair. He walked into the two-star general's office without knocking and placed the red binder on his desk.

"Sir, I think you might want to see this," he simply said.

The general was slow to look up. "What is it?" he asked dismissively.

The small man firmed his shoulders. "A target from the presidential directive we received two days ago."

The air force general/NSA director looked up slowly, his face filled with instant disdain. "We don't have a president right now," he said.

"I know that, sir. I'm talking about our leadership out in Raven Rock."

The NSA director scoffed.

The man nodded toward the folder. "It falls within the parameters of the priority search," he explained.

The general didn't care.

"Should I pass it on?" he asked.

The white-haired general snorted. "Do we have a choice?"

The man lifted up the binder. "Do you want to read it first?"

The general waved him off and repeated his first question. "Do I have a choice?"

The man waited.

"Will it matter if I read it? Will it matter what I think? Does it matter what any of us think anymore?"

The small man stared, his eyes blank as a snake's. *Yes,* he thought, though he didn't say the words out loud, *it matters quite a lot what you think. And who you support now. It matters more than you will ever know.*

His eyes remained expressionless as he answered, "Some of the targets they are looking for have popped up in Chicago. General Brighton's wife . . ."

The general glared in fierce anger. "Who friggin' cares! With everything else that we are dealing with, how can anyone consider this a priority right now!"

The greasy-haired man met the general's angry gaze and didn't blink. "There must be reasons we don't know about."

The general huffed, thought a moment, then grabbed a pen, scribbled his three initials across the routing paper, and handed the binder back. "Take care of it," he said.

The man took the binder, turned, and started walking toward the door. Pausing without turning back, he said, "The president has given us a directive."

The general was looking down at the papers on his desk now. "I know that, Spencer."

"You may not like it, I understand that, but some of us feel—"

The general didn't let him finish. "I know how you feel, Spencer. I don't care for either your feelings or your thoughts. Now go on, take the intercept and get out of here."

RAVEN ROCK (SITE R), UNDERGROUND MILITARY COMPLEX
SOUTHERN PENNSYLVANIA

At seventy-eight hours, fifteen minutes, Bethany Rosen, the former president *pro tempore* of the Senate, would go down in history for being the president of the United States for the shortest period of time: just more than three days from the time she was sworn in until she was dead.

After her death, it was time for what remained of the national civilian leadership to work further down the line. Next in the order of succession—fourth in line—was the Secretary of State, who had been killed in the nuclear attack on Washington, D.C. Next was the Secretary of the Treasury. Not being a fool, and having figured out—or, more likely, having had it whispered to him—what had really happened to the previous president, he utterly refused to be sworn in.

The Secretary of Defense was next. Problem was, no one knew where he was. Buried under the rubble of D.C., they were certain, along with two hundred thousand other souls.

Which brought them to the Attorney General.

Beautiful when a plan fell into place.

So it was that, after one nuclear explosion, two murders, and one very clear conversation in a small office deep in Raven Rock, they finally got to their man.

Albert J. Fuentes, current Attorney General, soon to be the next president of the United States, scheduled the swearing-in ceremony for six o'clock that evening. Once that formality was over, it would take them only a few weeks to put the necessary changes in place.

The cabal that had brought him to this point would give him very specific instructions. And they were certain the new president would comply.

The United States, as they knew it, was about to cease to exist. After years of waiting, hoping such an opportunity would one day present itself, Albert J. Fuentes and his friends were prepared to act. And while the new president would be the front man for the code of power, he would not be the brains. The real brains, the real power, went much deeper than any single man.

No, the young man Fuentes, a simple federal judge whom hardly anyone inside Washington had even known two years ago, would not be the one holding the real reins of power.

That night, at exactly 6:00 P.M., Fuentes placed his left hand upon a Bible and raised his right. Standing before a video camera, a few witnesses, the only surviving member of the Supreme Court, his wife, a couple of members of the Congress, and the press, he swore to defend the Constitution from all enemies, both foreign and domestic. Completing the oath of office, he shook a few hands, then got to work.

OFFUTT AIR FORCE BASE
HEADQUARTERS, U.S. STRATEGIC COMMAND
EIGHT MILES SOUTH OF OMAHA, NEBRASKA

The air force technician listened, took some notes, then hung up the secure telephone. "Some of our military guys got a trace on a couple of the individuals the SecDef was asking about," he said to the four-star commander looking over his shoulder.

The four-star leaned toward him, resting his hands on the younger man's chair.

"You sure it's them?" he prodded. It had been so long since he'd received any good news that he was immediately skeptical.

"We can't know for certain till we get them, but it sounds that way right now."

The general hesitated. "How'd you get the information?"

The technician nodded toward the telephone. "We stole it, same as they did. The Raven Rock guys took it from the NSA. We took it from the Rock guys as they passed it up the line."

The general swirled a cup of cold coffee in his hand. "Let me have it," he said, reaching for the report.

chapter sixteen

EAST SIDE, CHICAGO, ILLINOIS

The apartment was like a prison and they simply couldn't stand it any longer. At the quietest time of the afternoon, when the streets had fallen into a lull and the sun was dropping, a few of them fled outside.

The setting sun was pale gold, giving light but little warmth as it moved toward the western horizon, and there was a jarring hint of fall in the air. The sky was pink above the horizon and dark blue, almost purple, overhead. Everyone noticed it now, the different colors in the sky, the shifting shadows and translucent hues. The cold wind blew in from the great Lake Michigan on the north shore of the city and swirled around them, stirring dry leaves at their feet as it funneled between the high buildings. The sky was full of color but cloudless, the rain clouds having moved off to the east, where they had already mixed with a blast of arctic air—months early down from Canada—to form a line of heavy snow showers over Pennsylvania and New York.

Azadeh Ishbel Pahlavi, Mary and Kelly Beth Dupree, and Lieutenant Samuel Brighton sat on a rusted metal bench in a small, littered courtyard crammed between two of the high-rise apartments. Kelly slept, her head resting on Mary's lap. The afternoon was calm, and for the first time in days, they had time to think.

Though they didn't know it, very similar feelings had settled in all of their hearts. Together, they worried about the future of their terrifying new world.

The streets and sidewalks were full of people, people moving everywhere. Sam watched, wondering where they might be going, where they were getting food. He noted the different sounds: voices, footsteps, sometimes shouting, far off a sharp *crack*—maybe a gunshot—but never the sound of trains or cars. To their right, the elevated train tracks stood against the afternoon light, dark spindles of steel reminding them of what used to be just a few days before.

Sam wore his camouflage pants and shirt, which caught everyone's attention. At first glance, some of them probably thought he was an imposter, for though his hair was short and tight, his face was dark with five days' worth of beard. Seeing the holstered weapon under his left arm and the pack at his feet, most of them turned away.

Sam tried to relax, though it seemed his eyes were always moving, looking at each man or woman who walked by. Inside, his gut was tight. He was in America, but he felt like he was back in the Middle East and, like an American in Sadr City, he knew that he stood out. He also knew there were more illegal weapons in the neighborhood around him than there were in Sadr City, one of the poorest cities in Iraq. Funny, he thought, how much it was the same. Here, like there, unemployment was rampant, the homes in disrepair, the abandoned warehouses, old buildings, and crowded housing complexes providing a haven for criminals. Here, like there, it came down to clusters of families and tight groups of thugs. The Americans called them gangs, the Iraqis called them tribes—didn't matter, they were the same. Even the looks on the faces of the people were familiar: vacant stares, resigned acceptance, hopelessness, uncertainty, anger, fear, some open rage, a few shy smiles. It shocked him how similar the two places felt. Opposite sides of the world. Opposite cultures. Very different people. Still, so much the same.

Azadeh sat quietly on the bench opposite Sam. Mary sat at her side, her arm around her shoulder, holding her close. Sometimes Azadeh rested her head against Mary's arm; sometimes Mary leaned against her head. Dropping his eyes, Sam looked at Kelly Beth, who was asleep curled up on the bench, her legs tucked up to keep warm, her head on Mary's lap. She slept contently, her breathing slow and deep. Though healed from the ravaging cancer that had taken her to just a few hours from death, she was frail and recovering from the emotional and physical ordeal. Weak still, sometimes disoriented, she would need weeks to build her strength back, maybe months before she completely regained her health. Meanwhile, she needed food and water, proper sanitation, and lots of time to heal and rest.

And everything she needed, they couldn't give her now.

He looked down at his hands, then held them up to the light, thinking of that night along the road, hidden in the cluster of trees, running as if his life depended on it, looking for his family and finding them in the trees, giving a blessing to his brother, giving a blessing to this little girl on Mary's lap.

He moved his hands together, rubbing them gently as he thought.

Sometimes he could almost feel it, the heat against his hands.

They had been there, he was certain. His father. Someone else. Sara told him she thought it was Azadeh's father. He

149

didn't know if that was true, but someone had helped him give the blessings that rainy night two days before.

Mary stared down at her daughter, absently stroking her brow. Her face was peaceful, her black eyes calm.

"She's going to be okay now," Sam said to her as he watched the mother and her child.

Mary looked up and smiled gently. "Yes, I am sure she will." She spoke with unwavering confidence. "The good Lord didn't heal her just to let her die a few hours later. One day she'll tell her children of these wonderful days."

Sam compressed his lips and nodded with a barely perceptible move of his head. Stealing a glance at Azadeh, he felt his heart skip a beat again. Sometimes she made it hard to think. Her soft skin. Her dark eyes. Her thin neck and delicate fingers. He thought about her too much, and he hated that. He didn't need the distraction and neither did she. She wasn't American, not even Christian. The two of them were opposites in almost every way.

Still, sometimes he wondered . . .

He sucked on his teeth and said nothing, just leaned back and stared into the empty sky.

*　　*　　*

Azadeh kept her head slightly bowed, but her eyes hardly left Sam's face, noting the anxious movement of his pressed lips. He seemed to fidget at the silence, sometimes acting as if he wanted to speak. She noticed that about the Americans: They expected conversation even when they had nothing much to say. It was very different from her people, who loved the silence; many of her closest moments with her father had been without words.

Sam kicked his feet, nervously moving the small pack, then dropped his hands onto his lap.

She watched him and wondered. Did he notice how she looked at him? Did he notice her at all?

No. He was an American, an officer, a soldier. He was far beyond anything she had to offer. He was part of another world.

Still, there was something about him, something different, something . . . she didn't know, something stronger than bone and muscle. She didn't understand it, but this much was certain: She was glad he was her friend.

Feeling the touch of Mary's hair against her cheek, she brushed at the tickle. The wind gusted and she turned her face to the sun, feeling welcome and cared about for the first time since she had said good-bye to the old woman back at the refugee camp in southern Iraq. With the thought of Pari, her only friend in Khorramshahr, the memories suddenly came flooding back. She didn't want them to, but she couldn't control it. She might as well raise her hands to stop the wind as to hold back the memories once they had been released. The London doctor had tried to explain it to her before sending her to the States.

"How are you sleeping?" he asked her.

Azadeh didn't answer for a moment. "All right," she finally said in Farsi.

"Are you having any nightmares?"

"Sometimes."

"Do you find it hard to concentrate? Do the memories sometimes flood your mind?"

Azadeh looked up at him with pleading eyes.

The doctor saw it and noted her response on his pad. "The emotional devastation you've experienced is very similar to that of combat soldiers. Your emotions have been jarred. Sometimes the memories will come out like a monster, too powerful to hold back. Don't worry about it too much. They'll eventually go away."

151

So it was that, as she sat in the afternoon light, her face turned up to the sun, the memories washed like a sudden flood into her mind. She thought about her father, a man she loved more than any other person in the world. She thought of her old friend in Khorramshahr. The afternoon the flesh dealer had come to take her away. The first time she had seen Sam back on the hilltop overlooking her tiny village in Iran. The Iranian troops, their black uniforms and unmarked armored personnel carriers, the greasy smoke hanging in the air, her father's cries of anguish, looking into his dying eyes, the vertigo and crushing loneliness of knowing that she was alone.

*   *   *

The afternoon sun was low and cold, but Sam felt warm and safe and he started to relax. Watching Azadeh, her face soft and full of thought, his mind too drifted back to the first time he had seen her, the battle in the valley so very far away.

Closing his eyes, he relived the entire scene.

*   *   *

Sam took a step to the right to see past his men, and his shoulders slumped as he looked at the smoking tree. The lower branches had been scorched and all of the leaves had been burned to ash. The corpse lay in a heap at the base of the tree. "Anything else?" he demanded as he looked away.

"No, Sam, that's all."

"Awright then, let's go. There's nothing more we can do, and the Honcho wants to get out of here. Move to the chopper. Let's get out of this hell."

"Roger," the soldiers muttered. They all wanted to leave. There was too much death, too much darkness, too much destruction and despair. And it seemed to be for nothing. None of it

made any sense. His unit gathered their gear and moved down the hill in a run. Sam watched them go, then stood alone on the top of the hill.

A slight wind picked up, blowing up from the valley and lifting the smoke to the tops of the trees, bending it over the branches like the long, misty fingers of an enormous, dark hand. Sam turned his face to the breeze, hoping the wind would remove the stain from his memory and the smell of smoke from his clothes. He closed his eyes and listened, feeling the breeze on his face and the weight of his gear pressing against his shoulders and chest. The tiny radio receiver beeped in his ear as the other squads announced they were ready to go. He pulled out the earpiece and let it hang at his neck. He needed a moment of silence, a moment of prayer.

He bowed his head slowly. "Father," he began, then paused for a time. He wanted to say something, and he felt that he should, but try as he might, the words didn't come.

He didn't feel like praying. He felt like kicking someone in the head.

He paused, then finally mumbled the only prayer he could say, "Please bless them." He lifted his head.

Turning, he started to walk down the muddy road. He had gone only twenty paces when something spoke in his mind. He tried to dismiss it, but the feeling remained. He paused and looked back at the smoldering tree.

She crawled from the high grass on the other side of the road. She was young, wet, and muddy, with long hair and a tan dress. She moved toward the body at the base of the tree and knelt down beside it, holding her hands over her mouth. He saw her shoulders heaving and heard her muffled cries.

"Go to her," the voice said. "She is your sister and she needs your help."

Sam stared in frustration. "But what could I do?" he thought desperately.

The voice didn't answer and Sam didn't move. The sound of the chopper blades began to beat from behind him as the pilots spun the rotors up to operating speed. He turned to the landing zone to see that his squad had loaded up in the choppers and were ready to go. He heard his name being called through the tiny radio earpiece that hung at his neck. "Sergeant Brighton," his captain called him. "Brighton, let's go!"

He stared at the choppers, frozen in his tracks, then glanced back at the girl who wept in the mud.

"Go to her," the voice repeated.

The chopper blades spun, ready to lift in the air. His captain moved to the side of the lead chopper and stared up at Sam. The officer motioned to his radio and pointed to him. Sam slipped in the earpiece and heard his captain's voice. "Sam, come on, buddy, we've got to get out of here."

"Please, Sam," the voice pled. "I need your help now!"

His captain broadcast again through his earpiece. "Let's get out of here, Brighton! Come on, soldier, let's go!"

Sam reached for the transmit button. "Stand by," he said.

"What are you doing up there, Brighton?"

"Stand by!" Sam replied.

He turned away from the choppers and looked at the girl near the tree. She kept her head bowed and her hands at her mouth. Sam took ten steps toward her and she finally looked up, her eyes wide with fear. She started to back up, pushing herself through the mud. Sam lifted his hands, holding them away from his body in a gesture of peace. She cowered, her head low, almost bowing to him.

Sam took another step forward and she slowly raised her head. When she looked at him, his heart seemed to wrench in his chest. Her eyes were brimming with tears, which left a small trail on her cheeks. Sam caught a sudden breath. The feeling was so strong it was like a kick in the chest. He stared, then stepped back. "I know you," he said.

She watched him intently, cocking her head. Her face softened and she quickly wiped a rolling tear from her cheek. Sam saw the pain and desperation and he felt his heart twist again. He felt breathless and hollow, his chest growing tight.

He moved to her slowly. She backed up in the grass, keeping her eyes low, terrified to look at his face. Sam stopped a few paces from her and knelt down at her side.

He shot a quick look over his shoulder. His boss and two other soldiers had come up the road and were watching from twenty paces away. They didn't move toward him, letting him talk to the girl.

Sam moved a few inches toward Azadeh. "I'm sorry," he said. He spoke slowly in English, hoping she would understand.

She forced herself to stop weeping and lifted her eyes.

And Sam saw it, a flicker of recognition, as if she knew him too!

He gestured to the body. "Your father?" he asked, keeping her locked with his eyes.

She nodded in despair, then turned away from the tree.

"Where is your mother?" he asked her.

She only stared back.

"Mother?" he repeated.

Azadeh shook her head.

"You are . . . alone?"

She looked at him. "Now . . . yes."

Sam leaned slowly toward her and reached for her hand. "Look at me," he told her.

Azadeh kept her head low and Sam lifted her chin so he could look into her eyes. "Khorramshahr," he told her. "Do you know where I mean?"

She backed away from him slowly, her face uncertain with fear.

"A refugee camp," Sam repeated, pointing with one hand to the north. "Khorramshahr," he repeated. "Go there. We will help you."

Though she nodded slowly, Sam could see she didn't understand.

"Khorramshahr!" he repeated. "If you can make your way there . . ."

"Sam," Brighton heard his platoon leader's voice. The captain had moved to his side and he placed his hands on Sam's shoulder. "Sam, we have to leave. Come on, man, let's go." He pulled on Sam's shoulder, then put a hand under his arm, lifting him up and pulling him toward the road.

"Khorramshahr!" Sam called out to her before she disappeared in the grass.

✸   ✸   ✸

Opening his eyes to look at Azadeh, Sam couldn't help but notice how much older she was now. She had seen a lot, lived through a lot, since the first time they had met. Both of them were different now. The entire world had changed.

It was getting dark, and the noise and hustle from the street was getting louder as the shadows grew. Sam looked around anxiously, the hairs on his neck suddenly standing on end. He didn't know what it was, but there was a sudden dread inside him. Like a little kid, he was growing fearful of the dark. "Let's go upstairs," he said, standing suddenly.

Mary looked up at him. "This will be our last night in Chicago?"

Sam looked down at her and thought. "Probably not. I want to check our route before we leave. It might take a couple days. Better to know what we're walking into."

Mary motioned to the neighborhood. "I wonder if I'll miss this?"

Sam looked around at the chaos and ugly devastation, wondering how she could. "I'm going to go out tonight and check a few things," he said.

Mary nodded to the streets. "It doesn't get any better, not until we get a long way south."

"That's why we've got to take some time and figure out the best way out of here."

*　　*　　*

The apartment was as dark and quiet as a morgue. In fact, that was what it felt like—death, sadness, despair, and impending doom. Sara hated it. It was oppressive and claustrophobic. She knew her sons felt they were prisoners in the apartment, unable to walk around the neighborhood or even step out on the street. And though she tried to hide it, sometimes she felt the same way too.

She rolled over on the sleeping bag, listening to the breathing around her, then sat up. Her legs pulled up to her chest, her arms wrapped around her knees, she thought of her husband, Neil. For the thousandth time, she longed for his touch, his voice, his strength, his ability to make a decision, his optimism for the future, his courage, his willingness to help others regardless of what it meant to him, his eyes, his laughter, his sense of humor, everything he was or used to be. For the thousandth time, she wished that he were there. If she closed her eyes, she could almost smell him. She could feel him, his spine taut, his arms around her, his hands against her back, his stubbled face against her cheek. She closed her eyes as she imagined, then felt an overwhelming sense of peace.

"Patience," the Spirit told her. *"You have this to look forward to."*

Patience. She almost viewed it as a friend now. Life had taken them to an interruption, but not the ending. With such hope, she knew that she could wait.

She quietly stood. Moving into the tiny bathroom with its yellow tile floor and cracked walls, she shut the door and felt around for the candle and box of matches Mary had left out on the sink. Holding the half-burned candle beside her face, she looked at her image in the mirror, studying the features that stared back at her. She'd lost weight, she could see that in her face; she was too thin now, her cheekbones taut. Her blonde hair was pulled back and dirty and she wanted a shower in the worst way. But she was still beautiful. More, she felt stronger than she'd ever felt before. The light inside her eyes was just as bright and she had lost the hesitation that had haunted her during the first days after the attack. The floor was cold and she rubbed her hands against her arms, then looked back in the mirror, staring into her own eyes in the flicker of the yellow light. The pain was there, deep inside, but she knew she would be okay. She could smile now and really mean it. It was true; she had a lot to look forward to.

Wasn't it strange? Despite the desperation all around her, she had so much to live for.

"*Patience. Keep looking forward. You have a lot to be grateful for.*"

Puffing out the candle, she opened the bathroom door and moved toward the sleeping bag on the floor.

✳   ✳   ✳

As Sara passed the narrow doorway that led into the kitchen, something caught her eye. She stopped, frozen, her heart suddenly racing in her chest, then slowly turned her head.

Something was at the window.

No! It couldn't be!

There. It flashed again.

She caught her breath in fear.

It couldn't be. It couldn't be! She was on the *third floor.*

But she'd seen it. She knew she'd seen it. She hadn't lost her mind.

A pale face. A vicious smile. Dark eyes staring back at her.

She gaped at the window without moving. The empty pane was lifeless, dark, the faintest glow of starlight casting a pale sheen. She stared and held her breath again. Nothing moved. Her heart raced, the blood pounding in her ears. Behind her, she could sense her sons as they slept, their heavy breathing, sometimes movement, the soft brush of bodies against the sleeping bags. She wanted to run to them and cry in fear. But she was frozen where she stood.

She wasn't going crazy. She had seen him at the window, staring back at her.

Another chill ran through her. She could feel her own breath upon her face, moist and faint. It was cold inside the apartment now, and she shivered as she stared.

She took a step toward the window. Her feet touched the cheap linoleum, feeling every crumb and crack. The room was silent. It seemed so dark, darker than any other night. She kept on walking. Eight steps before she reached the window.

Something fluttered by! Black cloth. A hand. Suspended in the air.

Her fist shot to her mouth to stifle her cry of fear.

No! It couldn't be.

She didn't move. A full minute passed. She felt faint and dizzy, almost sick inside. She realized she wasn't breathing and took a gasp of air.

She wasn't dreaming. She wasn't crazy.

She took another step, forcing herself to breathe. Another

step. The floor creaked as she adjusted her weight to release the pressure against the floorboard. Behind her, Ammon coughed and rolled over. Somewhere above her, heavy footsteps moved down the tenement hall. She stared. The window was completely blank. Dark. Another step and then another. She never blinked, always staring at the window. Something drew her forward. She tried to fight it, but she couldn't resist. The window stared back at her, a sheet of black, flat and cold. It seemed to mock her, daring her to come. *Come closer. Come and see. There is something out here. Come closer. Do you dare?*

She kept moving forward, every sense raw and on edge. She was aware of every breath, every touch against her feet, the cold air against her arms, the utter lack of sound, the blackness of the night, the dank smell of the refrigerator that didn't work.

A final step. She felt the countertop against her hips and sensed the emptiness of the kitchen sink below her arms. The window was just two feet away. She leaned forward but saw nothing. She reached out to touch the glass, feeling the coldness of the outside air against the pane. Leaning a little closer, she looked down at the outline of the streets below.

He dropped down and stared at her, suspended in midair. His face was evil, black and brooding, his dark eyes flashing in the starlight. He smiled and pointed at her.

She was what he was looking for.

Sara's mouth hung open, her breath sinking in her chest. Half a second passed in silence. Finally, she let out a scream.

*   *   *

Twenty minutes later, Sam and Ammon tapped carefully on the apartment door. Mary let them in. Sam held his flashlight, its bright, white beam illuminating the night. Like all of his gear, it had been protected from the devastating pulse of

EMP by the underground subway. Sara sat on the edge of the couch, her hands trembling at her side. Sam's face was tense but not frightened, puzzled but not strained.

Sara watched her sons as they walked into the room. Luke was standing behind her, both of his hands resting on her shoulders. Mary remained close, never leaving her side. Sara caught a flash of dark metal in Sam's hand.

"What did you find?" Mary asked. She gripped Sara's shoulders as if bracing for bad news.

Ammon and Sam exchanged an anxious look. "You were right, Mom. There was someone outside the window."

The room was silent. "Are you kidding me!" Luke finally asked.

"See, I'm not going crazy," Sara said, her voice defensive. Mary knelt down by her.

"No, Mom, we always said that you weren't crazy."

"But you didn't believe me?"

"That's not true. We just didn't know what to think."

Sara reached over and placed a hand on Mary's arm. "He was there. Suspended in the air. Like he was flying," she repeated her story for the dozenth time.

"Well, not exactly." Sam held up the piece of metal. "But it would have looked like that to you."

"What did you find?"

Sam moved the flashlight to the piece of black metal in his hand. "This is a military rappelling device. They'd planted a bolt into the edging along the top of the roof, then rappelled over the edge using this brake and carabiner. It was the only way they could have looked inside the window."

"They! Who is *they*? What are you talking about?" Sara pleaded.

Sam hesitated. "I don't know who they were, Mom."

"Military rappelling devices? Bolts and carabiners?"

Sam held out the oval carabiner and braking device. "I know this gear," he said. "It's highly specialized military equipment used by Special Ops."

Sara stared at him, her face growing pale. "Are you saying there was a U.S. soldier outside our window?"

Sam thought for a long moment. "I'm saying there was someone. We don't know who. We don't know why. It seems crazy, but someone was out there. And they knew what they were doing. They were looking for something . . . someone . . . there was a reason they were there."

Sara looked away. For a moment, Sam thought she was going to be sick, she looked so ghostly white. He took a step toward her. "Mom, are you okay?"

He watched her as her head dropped.

"Mom?" he asked again.

She was silent a long time. The apartment was deathly quiet. "I know who they were," she finally said. She shook her head and closed her eyes.

Sam shot a quick look to his mother. He was the only one who knew.

Mary asked, "Who would be using this equipment? Why would they be here?"

Every eye remained on Sara. She turned and looked at Mary. "I have put you all in danger."

Mary shook her head. "You have saved me, baby."

Sara swallowed hard, then jumped up, ran into the kitchen, and threw up into the sink.

chapter seventeen

T he young lieutenant pulled his camouflage jacket around him and rolled over in his sleep. He was crammed in the backseat of a black Cadillac, the largest car abandoned on the freeway that he could find, but his feet were still jammed against the rear door and his legs were cramped from being bent. He had taken off his boots and placed them on the floor beside him; other than that he was fully dressed. He'd rolled up an extra pair of pants to make a rough pillow and spread his military jacket over him for a blanket, although it only covered him to his waist. His gear and pack were beside him on the floor, everything organized and tidy, just as it should be. Attention to detail. Keep things tight. Keep things clean and oiled and always ready for a fight.

The military issue 9-mm Beretta Special Forces handgun was under the front seat, within easy reach. The tiny, pearl-handled .22 he'd picked up in Baltimore was, as always, strapped around his calf.

Bono shivered in his sleep. It was cold outside. Really cold. Frost had formed on the front window, creating a maze of crystals that, in half an hour, when the sun came up, would reflect in tiny prisms of light. His breath formed a light mist in front of his face. The lieutenant rolled over, pulled the jacket to his chin, shivered, and slowly opened his eyes. He lay there for a moment trying to figure out where he was, the semi-darkness of predawn illuminating the car in gray light. Within a few seconds it all came back to him and he was instantly awake.

He got up, pulled on his boots, climbed out of the car, and stretched. A small ditch ran under the freeway and he climbed down to it, washing his face and shaving as quickly as he could. He hadn't shaved in days and it felt good to get the itchy stubble off his neck. Working his way upstream, he traced the water in the growing light until he found a pool where the small stream was calm and clear. He studied the water, looking for signs of vermin or other water life. He sifted it with his fingers, smelled it, let it drip against the light, tasted it, then sat back on his haunches and thought. He had iodine pills in his pack, but only a few weeks' worth, and who knew what lay ahead? The next water hole he found might be little better than a sewer, while this seemed fairly clear. Take his chances? Wait for better? He thought for a moment, then leaned over and drank deeply, filling his stomach as much as he could, then his canteen, then the plastic water bottles the air force sergeant had given him on the flight into Little Rock. Scrambling up the embankment, he walked back to the freeway and climbed up onto the roof of the car.

The sun was up now, its yellow rays slanting across the horizon, and he took a few minutes to look around. Interstate 40, the major artery between Little Rock and Memphis, ran east and west. Lines of dead cars cluttered the freeway as far as he could see. To the west, toward Little Rock, he could see multiple lines of smoke lifting into the calm sky. Thousands of people, all of them refugees, had moved into the country now, setting up makeshift camps of various shapes and sizes. The nearest campfire was two, maybe three hundred yards behind him. Looking east, he saw no fires. The roads between the major cities appeared to be mostly deserted. Still, he didn't plan on walking along the freeway. Too many people there. He pulled out his map and studied it in the growing light. The old State Road 70 paralleled the freeway a couple of miles to the south. Using his fingers, he measured the distance to the small ranch where his wife was staying with her parents. Twenty-five, fifty, seventy-five miles. He thought it over. He wouldn't run, but his walking pace was as quick as a slow man could jog, which meant he could cover maybe thirty miles a day if he kept it up. Two and a half, maybe three days to get there.

Just enough time to kiss his wife, hug his daughter, and turn around and head back to his military unit again.

He thought about his last conversation with his unit commander back in D.C. and the very specific instructions he'd been given. *"You have two weeks. Understand me, Lieutenant. Fourteen days. Not an hour more. I can't believe I'm doing this anyway, letting you guys even try to go home. But I want you back here, understand. I want you checking in in two weeks. We're in the middle of a war here, I don't think I need to remind you. Now go on, get out of here."*

Bono counted the days. One night in the military aircraft flying down to Little Rock. Two days walking south and east. Three days since he'd left D.C. A total of six days to get to his family, had to plan on six days getting back, which left him two days to spend with his wife and daughter.

Part of him swore in frustration at so little time; part of him smiled at the thought of two days with his family. Two days of heaven. Two days of bliss. Truth was, he would walk a year across the Gobi to spend two days with them. He'd crawl across broken glass and nails to spend an hour with his wife.

Jumping down from the roof of the car, he opened the back door, took out his pack, pulled out an incredibly dense military meal bar—two thousand calories of sweetened rust and nails, so far as he could tell—hoisted his pack, checked the weapon in the holster at the small of his back, turned southeast, and started walking with a long, determined gait.

The sun rose and it got warmer. Half an hour later, he started to sweat.

His stomach started growling.

He felt a little dizzy.

Sweat started dripping down his ribs.

Twenty minutes later, just as he climbed the embankment of State Road 70, he leaned over and started heaving in gushy, gasping gulps.

An hour later, he knew he was in trouble. Whatever was in the water, he felt like it was killing him.

Two gut-wrenching hours later, he wished it would.

chapter eighteen

What started as a cool morning, with temperatures just below the freezing mark, quickly heated up to a humid 73 degrees. The sky was clear, the air still, almost like it was waiting for something new to come. The sun rose higher in the pale sky, beating straight down on Bono's face.

Just before losing consciousness, the young lieutenant had made an important decision. Knowing he was slipping away, he'd crawled off the road, not wanting to be found by other travelers when he wasn't in a position to defend himself. Dragging his body painfully between the strands of a barbwire fence, he'd dropped into a thicket and immediately passed out.

The day wore on and the sun beat down, burning the left side of his face, his right side mashed into the thistles and dirt. He sweat, he threw up across his chest, he mumbled and called out, but he never regained consciousness. By afternoon, a violent seizure racked him and he almost choked on his tongue. Sporadic spasms came and went, convulsing him into a painful ball.

Along the road, half a dozen people moved east and west.

None of them saw him, though a couple of people thought they heard someone calling as they passed.

Afternoon came and a band of clouds started building in the west. Rain was coming. The sun dropped toward the western horizon and the temperature fell.

As twilight approached, Bono opened his eyes and shivered. Focusing his entire will and using every ounce of energy that he had left, he opened his pack, his hands shaking violently, his arms barely able to even move, and pulled out his field jacket. Fighting against the crippling pain inside his stomach and chest, he struggled to spread the jacket over his shoulders—it felt like it was made of lead—then dropped his head onto the dirt.

He was so thirsty. Brutally thirsty. His stomach muscles were tied in knots, painful spasms racking him. He heaved at the dryness, but there was nothing left inside him to throw up. He tried to swallow. His tongue and throat were so swollen it was like trying to swallow sand.

"*No, no, no,*" he almost wept, physical and emotional misery racking him. "*Please, whatever it is, I cannot die here. Please, help me to get home first. If it's your plan, then I accept it, but please don't let me die out here by myself. Caelyn will never know what happened to me. Please don't make Ellie spend the rest of her life wondering what happened to her father. Please . . . I do not ask this for myself . . . I only ask it for my family.*"

chapter nineteen

Sam tapped quickly, almost silently, on the apartment door. Azadeh stared at it anxiously while Mary let him in. He pushed the door back just a crack, slipped into the room before she could open it all the way, then grabbed the metal handle and shoved it closed again. All of them except for Luke and Kelly were waiting in the small living room. They all stared at him, waiting for his report. The soldier's face looked grim.

"What's the matter?" Sara asked him.

He glanced over his shoulder. "I was being followed!"

Sara's hand shot to her mouth and she sucked in an anxious breath. Mary looked at the window nervously. Being from the neighborhood, she knew better than the others what being followed might really mean. Ammon stepped toward him, the brothers communicating with just a look between them.

"Followed?" Sara asked. "Do you think it was the . . . you know . . . the same man who was at the window?"

Sam went into the kitchen and poured himself a drink of water from one of the plastic canteens they had brought. "No, Mom, it was just a couple of hoods," he answered after taking a quick swallow. "No biggie. I can take care of them. I lost them anyway. Still, I'd just as soon not advertise that we're all up here in this apartment." He took another swallow. He was thirsty. He'd been running. For the first time, Sara saw the shiny beads of sweat on his brow.

Sam motioned to his army jacket. "Funny how this gets such an interesting reception out there on the street."

Sara and Ammon followed him into the kitchen and the group eventually congregated around the tiny table, anxious to hear everything he had to say.

"Did you learn anything?" Ammon asked.

"Not a lot," Sam answered after finishing his drink. He motioned toward the window. "It's getting kind of crazy out there."

That much they knew. All it took was one look out on the street to see that the world that had existed just a few days before was gone.

"Are we going to be able to leave tonight like we planned?" Ammon asked. He was more ready than any of them to get out of the dreary place.

Sam shook his head. "I don't think so. Gangs have blocked off almost every street. They've dragged old cars, piled up garbage cans, old furniture, anything they can get a hold of to build a barrier."

Ammon almost swore. He simply couldn't stand the thought of another day trapped inside the apartment.

"It'll be okay," Sam said to assure him. "They've already started to fight among themselves. It reminds me a little bit of Serbia, but things will settle down. Still, we don't want to leave tonight. I think it's too early. Another day, maybe two, and I think things will be okay. If we leave at the right time and follow the route we talked about, I think we can get through the worst areas without too much problem." He shot a secret look at Azadeh. "If we are careful, and if we stay together, we'll be okay." He turned to Sara. "How's Luke doing? What about Kelly Beth?"

"They're both doing really well. It's just amazing."

Sam walked toward the window. "I met some policemen," he continued.

"Really!" Mary exclaimed, her voice hopeful.

"It's about time," Sara said. "Where have all the law enforcement officers been?"

"There aren't many of them reporting for duty, from what I could learn. Right now they're trying to operate with less than five percent of their total force."

"Five percent!" Ammon shot back. His face showed disappointment and disgust. "Cowards! Where did they all go?"

"Same as the rest of us," Sam replied. "Home with their families. Trying to survive. Trying to figure out where they're going to get some water for their kids, where they're going to find some food. And in some ways, I can't blame them. I wouldn't want to be a law enforcement officer down there on the street right now. A million crazy people, lots of them with guns. No rules. No expectations. No communications between officers. No backup. No police vehicles. No way to get around."

The group was silent. Azadeh started to say something and they all looked at her, but she fell silent, embarrassed.

"You saw some cops, though. That's a good step," Mary said. "Maybe we've turned the corner. If we can get some officers down there on the street, if people start to feel like things will soon be back to normal—"

"Miss Dupree," Sam interrupted, "I don't mean to be disagreeable, but things are not getting anywhere back to normal."

"But if we can get some policemen . . ."

"I'm not sure we can be counting on these guys to help us anyway. Maybe just the opposite. I watched them shaking people down. First thing they did when they stopped me was frisk me for any food or water. Second thing they wanted was to take away my gun. I told them, dude, you got to be kidding. They insisted. Well, maybe even more than insisted. I tried to show them my military ID, explain to them I was authorized to carry it, that it was a military-issue weapon. It took a while to get them to back off." He cracked a quick smile. "I had to be persuasive."

Ammon watched him carefully. There was more to this story. A lot more. Sam hadn't gotten the cops to leave him alone by sweet-talking them. He would discuss it with his brother later on.

Sam lifted the cup again, letting every drop of water drip into his mouth. Putting it down, he wiped the sweat from his forehead, wetting his sleeve. "We've got a new president of the United States," he said.

Stunned silence. No one moved. An unexplained chill fell over the room.

"A new president?" Mary asked him.

Sam nodded at her.

"A new beginning? A new start at order?" Mary's voice was full of hope.

A cold chill moved through Sara. It cut her, sending a dull ache around the base of her skull. *A new beginning?* She forced herself to breathe. *No, she knew that wasn't true.*

She took a step back, her face drained of color. She didn't breathe again for a long moment, her eyes dropping to the floor.

No one noticed her distress. They concentrated on Sam.

"A new leader for our nation?" Ammon asked him.

"Yep. A new Head Cheese."

"Who is it?"

Sam wiped another bead of sweat from his face.

The room fell still and cold again.

"Albert Fuentes," Sara said into the silence.

Everyone turned to her, but that was all she said.

Ammon shot a puzzled look to Sam, asking with his eyes. "Yeah, she's right," he said.

Ammon turned back to his mother. "How did you know that, Mom?"

She stood in the middle of the tiny kitchen, her hands shaking at her side. If she'd been staring at a monster—which she was—she couldn't have looked more scared.

Ammon took a step toward her. "How did you know that, Mom?" he repeated, his voice as gentle as a whisper.

Sara swallowed and looked away.

The room was still and silent.

"Your father told me," she finally said.

"*The totalitarian phenomenon is not to be understood without making allowance for the thesis that some important part of every society consists of people who actively want tyranny: either to exercise it themselves or— much more mysteriously—to submit to it. Democracy will therefore always remain at risk.*"

—JEAN-FRANCOIS REVEL

"*. . . because of the power of Satan who did get hold upon their hearts.*"

—4 NEPHI 1:28

chapter twenty

RAVEN ROCK (SITE R), UNDERGROUND MILITARY COMPLEX
SOUTHERN PENNSYLVANIA

It was a small group, two women and five men, not including the new president of the United States. With the
exception of the lean, thick-haired man who found himself
in the amazingly unfamiliar position of sitting in the president's
chair, the members of the group knew each other intimately,
having worked together from behind locked doors, aboard private jets, and inside luxury villas for many years. Along the wall
before them, a secure conference system brought in video feeds
from Paris, London, and Berlin. Altogether, thirteen people
were on the line. And though he sat at the head of the conference table, President Albert J. Fuentes didn't control the meeting, set the agenda, or have very much to say.

He was a weak man, a coyote of a leader, doomed to follow the pack, with no more intelligence or talent than the
average man out on the street. The only things he had in great
abundance were good looks, an empty character, and hot,
burning, soul-selling, back-stabbing ambition. He also had
camera presence, having started out as a television newsman,
reading other people's words from a teleprompter as if they
were his own.

It was a deadly but useful combination. And the reason why he just might be the perfect choice.

The old man sat on the same style of black leather chair as they all did, but he hunched lower, old and shriveled, almost pygmy-like against the enormous conference table. The others watched him carefully, listening to his every word. He gestured toward Fuentes. "This is him?" he asked.

The others only nodded.

The old man raised an eyebrow. "He's the best you got?" He smiled weakly as he said it. Fuentes thought that he was kidding. The others knew he was not. "I don't know. I really don't," the old man went on. "I feel like I'm on the iceberg watching the *Titanic* bearing down. It's a full moon. We'll see the bodies. This is going to be a freaking mess."

The newly appointed vice president, the man who'd chosen Fuentes, sat forward in his chair. He was intense, moody, brilliant, and one of the wealthiest men in the United States. He had already mastered money; now he mastered power. "It's going to work out," was all he said. There was significant, if unknown, meaning in his words.

Sensing their mood, Fuentes shifted angrily. He did not know the old man, had never seen him before in his life (and he knew everyone who was anyone, or so he thought), and his indignation rose. "I remind you, *sir*, that you are speaking to the president of the United States."

The old man didn't even answer as he stared at him.

"He'll do what we tell him to," the new vice president went on, speaking as if Fuentes weren't there. "And remember, he was the next in line of succession. We had to follow protocol. We couldn't push too far. I mean, we've already had to kill one of them, put another into a coma. We thought it best not to have to kill him, too."

"You're going to have to kill him eventually. Might as well do it now."

Fuentes' face grew white, his lips tight. Was it him they were talking about? He couldn't even tell. Surely not. He must have missed it. No one looked at him.

The vice president brought his elbows atop his armrest and put his fingers to his lips, building a small tent before his face. He patiently glanced at Fuentes. "I trust him," was all he said.

The old man pulled on his feeble chin. It was covered with white hairs, scattered and wispy, some of them far too long, as if it was hard to shave between the deep creases on his face. And something about him smelled. It wasn't strong and it wasn't necessarily unpleasant, but there was something odd, almost unworldly. Fuentes sniffed the air, trying to identify the odor. It was . . . old . . . stale air released from a sealed room within an ancient temple . . . an old book that hadn't been opened for many years . . . an old house . . . a rotting tree . . . it was, what? He couldn't tell. And maybe it was that simple. The old man just smelled old.

The man cocked his head to the right, then leaned toward Fuentes. "Do you love your country?" he asked.

Fuentes hesitated. What was the answer he was looking for? "There are things I love about it," he finally said.

"Do you think it can be rebuilt?"

"Of course I do."

"Do you think it *should* be rebuilt?"

The president of the United States looked down. This was where they had him. He answered carefully. "We have made mistakes. Plenty of them. There are many things we shouldn't have done. We've hurt the world, there is no question. Most of the world hates us now, and who are we to blame them, when we even hate ourselves? We've oppressed and robbed and plundered. Pumped our filth into the air. We've started wars to keep the oil coming, spilling blood to prime the pump . . ."

The old man raised a hand to stop him. "Yeah, yeah, I've heard it all before. Some of what you said is truthful, but most of it is crap. You've got to learn to see the difference."

Fuentes hesitated. "We've grown weak," he concluded. "We could be stronger, so much stronger, *if* we take the proper steps."

The old man pulled out a pack of cigarettes, tapped the box, extracted a filter, and held the cigarette between his dry lips. "Do you realize that you can't lie to me?" he said.

Fuentes kept his eyes down. Such an unusual thing to say.

"You can't lie to me," the old man said again. "You can't deceive me. I can see into your soul. I sense your deepest thoughts by the flicker in your eye. I know your heart by the way you look at me. I know everything about you. More than you even know yourself. You forget. I never do." The old man stopped, lit the cigarette, and sat back against his chair.

Fuentes started to fidget, brushing his hands across his face.

"You're forty-seven," the man continued. "You used to be a Republican but switched parties when your old boss told you there were better opportunities in the new administration for a man such as yourself."

Fuentes looked up at the old man, his courage building. That was no secret. Anyone who knew him would know about that.

The man drew a breath of smoke, then broke into an evil smile. "You tell your friends and family, even your wife, that you've got a lot of money, but the truth is, you've got nothing. Not a dime, as far as I can tell, and you've been broke for years. If it wasn't for credit cards, and a handful of overly generous friends, I think you'd be living on the street."

Fuentes frowned and started to answer but the old man cut him off. "That's okay, I can live with beggars. It's some of these other things I find more interesting." He pulled himself forward by the edge of the table. "When you were ten, you and one of your old buddies, what was his name, David Butter, yeah, I'm sure that's it, the two of you found a litter of kittens in the old barn behind your grandma's house. Do you remember that, Albert?"

The president sat lower in his seat, his face growing pale now and sick.

"You put them in a small bag . . ."

Fuentes shifted on his chair. A cold chill seeped into the room. "Stop it," he muttered quietly.

"You dropped them in the creek. Five little kittens. There was no reason. I've got to tell you, I think that's kind of sick. Then, remember back in high school, that sweet young thing you took to the prom—what was her name? Kristen, yes, I think that's it. A real cute little girl. So much younger than you were . . ."

Fuentes wanted to scream, but he was silent, overcome with gut-wrenching surprise and fear. *Who was this man? How did he know these things? Where did he get his information from?*

The old man stared at him. His lips were smiling but his eyes were blank and dark. "Funny, isn't it, *Mr. President*," the name was sweet syrup on his lips, "a man of your background and education; a young television reporter, then Harvard, then state attorney general, U.S. assistant attorney general and now president of the United-freakin-States. Yet you have so many peculiar habits. So many late nights on the computer. What are you staring at all that time! Why does your wife sleep in the basement? What is she afraid of, President Fuentes?"

The old man stopped and drew another smoke. Fuentes kept his eyes down. His hands trembled on the table and his breath was short and tight.

"Look at me," the old man said to him. "Look at me right now."

Fuentes barely raised his eyes.

The old man leaned toward him. "You're not who I would have chosen, but some things are beyond even my control.

181

When you're a member of the Donner party and someone throws you a bone, you've got to take it and chew on it, sucking out whatever marrow you can get, know what I mean? And that's where we are now. Someone threw you to us. Now we're going to chew.

"But I want you to remember: I know you. I have known you well for years. Yes, we're going to use you, but there are many things we have to teach you first, many things you need to know. Who I am. Who these others are. What we intend to do. It will come slowly, but we will teach you, and this is your first lesson: You can't lie to me. You can't deceive me. So please, don't even try. All it will do is hurt you. And we don't want to hurt you, friend."

Fuentes took a breath and held it, then looked up at the old man. "I understand," he muttered, though he understood not a thing at all.

"All right, then. We understand each other. Now, let me ask again. We have a chance to rebuild this nation, but in another way, after a different model, a model we'll control. Are you willing to support us? It all comes down to that."

Fuentes pressed his lips together and adjusted his perfect hair. Leaning forward, he lowered his voice to a dry whisper. "If you say you truly know me, then you already know I will."

The old man smashed his cigarette. "Let's get to work," he said.

*　　*　　*

They talked for hours, outlining a final agenda, naming key players and responsibilities, and setting up a timeline to put the plan in place. The last thing they had to decide was when the new president would address the people of the United States.

"It will take FEMA days to distribute the equipment throughout the country," the vice president announced. "It's a huge problem, getting working television receivers and satellite systems out to all the cities and towns. We don't want people to congregate any more than they have to—larger crowds are unpredictable and so much harder to control. We want a television in every small town. We're talking a couple hundred thousand systems . . . it will take a little time."

"Four days," the old man prodded.

They agreed that that would work.

Their business complete, the meeting started to break up.

"There is still one problem," the new vice president said as the group started collecting their things. They hesitated awkwardly, throwing a glance or two in Fuentes' direction.

"This is private," the vice said to his new boss.

The president was excused. He left without comment and the group sat down at the conference table once again.

"We think the SecDef is alive," the vice president announced. "Not only alive, but suspicious. And we can't find him anywhere."

The old man's eyes flashed in anger. "You will take care of him, I am sure."

The vice nodded. "He's an old friend. I think I can round him up."

"And what about King Abdullah?" one of the women wanted to know. His absence from the conference call had not gone unnoticed among the group.

The old man sat back and thought a moment about his good friend, the Saudi king. The group sat in awkward silence. They all knew what he would do.

"You're going to kill him?" the vice president asked.

The old man stood up from the table. "I don't think I'll have to. He's stupid. He's too aggressive. And always there's his foolish, blinding pride. I don't think I'll have to do it. We'll simply let him kill himself."

chapter twenty-one

EAST SIDE, CHICAGO, ILLINOIS

The sound of thudding footsteps rolled down the narrow hallway of the high-rise apartment building. Sam, lying atop a sleeping bag just a few feet from the apartment door, was immediately awake. He sat up and listened carefully to the sound of the passing footsteps, taking measure of them, his nerves on edge, his breathing light. Four people, maybe a few more. Adults. Most of them heavy treaders, probably men. None of them were speaking. They knew where they were going and what they needed to do. The sound faded, the stairwell door slammed, and they were gone. Sam checked his watch: 0345. He stretched, swallowed against the dryness of his mouth, and lay back down. Then, knowing he'd never get to sleep again, he stood.

Luke and Ammon were asleep inside their bags. Luke's breathing was heavy. It almost sounded sedated. Ammon was curled up, his sleeping bag pushed down around his waist. Sam's military boots and jacket were lying on the floor beside him. Moving quietly, he pulled on the leather boots, ran the laces behind the quick-lace eyelets, stood, and pulled on his

184

jacket. Turning for the door, he sensed her outline in the darkness and stopped.

"Hey, Azadeh," he whispered, not wanting to wake his brothers up.

She barely nodded to him, afraid to speak.

He moved toward the door. She followed closely. "Where are you going?" she whispered once she got very close.

"Thought I'd go up on the roof and take a look around."

She moved a little closer to him. "Can I come with you?"

Sam hesitated. "I don't know. It might be better if you stayed here."

She dropped her eyes. The whites, large as they were, were barely visible in the dark. "I've been inside this apartment for a very long time. Days. It seems much longer. If I could please just come with you, it would . . ." she hesitated, searching for the right word . . . "it would mean good things to me."

Sam smiled, wondering what word she had been searching for. "It's going to be cold up there."

She was already holding her coat and she stepped toward the door. He helped her put her coat on, then pulled the door back. The hallway was empty and he led the way toward the stairs.

*　　*　　*

The moon, a quarter full, waning and burning orange, was already low on the western horizon when they came out on the roof. With no city lights to drown them out, the stars filled the night sky, a million of them or more. A light wind was blowing from the south, and Sam sniffed the air. "A cold front is going to move through sometime in the next day or so," he said.

Azadeh nodded, pretending to understand though she had no idea what he meant. Sam watched her, knowing she was faking it, and explained. "A south wind at this time of year and up here in the north," he pointed to his left, "usually means a low pressure is moving through. The wind circles around a low pressure in a counterclockwise direction." His voice trailed off. He had lost her again. "It's going to turn cold in the next day or two," he said more simply.

Azadeh nodded. That she could understand. She shivered anyway. "It seems cold right now," she said.

Sam reached out and pulled her collar up around her ears. "I guess Chicago is a lot colder than Iran?"

Her hair was loose and it blew behind her, falling in shadows down her back. Her face was almond colored in the moonlight and her eyes were large and bright. Sam felt his stomach tighten as he looked at her and he tried hard not to stare. "I grew up in the mountains," she said. "My village was in the Agha Jari Deh Valley. Remember? You have been there."

Sam remembered very well.

"I am used to the cold." Still, she shivered. Sam knew that she was scared.

"It's going to be okay," he told her.

She looked at him and nodded. "I think it will." She brushed a strand of hair away. "I saw what you did on that first night, back in the car. I saw what happened to your brother. I saw what you did for Kelly Beth. I don't understand it. It makes me feel . . . awkward. Is that the right word? I don't think that it is. It makes me feel funny. There is a strangeness in my chest. It keeps me warm. It makes it so I can't sleep. I wonder what it means?"

Sam hunched his shoulders, struggling for his own words. He was not good at this and it scared him that he might say the wrong thing and screw it up. "It's going to take a while to understand it. But it has to do with God. With Allah. He is real. Do you believe that?"

"I know that He is real."

"Do you believe that He can hear us? Do you believe that He can answer our prayers?"

She looked away. "I have prayed my whole life."

Sam waited, noticing she had left his actual question unanswered. But her face was softer now and not so full of fear.

"God does answer us," he told her. "God always hears and answers our prayers."

"Are you a messenger from Allah?" Her voice was full of doubt and wonder.

"No, no, no." He started laughing. "I'm no messenger from Allah. I'm just a man, just a kid, really, at least that's how I feel. I'm just like you are, Azadeh, trying to figure this whole thing out."

"But the blessing? The prayer you uttered. You promised your brother he would live!"

Sam bit his lip and looked away. He had no idea what to say. This wasn't something he was comfortable with. He was a doer, not a talker, and someone else, anyone else, was far better at explaining this kind of thing. "It will take a little time, Azadeh, before you can understand," he finally said. "But that's okay. You've got all the time in the world."

He watched her, waited, and, when she didn't answer, he turned and walked toward the corner of the building, looking around. She followed, keeping a few steps behind. The city had fallen silent below them. The sky was alive and bright, the ground nothing but an empty black hole. Looking west, Sam could barely make out the outline of downtown, the skyscrapers reaching high enough to blot out some of the stars, leaving square shadows against the bowl of light. North, Lake Michigan was another black hole. No lights but the setting moon and stars. No noise now. Perfect quiet. He took a breath and held it. It was almost beautiful. So peaceful. So serene.

Azadeh moved beside him and touched his shoulder, pointing east. "Look at that!" she whispered in surprise.

Sam turned and looked. Lights! Man-made lights along the shoreline! They were clustered in a row that seemed to stretch two hundred feet or more. A long way away, maybe four or five miles. Lights. That meant electricity. Which meant . . . what? He didn't know. Civilization? Maybe. At least it was a start.

He stared, his mouth open, then grabbed Azadeh by the hand and said, "Let's go."

chapter twenty-two

EAST SIDE, CHICAGO, ILLINOIS

It was getting lighter now, sunrise less than an hour away. They were heading east. The streets weren't empty, but they were relatively quiet: a few clusters of people here and there, a few fires—an old warehouse had burned down, but it was only smoldering—and a row of barricades, which Sam helped Azadeh climb over. They walked another forty minutes. A couple of miles away from the shoreline, the streets became noticeably more crowded. Word had started spreading. *Lights along the shoreline!* Getting closer, Sam could smell the lake: seaweed, wet sand, humid air. Azadeh stayed close to him, her hair tucked underneath the hood of her overcoat, the buttons tight around her waist. Moving toward a large intersection, they turned right and immediately stopped.

Two blocks ahead of them, an enormous crowd had gathered. Noise. Sometimes screams. Fights were breaking out. Smoke—it looked like tear gas. Behind them, they heard the pounding of footsteps as a group of people ran toward the massive crowd. Sam immediately pulled Azadeh to the side, pressing her against the wall of the nearest building, letting the screaming crowd go running by. A dilapidated antique shop was on his right. He approached it, broke the window on the door with his elbow, reached in and turned the lock, pushed the door back, and pulled her inside. The room was dark, although there was a hint of light now, the eastern sky turning light pink and orange. The shop was musty and mostly filled with junk. "Stay here!" Sam commanded. "Look around and see if you can find a back room. There has to be a rear entrance to the building. Find it, then stay here. If anyone comes through the front door, and I mean *anyone,* you run out the back. You understand me, Azadeh! Go out the back. There has to be an alley back there. Find a place to hide and wait for me."

"Don't leave me here," she whimpered. "Please don't leave me here alone!"

"Azadeh, you'll be okay. No one's going to come in here. If they do, do what I tell you and go running quietly out the back. But it's important, Azadeh, that you not talk to anyone. They will know where you're from. Normally, that's not a problem. Might not be a problem now, but we can't take the chance. These are not normal times. There is no normal anymore." He stopped and looked toward the broken window. Another crowd of people ran noisily down the street. He turned back to face her. "Are you okay?" he asked.

"I'm okay. I stay here. If anyone comes, I go out the back door and wait for you."

"That's right, babe." He stopped and looked around, suddenly embarrassed. He knew that he was flushing. His dad had called his mother *babe,* but Sam had never called a woman that.

He held her shoulders. Then he turned, walked toward the door, and disappeared. She followed him to the doorway and looked out, but he was quickly swallowed up in the shuffle and panic of the growing crowd. She stood at the door a moment longer, looking out through the broken glass, then turned away, slipped behind the counter of the small antique shop, leaned against the wall, and slid down to the floor.

chapter twenty-three

TwENTY-ONE MILES EAST OF LITTLE ROCK, ARKANSAS

The rancher found him lying in a ditch, surrounded by his own vomit and coated in sweat. He watched him from the saddle of his horse without moving toward him, suspicious, even angry at finding the stranger who had passed out on his property. Probably a drunk. Maybe someone running from the law. Maybe worse. Maybe he was one of those men who'd joined up with the tribes that were forming in these parts, some of them violent, most of them crazy, all of them growing desperate. He held his horse back and watched the stranger closely, noting the sickly face and short hair. Seeing the military clothes didn't help to ease his suspicions, for he doubted they were real; lots of losers hung out in second-hand fatigues they'd picked up at the army surplus store. He'd known more than one or two liars who claimed they were in the army when the closest they had ever come was walking by the recruiting station on their way to the Red Cross to give a pint of blood for thirty bucks.

A little pressure against the mare's ribs was all it took to move her forward. She stepped over a narrow ditch and stopped again and he leaned forward, crossing his arms atop the saddle horn. For the first time he noticed the three-day assault pack, coyote-tan and clean, then the insulated pouch of water. He studied the equipment hanging with carabiners from both sides of the pack, all of it well maintained and clean. For the first time he considered that this guy might be real.

Quickly dismounting, he dropped the reins—the young horse was as trustworthy as his dog and wouldn't go anywhere. He patted her neck without thinking as he passed and moved quickly toward the stranger.

The young man was almost lifeless, his breathing shallow and slow. The rancher leaned toward him, then pulled back from the smell. Turning his face, he took a deep breath, then pressed two fingers against the young man's neck, feeling his pounding pulse. Lifting the soldier's head, he started talking to him. "Hey there, buddy. Can you hear me?" He gently patted his cheeks. "Are you in pain? Can you hear me?"

The dark-haired soldier didn't move. The rancher quickly wiped his right hand across his jeans to clean his fingers, cradled the soldier's head, and opened his right eye. The pupil quickly dilated but stared past him, still not seeing. He could feel the soldier's cold and clammy skin under his careful hand and he gently laid him down again.

Whistling, he called his horse. The young animal, dark with white socks, lifted her head and stared at him but didn't move until he whistled a second time. The rancher held his breath against the smell of human waste and vomit and strained against the soldier's weight. Sensing his burden, the horse almost knelt, making it easier for him to lift the soldier across the back of the leather saddle. Working quickly, the rancher gathered up the backpack and small sleeping bag and tied them to the saddle with leather straps. He pulled the reins over the black mare's neck and she lowered her head, allowing them to fall across her head. The rancher held on, then started jogging. He wasn't young anymore, and he was a little over-weight to boot; it was only a couple of minutes before he was panting like a dog. The horse easily kept up with his pace, moving gently to keep her load from bouncing on her back.

Looking back, the rancher watched her smooth gait and reached back to pat her neck again. A good animal. Smart. Sensitive. One of the best horses he'd ever owned.

* * *

Fifteen minutes later, he led the horse and unconscious soldier through a wooden gate at the back of his yard. A large wooden barn, built by his grandfather, was on his left. Metal buildings and granaries were on his right. The area around the outbuildings was paved with asphalt and cement. The farm-house, a large, brick rancher with a four-car garage and peanut-shaped swimming pool, was straight ahead. A little boy watched him from behind a low fence that separated the farm buildings from the grass, then turned and ran inside. Seconds later, a middle-aged woman exited the house and ran toward her husband. "My goodness, Reed . . ." She stopped short. "Are you okay? *Who* is that . . . is everything all right?"

The rancher dropped the reins and moved around to the other side of the horse.

"What in the world happened! Is he okay?"

"I don't know, Jazzy. Found him near the highway. He'd crossed the fence onto our property and passed out down by the old well."

She took a careful step toward her husband, her dark eyes scared. She was middle-aged, but tan and pretty. Her nails were carefully manicured and her hands were smooth—not the hands of a woman who spent much time out on the farm.

All she could see were the stranger's legs hanging from her side of the saddle. She followed her husband around to the other side of the horse. "Oh my . . . oh my . . ." she whispered upon seeing the uniform. "Reed, is he a soldier?" Her face turned pale, a deep sadness falling across her eyes.

The man grunted as he pulled the stranger off the back of the horse, draped him across his shoulders, and headed for the grass.

Jazzy smelled him and turned away, then yelled toward her youngest son: "Bruce, get a couple buckets from the garage. Fill them from the pool. Go on! Go on! Get 'em now!" The little boy, maybe ten or eleven, had wandered close. So far he hadn't said anything, but now he turned and ran again.

Reed laid the soldier on the grass at the back side of the house. His wife followed and immediately started taking off his filthy clothes while Reed worked on his boots. The young boy showed up with two sloshing buckets and a wet rag. The woman gently placed the rag over the unconscious man's forehead. He mumbled but didn't wake.

* * *

Twelve hours later, Bono opened his eyes. It was dark. It was quiet. The bed was soft and warm. He looked at the darkness in utter confusion, then started to push himself up from the pillow, panic surging through his veins. He fell back, his head pounding like a hammer as he grunted against the pain. Taking a deep breath, he gathered his strength and tried to lift his head again.

"Shhhh," he heard a soft voice. "It's okay. You're all right. Don't try to get up just yet."

A dim glow from a small candle filled the room and, as his eyes adjusted to the darkness, his surroundings slowly came into focus. A woman was staring at him, her hand upon his arm. "It's okay," she repeated, her voice as comforting as anything he'd ever heard. "You can relax here. I'll stay beside you. Everything's going to be okay."

Bono fell back against the pillow. "Where am I?" he muttered through a dry mouth.

The woman lifted a cup of water. "You need to drink," she said.

Bono strained to lift his head, desperately thirsty, and she pressed the cup against his lips. He drank several gulps, then leaned back. "Where am I?" he repeated.

The woman started to answer, but Bono was asleep again before she could explain.

*　　*　　*

"It's impossible to say for certain," the rancher said. "It could have been a number of things." He appeared to hesitate and didn't explain any further.

Bono sat at the kitchen table dressed in a thick blue bathrobe and white slippers that were a size too big. He was still weak, but an empty soup bowl sat in front of him and he was starting to feel a little better as the food had time to seep into his blood. He eyed his new friend and wondered in amazement at the unlikely coincidence, then turned to stare at the pictures on the kitchen wall: the doctor with his family, his horses, pictures of all the things he loved. The man sitting before him had saved his life not because he was a rancher but because he was a surgeon from Little Rock who had fled the city to their family ranch after the EMP attack.

"Had to be something in the water I drank?" Bono said.

The doctor hesitated, then stood up from the table and walked toward the sink. "I'm guessing it had to be."

"Does this mean, you know, I've got some kind of worm or snail or something disgusting growing inside me?"

The doctor laughed. "I don't suppose you're any worse off

now than you were when you got back from Iraq or Afghanistan or wherever else you've been."

"It wasn't Giardia," Bono said, still trying to diagnose himself. "Way too fast to be a parasite."

The doctor turned around. "Without the ability to do some proper blood and lab tests, we'll probably never know."

"So I don't need to worry about it?"

The doctor shook his head. "I didn't say that, lieutenant. I didn't say that at all. In a perfect world, we'd do a little more research to try to figure out what it was. But I don't think it's going to kill you and I don't think it will necessarily have any long-lasting repercussions or side effects. I may be wrong, but we can hope."

Bono sipped at a cup of chocolate milk, staring at the bright blue mug. One of the doctor's neighbors had a herd of cows. How valuable was that? Gold. Even better. You couldn't drink gold. Better to have a cow.

"How far up the stream did you walk before you drank?" the doctor asked.

"A little ways," Bono answered sheepishly, recognizing his foolish error.

The doctor sat down at the table. "You didn't purify it, boil it, use iodine tablets or anything?"

Bono lowered his head. "I was in a hurry."

"Look, lieutenant, it could have been a couple of things. My best guess, if you were to backtrack up the stream a ways, you'd find a dead animal in the water. A raccoon, skunk, rat, fox, who knows, but I'd bet my left arm—and I pretty much need my arm for surgery, so you can see I'm fairly sure about this bet—that there was a rotting carcass somewhere not too far upstream."

Bono's face turned to ash and he pressed his lips together, looking sick again.

The doctor couldn't help but notice. "You know, back in ancient days the Persians used to poison their enemies' water by throwing in dead dogs and rats, the first example of biological warfare that we know of. Entire armies are recorded as having been brought to their knees. Anthrax, Ebola, salmonella, lots of bad things."

The doctor paused as he thought. Something about the story still didn't add up. "I want to be sure I understand. You drank the water when?"

"I've been here one night is all, right?"

"Yes. I found you yesterday just before nightfall."

"Then I drank the water yesterday morning. I was very sick by early afternoon."

It can't be, the doctor thought. *The incubation time for any of these contagions is much longer than just a few hours. The timing isn't right. It doesn't add up!* He thought for a long moment, then let it go. "You're lucky you survived it," he told Bono. "Frankly, if I hadn't found you, I don't know if you'd have made it through the night. You were about as dehydrated as anyone I've ever seen."

"I wanted to die," Bono said. "I felt like I was throwing up everything I've ever eaten since the second grade. Given the choice of going through that again or dying, just hand me a gun."

"But you're feeling better now?"

Bono took another drink of chocolate milk. "You have no idea," he said.

The doctor pointed to his abdomen. "A little sore, I imagine?"

"Feels like a freight train drove across my chest."

"You're going to be sore for a while. And weak. It will take a few days to get your strength back."

Bono pushed back from the table. The sun was just

coming up and the room was lit now by soft morning light. "Thank you," he said for at least the third or fourth time.

The doctor, owner of Arabian Acres Ranches, only grunted.

Bono stood. "I've got to go," he said.

"You should stay and rest a little."

Bono felt his legs grow weak, his knees seeming to buckle under his weight. "I can't, sir. I really can't. I've only got a few days."

The doctor lifted a hand. "I understand," he said, watching the lieutenant wobble as he grabbed the kitchen table, "but I don't think you're going to make it."

Bono started to turn, then suddenly changed his mind, falling back into his chair and closing his eyes to stop the room from spinning.

"It's an awful long walk to Memphis," the doctor said, his eyes narrowing with concern.

"How far is it if I crawl?" Bono tried to laugh. "That's the only way I'm going to make it unless the world quits spinning."

The doctor raised an eyebrow. "I don't think you're going to make it," he repeated. "I don't think you could walk around this house."

The doctor's wife, Jasmine, entered the room with a bucket of small tomatoes, some of the last to be taken from her garden. She glanced at Bono and patted him on the shoulder as she walked by. "You look better," she said as she moved toward the kitchen sink, where she dropped the tomatoes and started washing them in another bucket of water she'd brought in from outside.

"You've been so good to me, Jasmine. I want to thank you," Bono said.

She kept her eyes on her work. "We don't have much, but

I'm going to make you some sandwiches to hold you over on your journey."

"You don't need to do that. Really, I've got supplies. I'll be okay."

She quickly turned toward him. "Have you told him, Reed?" She eyed her husband.

The doctor looked away. "It didn't come up," he said quietly without looking at his wife.

She lifted another tomato and dropped it in the bucket of water. "Tell me, Lieutenant Calton, did you ever run into a Captain Bradley?" she asked. "He was an Apache pilot. Flew with the Third Battalion of the One Hundred and First."

Bono thought, then shook his head.

The brown-haired woman with the soft hands turned around to face him. "That's too bad," she said. "Arnie was a good man. Too young. Too kind sometimes. Too trusting. Not careful enough. But he was a good boy, our son. He was killed eighteen months ago in Afghanistan."

Bono stared at her without speaking. "I'm very sorry," he said.

Jasmine turned back to her tomatoes. "So are we." She pulled some homemade bread from the cupboard. "We don't have a lot, you understand, but I'll put together what I can."

Bono started to argue but could see it wouldn't do any good. And he was thankful anyway, and willing to accept her generosity. He watched her spread some peanut butter and homemade jam across thick slices of bread. Standing again, he said, "Thank you, sir," to the doctor, his voice determined. "Thank you for what you've done, but I really have to go."

The doctor stood beside him. "You'll never make it in your condition."

"Maybe not, sir, but what choice do I have? I think if I start slow and pace myself . . ."

"I really can't allow it."

Bono stared at him without replying. Turning, he headed to the kitchen door. His clothes were drying on the fence outside.

"Let me ask you something," the doctor said as Bono walked away. The officer turned back. "Do you know how to handle a horse?"

Bono hesitated. "I rode a horse in Afghanistan."

"If I give you a good animal, will you take care of her?"

Bono's eyes moved from the doctor to his wife and back again. "I promise you, I will."

The doctor nodded. "Figured you would."

chapter twenty-four

EAST SIDE, CHICAGO, ILLINOIS

It was almost two hours before Sam returned. By then the sun had risen, bringing light to the day. He stood in front of the broken window on the door, his back to it, looking out on the crowded streets. Then he quickly pushed the door open and backed in. "Azadeh," he called softly.

She was nowhere to be seen.

"Azadeh," he called a little more loudly. Still no answer. He pulled the Beretta from his holster. The handgrip was already warm. He'd been holding it before. "Azadeh." This time he whispered, his nerves on end. He listened, waited, then slowly started moving toward a door on the back wall. Passing the store's counter, he found her asleep on the floor. "Azadeh," he whispered, kneeling down beside her. She opened her eyes and looked up at him, confusion in her eyes, then sat up instantly, wrapping her coat around her waist. "I am so sorry. I am so sorry. I must have fallen asleep." She rolled over to her knees.

Sam put a hand on her leg to reassure her. "It's okay. I'm glad you got some sleep."

She stood up. "I am ready."

He looked at her and laughed. "Ready to what, Azadeh?"

She looked confused again and then embarrassed. "I don't know. Whatever you tell me to do."

He put his arm around her. "Come with me," he said.

She nodded toward the street. "What did you find?"

"I'll tell you as we walk."

"It is good though, no? It is good. Lights? Electricity? Many people go there. They are all excited. I think it must be good."

Sam shook his head sadly and pulled her toward the door. "I'll explain everything, but we've got to leave right now."

Azadeh's face fell. "You are not happy?"

"I'm afraid not."

"It is not good?"

"No, it's not."

*　*　*

They moved against the flow of people who were rushing toward the shoreline. The crowds were larger now, and more desperate, most of them running, pushing, screaming, cursing, whatever it took to make their way along. Almost all of them carried something to hold water: buckets, plastic containers, empty milk jugs, water packs. One man carried an old metal sink and Azadeh stared at him, her eyes wide in disbelief. There were children with their mothers, babies in tired arms. All of them were moving down the street toward the shore-line, leaving Sam and Azadeh to push against the tide, like fish trying to swim upstream. Four or five blocks farther west, the crowd thinned out and they could finally talk.

"What happened back there?" Azadeh asked him as they walked.

Sam kept his eyes moving. "The United States government has brought in a portable water purification facility. They got it from Canada, apparently. Shipped it across the Great Lakes. It's got its own power generator, pumps, filters, distribution outlets, the whole bit. They're pumping water from the lake, purifying it, and making it available to anyone who needs it."

Azadeh looked relieved. "That is good, no? Water . . . we all need it."

Sam adjusted the water pack on his back. Azadeh reached out and pressed it, feeling its weight and pressure, noting it was full. "What is bad about this, Sam?"

He frowned, a fist of worry growing in his gut. Everything was tumbling around him and he didn't know how to explain. He thought back on what he had seen and heard at the water station. Someone had shoved him; others pulled him back. The water master had stared at him, his face a threatening scowl. "Where you from?" he had demanded. Sam was slow to respond. What difference did it make? The city official had glared at him and said, "You're the wrong color." Sam couldn't believe it and he stared, his mouth open. "Where do you live? What neighborhood? We need to ration. What *family* are you from?"

*   *   *

Walking with Azadeh, he felt another cold chill run through him and he wondered how he could explain it. Azadeh looked at him, her eyes wide. She reached out and touched his arm. "Sam, are you okay?"

He shook his head. "There were soldiers there. They were from a unit I didn't recognize. They wore dark uniforms and red headgear." He stopped talking. He was angry. And confused. His face screwed up tight.

Azadeh froze, her mind flashing back to the soldiers with black uniforms on the mountain in Iran. Her father tied up to a tree. The gasoline. The matches. She felt suddenly sick inside. Sam stopped beside her, glanced behind them, then pulled on her elbow, picking up the pace. "There were other soldiers," he went on. "Light blue uniforms with the U.N. symbols on their helmets." He paused again. "And other soldiers too."

Azadeh didn't understand. "Other soldiers?"

"Yes, Azadeh. Soldiers from other countries. Some of them appeared to be from private security organizations." He huffed in disgust. "Yeah, I saw them in Afghanistan and Iraq. A bunch of blowhard wannabes with big guns but little brains. It isn't good, Azadeh. It isn't good at all." He gestured to the crowded streets around them. "There should be U.S. soldiers everywhere. Every corner. Every street. If not active duty, there should be National Guard soldiers here." He paused, as if realizing it for the first time. "I haven't seen any U.S. soldiers since we got here." His voice was low. "Where *is* everyone! Why aren't they around?"

Azadeh didn't answer. Of course she didn't know.

"Our leaders have chosen not to deploy our own soldiers. Why wouldn't they deploy *our* soldiers? It doesn't make any sense."

Azadeh hurried by his side. "There were soldiers, though." She gestured to the water station. "Maybe from another country, but still, that is good."

Sam turned and looked at her. "No, Azadeh, it *isn't* good. If anyone should know that, it is you. There are good soldiers and bad soldiers."

She nodded slowly and dropped her eyes. That was something she understood. "But this is America, Sam. There are no bad soldiers in America."

Sam reached out and pulled on her hand. "There are now," he said.

chapter twenty-five

Sam and Azadeh were still five or six blocks from the apartment where the rest of their family was just waking up. A six-story, gray brick building was ahead of them on the corner. The main doors were open and a gang of men were waiting, watching them. As they approached the building, the gang moved off the stairway and onto the street, moving quickly toward them. Sam leaned into Azadeh as they walked, nudging her toward the other side of the street. He kept his eyes ahead, avoiding eye contact with the men. She kept her eyes down, too scared to look up. Her dark hair flowed over her shoulders, blown back in the morning breeze that was funneling down the street. The men adjusted their direction to intercept them. Underneath his jacket, Sam's hand moved toward his gun.

"Hey there," one of the men called to them. "Hey there, woman. Where you from?"

"Keep walking," Sam whispered.

"Hey! I'm talking to you!"

"Don't say anything!" Sam whispered, nudging her again.

They were on the opposite sidewalk now, pressed against the dirty building on the other side of the street.

Three of the men doubled their pace and moved out in front of them, two hemmed them in on the side, a couple more stood at their back. The apparent leader of the gang stepped up beside them. Reaching out, he grabbed a fistful of Azadeh's hair. She held back a scream, but knocked his hand away. Turning quickly, Sam swept her to his side, pushed her against the building, and moved to stand in front of her, positioning himself between Azadeh and the gang leader. The Beretta M9 was in his hand now but he kept it hidden between his jacket and his ribs. "What's the problem, buddy?" he demanded of the men. The hoodlums gathered around him. Too confident. Too cocky. They weren't afraid of him. They didn't have their guns out, but it was obvious that they were armed. Most criminals kept their weapons in the front of their pants—easy to conceal but also easy to retrieve—and their pants bulged in all the right places.

Sam kept his Beretta hidden. If he had to use it, he was dead. He couldn't kill them all—a couple of them, maybe more, but he wouldn't get them all before one of them shot him in the head.

He stood his ground, his shoulders square, his eyes unflinching, his body between the men and Azadeh. Pressing against him, she kept her head down and stifled a cry of fear.

The gang leader looked past Sam, taking in the girl, his eyes a dull and angry fire. It wasn't lust that burned inside him, it was black ache for revenge. "Where you from, pig!" he demanded.

Azadeh didn't answer.

"SPEAK TO ME!" he screamed.

Sam leaned toward him. "Look, man, she isn't part of the problem, okay? I know you want to hit them—hey, we all do.

Believe me, no one wants revenge any more than me. But this isn't anything to do with her. She's been here in America for a long time. She's . . ."

" . . . one of them!" the man sneered. "And we're going to kill them. Every freakin' Arab in our country. None of them will live."

"She isn't even Arab!"

"I know an Arab when I see it. They all look the same. They smell the same. I can smell her Arab stench from here."

"She's isn't Arab, she is Persian."

"Persian. Arab. They're all the same. And all of them are going to die."

Sam forced himself to stay calm, keeping an even voice. "Listen to me, buddy. Maybe you don't see them as different, but think about this, okay? There is innocent and there is guilty. And this girl has done nothing wrong."

The man shook his head in heedless rage. "Don't play your stupid games on me!"

"She is just as much a victim here as you are . . ."

"Are you freakin' kidding me! You and I are the only victims, baby. But that's about to change."

A crowd began to gather, pressing closer and closer to the men. Faces of desperation. Faces filled with anger and the deep lust for revenge.

A sudden motion in the street caught Sam's eye and he looked past the pressing crowd around them. Four soldiers in dark uniforms were moving down the street. They walked together. Too close together. Was that fear Sam saw in their eyes? He studied them quickly: heavy uniforms, Kevlar body armor, dark glasses, leather gloves. One of them carried a Minimi light machine gun. Standard model, 5.5 mm. Another, the lowest-ranking sergeant, carried a NATO squad support weapon. Sam caught the first soldier's eye, then motioned desperately toward him.

The soldier stopped, looked at him, and took his protective glasses off, but he didn't say anything.

"Who you with?" Sam demanded. It was a soldier's question with many meanings: What unit are you with? Who's your commander? What's your specialty? What's your army? What nation are you from?

The four soldiers stared but didn't answer.

"Look, guys, I could use your help here," Sam yelled, incredulous that they hadn't acted to do anything. The gang members seemed completely unconcerned. None of them made any effort to hide the handguns that were stuffed inside their pants, and Sam saw the knowing look they shot each other.

He took a quick step toward the soldiers, his heart sinking in his chest. "My name is Lieutenant Brighton. United States Army, Special Forces."

The soldiers only stared.

"As one soldier to another . . ."

"They're not going to help you," the gang leader sneered.

Sam called to them again.

The gang leader wrinkled his nose in disdain, then turned around to face the soldiers. "Hey there, boys. We ain't got no problems with you here."

Sam hissed in desperation. "Can't you see what's going on?"

The nearest soldier motioned weakly. "No Englis," he stammered, as if that excused everything.

"You don't have to speak English," Sam shot back. "All you have to do is not be stupid!"

The foreign soldier looked away. A second one stepped forward, then turned and looked anxiously up the street. Sam saw the nation flag that was Velcroed to the shoulder of his uniform. Uganda. *Are you kidding me?* "Listen," he commanded, "I need you to—"

The foreigner raised his hands again. "No Englis," he repeated.

"No English! Man, don't be so stupid."

The gang leader laughed and then whispered, "They're not going to help you, soldier boy."

Sam swore, then turned and shot a deadly glare toward the dark man. Laughing again, the leader said, "The soldiers are our brothers now. After a hundred years of police oppression, we've got brothers in uniforms. To show our appreciation, we sent them up a couple of our women. They've been very friendly ever since. And ya know what—once we established we were brothers, I found out their instructions are pretty clear. Protect the food. Protect the water. Other than that, they can't do nothing. U.N. regulations, they tell me. They're peacekeepers. That's it. That's all they do. You got the water boys of soldiers here. So I don't think they're going to help you. Don't think they're going to help anyone at all."

Azadeh looked at them, her eyes pleading.

The gang leader saw her eyes move. "They ain't gonna help you, girlie," he leered. "Can't do a stinking thing for you." He turned to Sam. "What do you soldiers call it? Rules of engagement? Is that right? Well it seems the U.N. has *very* limited rules of engagement for their soldiers." He cursed in sarcasm. "Might as well send over a bunch of kindergarten teachers. Funny thing is, these goobers are working under the same stupid rules over here that they've been working under everywhere. They can't be cops. No law enforcement duties. They can't fight. They are *peacekeepers,* baby. They're not ready for any war. They're not here to participate in any conflict. Now, uptown, I hear things are a whole lot different. Thousands of real soldiers on the streets. But that's only for the rich boys. The white boys. We don't get no protection down here in the d'hood. So what? We get along. Things ain't no different than they've ever been, even with these baby-blue U.N. soldiers all around." He turned and spat. "Seems kind of stupid, if you ask me, but I'm just a po' boy. What do I know?"

He turned and stared at Azadeh. Her head was low, her shoulders slumping, her hands quivering at her side. She felt his eyes boring into her and pressed against the wall again.

"Kinda crazy, ain't it," the gang leader sneered. "Here they are, four good soldiers, and they won't do a freakin' thing to stop me. I could rape and kill you right here on the street, and they won't even raise their guns. Sure, they might go back and file some kind of worthless report. *U.N. Form 1592. Observance of the Locals.* But that is *all* they're going to do." He bent his head and leaned to Sam, looking at him below his upraised eyebrows. "Amazing, ain't it, buddy. Welcome to the Twilight World."

Sam motioned toward the soldiers. "Listen to me, captain . . ."

"No Englis," the squad leader said again. Then they turned and started walking away, shoulder to shoulder, four scared men, all weak and worthless, going through the motions but too frightened of their own shadows to accomplish anything.

The gang leader watched them go, then spat a wad of dark phlegm at Sam's feet. "You thought they were going to help you. Disappointed, you gotta be."

The four soldiers disappeared into the crowd.

Sam's chest was quick and tight. He kept his hand behind his back, the Beretta warm inside his grip. "Look at me," he whispered as he leaned toward the man. "Do you see this uniform? You see these jump wings and combat badges? I've spent my entire adult life over there. I've dedicated myself to killing the enemy, and I've killed a bunch of them, I guarantee. But this woman behind me, she isn't one of them." Sam gestured to the filthy streets and chaos, then lowered his voice a little more. "She had nothing to do with this, man. She's just like you. She's just like me. She's just trying to live through this, you know what I mean."

The gang leader didn't soften. "She's one of them. Anyone can see that. You might be stupid enough to believe she's not here to cause us problems, but me and my crew ain't so stupid anymore. It's time to clean our own house." He stopped and glared at Sam. "We got each other," he nodded to his brothers, "and that is *all* we trust. Now, you got a choice here, white boy. You give her to us and we let you go. Or you can be a superhero and try to save her and we'll kill you both right here. What's it gonna be? You got three seconds to decide."

A flash of movement in the smoky morning pulled Sam's eyes away. Four of the men drew their weapons and pointed them at his head. In a simultaneous burst of motion, he pulled out his Beretta and shoved it into the leader's face.

"You'll never get us all," the leader mocked.

"Maybe not, but I'll get you."

"Go ahead and kill me! Do you think I freakin' care? We're all dead. We know it. I'd just as soon die from your bullet as from starving or puking my guts out on the street." He moved an inch closer, pressing his forehead against the muzzle of Sam's weapon. His face was loose and lifeless, his bare teeth sticking against the front of his dry mouth. "One thing I can promise you, soldier boy. You kill me, and your little princess there is going to suffer a long, long time. We could keep her alive for weeks, but it will seem like years. Or we could do this simple. You give her to us now, we kill her easy and let you go.

You do something stupid, and we kill you, then make her *wish* she was dead. Now I'm not gonna do it for you, you army pukes know how to count. You got three seconds."

Sam hesitated, his face turning white with terror. A moment passed in silence. He closed his eyes in dread. Another moment of pure silence.

"Guess that's it," the gang leader said.

Sam deflated, swallowing hard against the knot inside his throat. He lowered his eyes and then his weapon. Cursing, he pounded his fist against his hip. Growing limp, he turned to Azadeh.

She nodded and started crying, seeing the defeat inside his eyes.

"I'm so sorry." He leaned forward until their foreheads touched. They looked at each other, Azadeh pleading with her eyes. "I'm so, so sorry," he told her. "I've got my family, my mother, all the others I have to think about. I'm so sorry to have to do this. It's an impossible decision, but what choice do I have?"

She didn't answer. It wasn't the first time she had been betrayed. Glancing toward the furious men, she knew it would be the last.

"I've got to think of the others," Sam concluded, his voice strangled in anguish, teardrops rolling down his cheeks. He lowered his head, unable to look at her, then leaned into her face, brushed her hair away, and whispered in her ear. "Be cool," he said.

Lifting her head, she looked up at him.

"Be cool," he said again.

Turning, he glared at the gang leader and then started walking, pushing his way through the crowd of men. They held their shoulders against him and he had to turn sideways to work his way past. Sneering at his cowardice, they cursed and let him go.

Focusing on Azadeh, his face contorted in rage and pleasure, the leader slapped her hard across the cheek. "I have a family," he roared in pent-up fury. "My little girl is gonna die now. All of us are gonna die here and it's all because of you. You and others like you."

Azadeh stared at him, her eyes wide in terror, a hand across her split lip. Then, looking past her tormentors, she watched in shock as Sam disappeared down the street. Her eyes blurred. It was over. She was defeated. And she didn't care that much anymore.

chapter twenty-six

Sam ran as fast as he could, pushing through the crowd, throwing bodies left and right. He felt the gushing anger all around him as he ran, heard the cursing voices, felt the hands that pulled at him from every side, but he didn't stop. He had a few minutes, maybe less, and every second counted.

He ran a block. The streets were crowded now, more so than earlier in the morning, much more than on the day before. He reached an intersection and stopped, looking left and right. Which direction did they go? Which direction? He didn't know. He ran to the nearest light pole and pulled himself up a couple of feet, his eyes moving desperately.

There. Ahead of him. He saw their helmets. He dropped and ran again.

They didn't hear him coming as he ran up from behind, the sound of his footsteps swallowed in the noise of the moving crowd. They were together, still abreast, and he aimed for the center one. Grabbing the soldier by the shoulders, he spun him around.

The other soldiers stopped. Sam's Beretta was pointing at

the captain, the muzzle right between his eyes. The man's mouth hung open, his eyes wide, his hands lifting at his side. The other soldiers made half an effort for their weapons, which were hanging from leather straps around their shoulders, but Sam flashed his gun toward them, freezing them like ice. "Don't, don't!" the squad leader pleaded in heavily accented English.

"*No Englis,*" Sam reminded him. The soldier winced. Sam knew that he had lied; all NATO/U.N. soldiers had to pass a rudimentary English test.

"Don't kill me!"

"Don't be stupid!" Sam sneered at him. "If I had wanted you dead, I could have killed all of you by now."

"We didn't . . . we didn't hurt any of the women . . ."

Sam angrily shook his head. "This is what the U.N. sends for soldiers!"

"We don't . . . carry any money."

Sam jabbed the gun a little closer, making it obvious that he didn't care.

"What do you want?" the man pleaded in frustration. He was starting to understand that Sam wasn't there to kill him. Still, his hands trembled at the side of his head.

Sam pointed to the automatic weapons the men were carrying. "Your weapons!" he demanded, pressing his Beretta half an inch closer to the man. The soldier had to lean back to relieve the pressure of the metal against the tender skin between his eyes. "Your guns!" Sam cried. "I want them now!"

The soldier didn't hesitate, slipping the long machine gun off his shoulder and extending it to him.

Sam grabbed the machine gun, turned toward the next man, grabbed his weapon too, then lowered his Beretta and turned and ran.

Minutes, maybe seconds, was all the time he had.

*   *   *

Sam needed one thing. One simple thing. But he needed it desperately and he needed it now!

Cover. A place to shoot from. A way to stop the men who were after Azadeh before it was too late.

A large building loomed behind him, the front door open. A high school, it looked like, though it was remarkably beaten down. A large crowd had gathered on the corner where the wide cement steps met the street. A fence ran around the building and Sam dashed through the metal gate. Pushing everyone aside, he ran up the steps, taking them three at a time, rushed into the entry, and hesitated. The hallways were crowded with refugees—why the school was a better place to huddle than their apartments, he didn't know. The crowd stared at him: blank eyes, lots of children, mothers and their babies. No one reacted to the sight of a crazy man and his guns. Sam studied the crowd in seconds, turned left, ran up another flight of steps, then turned left again. A long hallway, dark and empty. It was cold enough to see his breath. A line of doors on his left and right, dim light bleeding through the milky glass. He chose the first door, jerking on the handle. It was locked. Pulling out his handgun, he shot it open, pushed it back, ran into the classroom, slid down by the window, broke the sheet of glass with his Beretta's muzzle, brushed the extended shards of glass away, and looked out.

They were a long way down the street, almost a full city block away. The men had her surrounded. She looked at them in terror. The leader slapped her face, but she stood firm, not cowering. She had moved out from the wall. She was ready. She was going to fight them, standing right up to the end. As Sam watched, the leader reached over and grabbed her by the throat. He had a knife. The others started cheering. A couple of them stepped back, giving their leader room.

He didn't hesitate. He didn't think. Every action was instinctive and sure.

Lifting the machine gun, he felt its heavy weight. The weapon he had stolen was a Minimi Para, a short-barreled "paratrooper" version with a telescoped buttstock and a bluish metal clip. Looking down the street, he realized it was too far. The gun wasn't good enough. Not from this range, not for this kind of thing. He stared down the barrel at the group of men, catching flashes of Azadeh's face between their shoulders as they moved about. He cursed in fear and frustration. The Minimi wasn't accurate enough, not with all the men around her, all of them moving, all the other people on the street. He estimated the distance. A hundred and twenty meters. More than a football field away. Too far. Way too far. The air was windy and filled with smoke and blowing debris. He swore and lowered the barrel. The gun simply wasn't accurate enough for this sort of thing. It was made for power, not finesse, to intimidate from short range, not to make a pinpoint kill. Still, he knew he had to act. The Minimi wasn't what he wanted, but it was all he had. Lifting the gun again, he aimed, wishing for his own sniper rifle—did the U.N. soldier ever clean and sight this thing? He adjusted for the wind that blew down between the buildings, did a final estimate of the distance between them, pulled the barrel of the light machine gun a fraction of an inch up and left, then fired a single shot, his shoulder recoiling from the pressure as the hot gases ejected the spent shell and pulled another round into the chamber.

The gang leader's leg collapsed, his kneecap shattered. Half a second later, the sound of the gunshot reached him. He cried in agony and fell onto the dirty street.

Sam shot a full burst now, aiming over the attackers' heads. Brick and mortar and dust and shattered pieces of metal exploded all around them as half a dozen shells impacted the side of the building next to where they stood. Some of them screamed. All of them dropped to the ground, their guns aimed in various directions. Azadeh fell, throwing her arms up to cover her head between her knees.

The crowded street exploded with crying, fleeing people. A couple of the men hunkered down and shot, sending random bullets into the air. Then they froze, looking for the shooter, not considering the vital need for cover, foolishly leaving themselves exposed out on the street. Sam aimed again, this time more carefully, and fired another gunshot. Another man went down, a quarter-size hole through the middle of his chest. Another screamed, threw down his weapon, and turned and ran. The remaining men continued shouting to each other, pointing left and right. Their eyes jerking in frantic motions, they searched up and down the street. Sam remained hidden in the second corner window of the building, a full city block away. *If they can see you, they can kill you.* He barely raised his head above the windowsill.

Another shot, this one another warning a few inches over the tallest man's head. Cries and screams of fear and pain and anger. One of the men moved and hid behind another. A couple of them took up firing positions, but their handguns were no match for the shooter—that was painfully clear.

Another shot, this one between them.

That was it. They got the message. This wasn't a fight they were going to win.

The men scattered and ran. Some fled up the sidewalk, heading north. A couple ran into the crowd, bending low between the panicked people who were running up and down the street.

Sam waited until the shooters had disappeared, then lifted his head above the window and called out. "Azadeh, can you hear me?"

She slowly stood. It was too noisy. She didn't hear him call. Screams and cries and people running on the street surrounded her. Her eyes darted left and right.

Sam called again, but she didn't hear him.

Standing in confusion, she hesitated, then quickly turned and ran, moving down the street toward him, back in the direction from which they had come.

"Good girl, good girl," Sam coaxed her even though she couldn't hear. "Don't look back, just keep on running. I'll be waiting for you down on the street."

He watched. She was getting closer. He did a final check for the gang members, then called her name again. She looked up at him, finally hearing his voice. He motioned to her and she understood.

Leaving the window, he ran back through the hallway and down the stairs and met her on the street.

Fifteen minutes later, they pushed into Mary's apartment building and made their way up the stairs. Knocking on the door, they waited desperately until Mary let them in.

"Where have you been?" Sara asked in a worried voice as they rushed into the room.

Sam and Azadeh glanced at each other but didn't say anything.

They had already decided there were a few things the others didn't need to know.

* * *

Across the street from the apartment building, a soldier in a dark uniform watched through a long-range scope. The glass in Mary's apartment had been tinted with a layer of opaque film to keep the sun out, but he still could see enough, and he reached up to the radio transmitter at his neck.

"I've got them," he said.

"Are you certain?" the controller asked.

"Yeah, it's them."

"Stand by," the controller told him.

Three minutes later, he came back. "Stay in position. Keep a tag on her."

"For how long?" the soldier asked.

"Until we tell you."

The soldier answered, "Roger," and sat down for the wait.

chapter twenty-seven

VIENNA, VIRGINIA
TWELVE MILES WEST OF WASHINGTON, D.C.

B rucius Theodore Marino stood in the bedroom window looking out on the street. A dozen stalled cars still
cluttered the road, though most had finally been
pushed out of the way, the worthless metal carcasses left at
awkward angles along both sides of the curb. The houses in
the neighborhood were old, a mix of red-brick, two-story Vic-
torians and old southern plantation homes with white siding
and green or black porches that wrapped around from the
front doors to the sides. The street was narrow, with old trees
draping their branches over the pavement, almost forming a
tunnel of branches and leaves. All was quiet—it was still very
early in the morning—and he couldn't see anyone on the sidewalk or the street.

Which meant almost nothing.

He knew that they were near.

He stood, feeling the oppressive lack of sound. He wasn't
used to silence and certainly not used to being alone. He had
staff: security men, personal aides, drivers, butlers, maids, and
chefs. He had three full-bird colonels whose only jobs were to
attend to his travel schedule, and four-star generals climbing

over themselves to see that his will was done. He had black sedans, underground bunkers, military helicopters, and jet aircraft at his beck and call.

No, he wasn't used to the silence, especially the silence of being alone.

But he was alone now. Alone in a way that he'd never been before.

He stood behind the lacy curtain, then moved slowly to his right, looking farther up the street. The residential lane ended with a T at Lawyers Road, which cut through Vienna from the northwest on its way toward D.C. Ironic, he thought, he'd spent his entire life working as, with, for, and against various lawyers. He worked, ate, slept, partied, ran, philosophized, argued, skied, hunted, and drank with various lawyers—pretty much spent his entire life with members of the second oldest profession. Yet, he would happily admit that he hated them all. Shakespeare's notion was genius: They should kill the lawyers first.

His grandfather had been a lawyer. His father had been a lawyer. He was a lawyer, graduate of Harvard Law. But his son would never be a lawyer. He would simply not allow it. Not unless they killed him first and buried him somewhere underneath Lawyers Road.

How a lawyer and business leader found himself the civilian commander of the greatest military force in the world, Brucius didn't know. Looking back on his life, he sometimes wondered. Trading the boardroom for the bunker—was it a worthy sacrifice? "Hey, with a crazy name like Brucius, what'd you expect?" his wife had used to tease. "Where'd your mom come up with that one?" He figured that was as good an explanation as any other: It was all his mother's fault.

Frowning, he looked out, his heart racing, his palms sweating at his side. He heard footsteps behind him and quickly turned around. His daughter knocked once and entered the small bedroom. "Dad?" she said in a questioning voice. "You're up early."

"So are you."

She glanced at the still-made bed. "You didn't sleep at all last night."

"I slept some." He nodded to the leather chair.

She frowned in displeasure, a growing look of concern on her face.

"Where's Kyle?" her father said, asking about his son-in-law.

"We heard they're setting up a government aid center at the Metro station in Falls Church. He's going to walk down and see if we can get some baby formula and milk."

The man's face crunched at her words, a crush of pain and guilt sweeping over him.

He could get them milk. He could get them baby formula. He could get them anything they wanted and he could get it right now. He could make sure his daughter and her family lived. He was, after all, one of the most powerful men left on earth. And he could have more power. He could have anything he wanted.

All he had to do was come out of hiding.

All he had to do was go along.

She watched her father's face and stepped toward him. "Daddy, are you okay?"

He tried to smile at her. "It's eight or nine miles to the Metro station in Falls Church."

"Kyle's in good shape. No big deal for him. And if we could get some formula, that'd be a really good thing."

Her father's face contorted in pain again.

"Dad, are you okay?" she pressed a second time.

He nodded at her sadly. "I'm fine. Really."

She shook her head in frustration. "I don't think you are, Dad. I don't think you're fine at all. Look at you. This is absolutely crazy! Do I need to remind you who you are? Do I need to remind you of the position you hold? I don't know what you're afraid of, I don't know *anything* anymore, but surely the government can protect you. If things are as bad as you say they are, if you don't trust your own people, there has to be someone—the Secret Service, maybe—someone you could trust to keep you safe."

He waved a hand to dismiss her, then turned away, glancing back toward the window. She took two steps toward him and paused. He looked old, many years older than he had seemed just a few weeks before. She held her hand to her mouth, then folded her arms. "You're scaring me, Dad. You're scaring me very badly."

He turned and walked toward her, put his hands on her shoulders, and looked deep into her eyes. "I'm sorry, honey, more sorry than you'll ever know. I don't mean to scare you. I don't mean to do anything. A few more days, a few more hours maybe, and I'll be out of your way."

"Out of my way, Dad? What does that mean? You think I consider you a problem, something I need to get out of my way? This is crazy, Dad, crazy. I'm really worried about you now."

He tried to smile again, a weak effort she didn't buy. "No reason to be frightened for me," he said in a quiet and perfectly unconvincing voice.

"Are you kidding? Either there's a really good reason or you've completely lost your mind. You skulk around, hiding from your shadow, refusing to let me answer the phone. Everything's a secret. I can't open my front door. For heaven's sake, Dad, you're scared to death, and yet you dismiss your security detail, telling them all to go home. You leave your own house and go into hiding, coming here to stay with me and Kyle. Yes, Dad, I'm frightened for you. I'd be stupid not to be."

The baby started crying from the nursery down the hall, low at first, a few grumbles that were muffled by the door, but quickly growing with displeasure as the infant sought something to eat.

The young woman tried to pull away from her father's grip. "The baby," she whispered when he didn't let her go.

He tightened his hands against her shoulders, looking into her brown eyes. "I'm so sorry," he repeated. He said the same thing to her at least once or twice a day.

She looked at him, her eyes tearing with concern. "*Don't you* say that to me, Daddy. Don't you ever say that, okay? You've got no reason to be sorry. Don't you ever tell me that again."

✳   ✳   ✳

A small crowd of boys had assembled on the corner, watching in disbelief. A car that was working! They stared as the black SUV drove quickly up the street.

The driver pulled over two blocks from the objective and turned off the ignition. The four men sat for a moment talking, then got out. One of them turned and walked toward the group of teenagers. He said something to them and they scattered. Rejoining the group, he talked another moment with the men before three of them started walking, leaving the driver to guard the car. Very little about the men was subtle. Black suits. White shirts. Dark glasses. Black Bacco Bucci lace-up shoes. The driver had a blunt-nose, single-hand machine gun hanging from a strap around his shoulder. A thin wire ran under his dark suit to the receiver in his ear.

No, they were not subtle. But the fight was out in the open now, and they didn't care about niceties anymore.

The war had started. It was upon them, the first battle taking shape. Both assassins and saviors were on the move now, their forces rushing together, opposing soldiers crashing toward each other on the street.

The first casualty or survivor of the battle would be the Secretary of Defense.

Whether he lived or died depended on who got to him first.

The three men walked a hundred yards together. At the corner, they split up. One of them turned east. The other two stayed together, walking toward Lawyers Street.

chapter twenty-eight

The single man walked toward the rising sun. Approaching the road that ran behind the target, he glanced back toward his comrades, but they had already disappeared. He turned. Walking quickly, almost jogging, he moved down a narrow driveway, then jumped a low fence and made his way through the backyard. A dog yelped at him, but he ignored it. Twenty feet from the back fence, he started running, then jumped, his powerful legs driving him up. Pulling himself over the fence, he dropped onto the other side.

A huge backyard lay before him. Lots of shrubs and oak and sycamore trees. Grass and a small goldfish pond. A large hedge along the swimming pool. He bent to his knees beside the vinca plants and studied the house. No movement. He listened. No sound. To his right, the lawn sloped away, allowing a walkout basement at the back of the house. He listened once more to the voice inside his tiny earpiece, then crouched and ran toward the door.

*   *   *

The Secretary of Defense watched as his daughter pulled away from him and turned for the bedroom door. Standing in the center of the room, he listened as her footsteps faded down the hall. The baby was insistent now, crying loudly, the hunger driving him, and Brucius could hear his daughter's soft voice as she tried to soothe him, then the creaking of the crib's wood frame as she lifted the child into her arms.

He stood for a moment, staring toward the window, then moved to the bed and sat down. His shoes had been pushed under the mattress rail and he leaned over, put them on, and tied them quickly. Straightening his back, his hands on his knees, he listened to the silence once again. The baby wasn't crying now and he wondered how, without formula, she'd made him stop. Standing, he opened the bedroom door and moved down the hall toward the nursery. Pushing back the door, he looked inside.

No one was there.

The bedroom window was open, a quiet breeze blowing the light curtains back.

He called his daughter's name, then heard footsteps downstairs in the kitchen and quickly moved down the hall.

"Jenny, you down there?"

No answer.

He descended the stairs, stopped at the bottom and listened again, then walked toward the kitchen. Morning light filtered through the hallway window, and shadows from the swaying oak tree in the backyard moved across the back porch. He thought he heard his daughter's voice and walked into the kitchen.

The room was empty.

The back door was open. He glanced out. No one was in the yard.

He instantly panicked, running into the living room. No one. The house was quiet and empty. It seemed he was alone. He couldn't be! Not so quickly! *How could they have gotten in!*

"*Jenny! Jenny!*" he cried. "*Kyle! Are you here?*" He ran to the front door and found it locked. He looked through the window to the front yard. Not a soul in sight. He ran toward the basement, calling their names. Pushing the door over the narrow steps, he peered into the dark. A cool flow of air blew up against his face.

*   *   *

The two men stopped at the intersection of Lawyers Road, standing beside a six-foot fence. The target house was halfway down the block and they studied the scene before them: rows of handsome Victorian and plantation homes, heavy trees, their leaves gold and orange and ready to fall, a dozen dead cars pushed to the curb, a quiet road, a quiet breeze.

Not a soul in sight. A quiet morning.

The leader listened to the receiver shoved inside his ear canal, pressing it more firmly into place, then cocked his head.

They couldn't take the target until they killed the others who were also after him. They couldn't kill the others until they found them. And they didn't know where they were.

Eighteen thousand feet above them, a pilotless drone moved silently through the empty sky, its sensors looking down, its hypersensitive radar, visual, IR, and ultraviolet sensors scanning the two-block radius around them inch by inch. Far away—from what location, the leader didn't know, perhaps an unknown base inside the U.S., but more likely from a CIA site overseas—a military pilot controlled the drone, flying it by satellite-remote control, the drone's sensors relaying what it sensed or saw. And the Predator reconnaissance aircraft saw everything. It could count the squirrels in the trees around them from the heat their bodies bled into the morning air, detect the coolness from the water trapped in rain gutters from the downpour the night before, sense the vibration on the front windows of the various homes enough to know if anyone was speaking inside. The man looked up, feeling naked, knowing the Predator could read the heat that escaped through his shirt collar accurately enough to estimate the heartbeats in his chest, knowing it could fire its Hellfire missiles at him and he would never know, the explosion killing him seconds before he ever saw or heard the missiles coming at him through the air.

And they would do it. If they had to, they would sacrifice the team to get the target. Everyone was expendable these days.

His earpiece crackled and he listened once again. Kneeling, he moved away from the fence, staring, his eyes squinting. "No tally," he cut in angrily.

Further instructions from the Command Center spoke through the receiver in his ear. "Fifth house down?" he asked.

He listened.

"Copy that," he whispered as he moved his focus farther down the road to a house across the street. "Tan house. A black Audi in the front. Two oak trees in the yard." He demanded definite confirmation before he moved.

He listened once again, then nodded. He watched. He waited. He saw just a hint of movement, but it was enough to let him know. He crawled back and pointed for his partner. Two hundred feet down. Across the street from the target's house. The front door partially open.

"Tally," his lieutenant said. Before he moved, he checked his weapon. His machine gun pistol was set on double shot, allowing him to fire two bullets with a single pull of the trigger, inflicting the far more lethal "double tap." The Heckler and Koch MP5k 9mm machine gun pistol had a twenty-round clip and pivot stock, which he kept folded, allowing him to conceal the perfectly maintained pistol at his back. Checking the clip a final time, he started walking down the street. The MP5k was stuffed inside his jacket, but only partially hidden, the blunt stock bulging at his back. He moved down the sidewalk without hesitating, his stride long and confident, his eyes staring straight ahead. He crossed the street just beyond the target's house and started jogging. Past the first oak tree. Toward the front door. Coming upon the front steps, he slowed to a furious walk. The front door pushed back and a single man walked onto the porch. Dark glasses. Work clothes. Something was out of place: a flash of gold. The Rolex on his wrist—what a stupid mistake. Without breaking stride, the suit man reached behind his back, pulled out the MP5k, the blunt-nose machine gun heavy in his hand. He touched the clip, aiming as he walked, his eyes unflinching, his hands sure. The man on the porch reached to his left side, but not nearly quickly enough. The assassin fired a set of rapid shots into him, the custom-built silencer spouting smoke and a muffled hiss of hot gas. The bullets penetrated the man's face, splitting his jaw in two. The assassin didn't even slow. Onto the front porch. Past the dead man. Through the partially open door. Another double tap, then silence, then movement near the window. The man reappeared at the door, looked around, bent over, and pulled the body inside, leaving a smear of dark blood across the white porch. He kicked the feet into the foyer, stepped out, and shut the door.

The other man watched from the end of the street, then started walking toward the house where the target had been hiding for almost three days.

* * *

The SecDef stood at the top of the basement stairs, his face frozen in fear. The cool breeze that blew up from below smelled of must and rotten leaves.

The basement door was open!

They'd found him!

They'd gotten into the house.

He almost screamed in fury, a guttered growl. "You leave them alone!" he screamed to the empty house. "You leave them be, you hear! It's me you're after, not my children. If you hurt them, I will kill you. I'll kill you, every one!"

*   *   *

The two men moved up behind him without a sound, their shoes silent against the granite floors. "Secretary Marino," the first man said.

Brucius spun around. He was just over fifty, but he was strong and tense as wire. He almost leapt toward them. "Where's my daughter! Where's my grandson!" he screamed.

The two men in black suits backed up as he ran toward him, both of them holding their hands disarmingly in the air. "Stay! Stay there, Mr. Secretary! It's going to be okay."

Brucius grabbed the first man by the throat and squeezed, pinching his Adam's apple between clenched fingers. "Where's my daughter and her family? If you hurt them, you dirty little . . ."

The man swung an uppercut and hit Brucius hard, catching him on the jaw with a blow that dropped him to the ground.

Brucius choked, his mouth smearing with blood from his split lip. "Where . . . is my grandson . . . if you hurt him . . . I'll . . ."

The man dropped to one knee beside the Secretary of Defense. The other man looked suddenly to his right and placed his right hand to his ear, listening to a voice that no one else could hear. He ran toward the front window and pressed against the wall.

"Get up," the first man commanded, dragging the secretary to his knees.

The second man peered out the window, then pulled back

and dropped to the floor, crawling past the window on all fours. He joined the other man and motioned him to stay low.

The first man listened to the receiver in his ear, then turned his head as if being directed where to look. A flash of movement passed across the back window and he shoved the Secretary down, almost smashing his head onto the floor. The second man pulled a blunt-nose machine gun from under his jacket, impossibly small, black, and cold, the metal glinting in the light. He pressed a toggle near the trigger, selecting single fire, then hunched toward the kitchen window and looked out. The backyard was huge, with half a dozen mature trees, a small pond, and a couple of shrub-lined paths.

Plenty of places for a shooter to hide.

The third man suddenly emerged from the foliage of the yard, running toward the house. He crashed through the back door, almost breaking it from his hinges as the full weight of his body pushed it in, then nodded to the others without saying anything.

Seconds passed. Outside, the sound of a racing automobile pierced the air, incredibly out of place against the backdrop of silent roads and the silent world. Brucius glanced toward the front window. He reached out, part of him wanting to run, part of him still too scared to move.

The black suits listened to their earpieces, turned to each other, nodded, and ran, hauling Brucius T. Marino, U.S. Secretary of Defense, between them as they moved.

"Where's my daughter!" Brucius screamed as they dragged him toward the front door. "Where's my daughter! Where's my grandson!" He struggled against them, pulling back. He was a powerful man, a little fat, thick arms, lots of weight, and the two men struggled mightily to pull him. Approaching the front door, Brucius fought again, finally pushing to his feet. The first man stopped and leaned toward him, pressing his mouth against the Secretary's ear. His breath was hot against him. "Do you want to live!" he hissed.

Brucius pulled back and stared at him.

"If you want to live, Mr. Secretary, if you want your country to have *any* hope of survival, then you need to shut up and do exactly what we tell you."

Brucius studied him, his eyes defiant.

"If you love your country, Mr. Secretary . . ."

The first man pulled again.

"Okay!" Brucius gritted between his bloody lips. "I'll go with you, I'll go with you, I'll do anything you want. I just want to know about my family. I need to know you haven't hurt them. I need to know that they're okay. They had no choice. They weren't a part of this."

The first man grunted at him.

Outside, the screech of tires. The black SUV came screaming down the street, then veered across the front lawn, almost smashing into the porch. The two men waited at the open door, holding Brucius, their eyes moving up and down the street. There might be others out there. They didn't know for certain and they couldn't take the chance. The third man took a final look, ran through the front door and across the porch, and jerked the SUV's back door open. The others waited, looked a final time, then ran out in a crouch, the Secretary huddled between them, their arms across his shoulders, their bodies positioned to protect him from sniper fire.

They shoved the Secretary through the back door, almost throwing him inside, then jumped in and pulled the door closed.

The driver gunned the engine, his tires spinning, dirt and grass spitting across the yard.

chapter twenty-nine

Brucius Marino, the Secretary of Defense (at least he used to be, who knew what he was anymore?) sat alone in the middle of a darkened interrogation room. It was small and square, with a cement floor (painted white) and a single solid door. He rested his arms on the simple metal table and stared across the room at the one-way mirror mounted on the wall. Were they there? Were they watching? He didn't know.

They had taken his watch, his socks, the laces out of his shoes, his belt, and his wallet, then strip-searched him, examining every inch of his body from his toes to his hair. They had embarrassed him, taken his dignity, and he was furious at them now.

Furious. And weary.

Angry. And scared.

He was cold—the room was chilly—and he gently rubbed his arms. His hands were bandaged, but they ached, the cuts and sutures deep. He didn't know what time it was, but he guessed it had been at least twenty-four hours since they had come for him, though it was impossible to tell. He'd been

235

without food, without water, without sleep, and he'd never left the room.

He slumped. Fatigue and disorientation were setting in. He waited, his mouth foul, his breath dry, then lowered his head onto his arms and fell asleep.

*   *   *

The door pulled back, allowing a square of light to fall upon the floor, the patch of white broken only by the shadow of a black man standing there. He was small, with silver glasses framing his almond eyes and graying hair around his temples. "Mr. Secretary," he said as he walked into the room and closed the door. "Brucius, are you awake?"

Brucius kept his head down though his eyes opened at the voice. For a moment he didn't move, allowing time to clear his thoughts. Then he slowly lifted his eyes. "Hello, James," he said, his voice acidic and tight.

"Mr. Secretary, you've got to forgive me, the treatment, the isolation. Believe me, it was the last thing we wanted to do. But we just felt . . . Brucius, we felt as if, under the circumstances, we didn't have any choice."

Brucius raised his head and lifted a hand to cut him off.

His angry eyes cut through the other man like broken glass, and the black man almost looked away. "Mr. Secretary," he went on, "please try to understand, we had no choice. We really didn't know. It's impossible to know right now who is with us or against us. The nation is hanging by a thread, and we couldn't take any chances until we knew for sure. I'm sorry, it has pained me to see this happen, but I think you'll understand. The enemy is deeply embedded. Until we identify them, we have to take every measure to be sure."

Brucius leaned back and frowned. "Instead of apologizing, why don't you tell me what's going on?"

The black man moved toward the chair on the opposite side of the table, motioned to the Secretary, who nodded consent, and sat down. "You got my family, right?" Brucius demanded.

"Yes. They're okay. We'll be flying them out here . . ."

"Where are we, James?"

"Offutt Air Force Base."

Brucius nodded. "Offutt . . . of course. Okay, you got my daughter, her husband, and their little boy?"

"As I was saying, they'll be flying out here tonight. We've had to take some countermeasures to make certain we could relocate them without being traced." He glanced at his watch. "A few hours, Brucius, and I think they'll be here."

"What time is it? What day?"

"Seventeen thirty-three local, sir. Tuesday afternoon. It's been almost thirty six hours since you arrived here."

"Thirty-six hours." Brucius sat back and pushed his hands through his dark hair. He watched the black man with small, deadly eyes, the anger rekindling inside him. "That's a long time to work through your suspicions, my friend. Long time to figure out if you could trust me or not."

The black man didn't say anything.

"James, I thought that we were friends."

The man thought before he answered, "The ugly truth is, Mr. Secretary, I might be your only friend."

Brucius huffed.

James tilted his head. "You know that you can trust me, Brucius. In your heart, you know you can. That's why, in the pitch of the battle, you trusted my people. I didn't force you to go with them. You could have stayed. "

"And if I had?"

"Then you'd be dead now. So would your family. Everyone you love."

Brucius dropped his eyes and swallowed.

"Those men who were coming for you at your daughter's house in Vienna, they weren't coming to defend you. They were coming there to kill you. Is there any question in your mind which side *they* were on? Yeah, I know back in the old days of, say . . . oh, I don't know, a week or so ago, a personal assault on the SecDef would have been inconceivable. But things are different now.

"The good news, if there's any good news in this mess, is that we beat them to you. Still, it was close. Really close. We barely got you out. A couple of seconds later, and you all would have been dead."

Brucius pressed his lips together. "I need a drink," he said.

James nodded to the mirror. The two men stared silently at each other, their faces blank. A minute passed in silence until the door pulled back and a military staff sergeant walked into the room, a plastic tray in hand. Sandwiches. Chips. A twenty-ounce diet soda. He twisted the lid for Brucius and poured soda into an ice-filled cup, then retreated, closing the door behind him. The Secretary of Defense drank the entire glass, picked up the bottle, reloaded, drank again. Light fizz misted his upper lip and he placed the half-empty glass down.

"Okay," he said. "You're my friend. That's why I chose to come here. But you've really got some guts, pulling off such an operation and keeping me here like this."

James nodded, almost smiling. "You think so?"

"Yes, I do."

"I take that as a compliment."

"Don't be so sure." Brucius took another sip. "You might have guts, but that doesn't prove that you're no fool. I've always told you, James, God knew what he was doing when he put you in that small body. You're like a Chihuahua, snarling and yelping all the time. You snap at everything. Everyone's the enemy. But yelping irritates a lot of people. I suspect you've angered some more now."

"I hate Chihuahuas," James said. "I want to kick them. They're obnoxious, noisy dogs." He reached across the table, opened the bag of chips, and stuffed a couple in his mouth. "And let me tell you something, Brucius, this Chihuahua saved your life. Saved your daughter and her family. You owe me. I'll remember that. And I'm good at keeping score."

Brucius finally laughed. "Add it to my bill." He drained his glass. Leaning back, he looked around, the two men sitting a moment again in silence.

"I've been elevated, Brucius," the black man said. "The director was killed in the attack on D.C. I'm the director now."

Brucius smiled with satisfaction. "Congratulations," he said.

James nodded humbly, his modesty sincere. "I wish it hadn't happened. At least not the way it did."

"James Davies, FBI Director. Sounds good, don't you think?"

James pressed his lips and hunched his shoulders. "I don't care that much."

Brucius watched him, sucking a piece of ice as he thought. He'd known the man sitting opposite him for almost thirty years, going back to their days at Yale. Skull and Bones. Time on the Yard. Coeds, parties, debate, and basketball. He knew James as well as he knew any man. If any of a number of men had told him they didn't care about being promoted to FBI Director, he would have called them bald-faced liars, or worse. (And he'd called others much worse, for his temper, like his intelligence, was way off the charts.) But James was different. He'd always been different. And what he said was true: He really didn't care. All he cared about was serving his country.

He was one in a million, and Brucius's feelings for the black man fell short only of the relationship he'd had with his wife.

A sudden pain shot through him when he thought about her, and he did the same thing he'd done a thousand times since that dreadful day in D.C.: He shoved it down, pushing the thoughts of her away. Someday he would think about her, he'd memorialize her in a meaningful way, but not now. He couldn't. It was too painful. And he was in the middle of a war.

He rubbed his fingers against his temples and cleared his throat. "Okay, you're the FBI Director. That's good, James, very good. We need you right now. Now, are you going to tell me what's going on?"

James took another bunch of chips. "There's something else you should know first," he said as he crunched.

Brucius waited.

"You're next in line to be the president of the United States."

The Secretary scoffed. "Next in line. I don't think so. You've got the vice president . . ."

"Killed in the explosion . . ."

"The Speaker of the House of Representatives . . ."

" . . . who, as we speak, is lying in a hospital in Leesburg, Virginia, with severe neural and cerebral damage. The doctors tell us she'll remain in a vegetative state until her body gives out, which won't take much time, based on her other injuries and the strain on the medical services we're experiencing. Scarce as our resources are, it's going to be difficult to continue providing life-sustaining measures to a person who has no detectable brain function remaining."

Brucius's face drained of color, his lips turning gray. "I knew she'd been injured, but the report I'd been given was that she was expected to recover. I had no idea . . ."

"She won't recover. There were complications. Complications that seem very difficult to explain."

Brucius stopped moving, his eyes and face motionless. "I heard rumors. I didn't believe them. I didn't know . . ."

"Of course you did, Brucius. That's why you went into hiding. You knew very well. That's why I had to hunt you down."

Brucius started to answer but James cut him off. "There's no explanation for the neurological damage based on the injuries that she sustained. We are certain she was poisoned."

Brucius Marino, son of Italian immigrants, son of a man who'd worked his way through law school delivering papers and booking at the tracks, son of a man whose mother had died when he was born and who had taught himself to read English before he was even four, took a breath and groaned, then stared down at his hands. "Bethany Rosen would be the next in line . . ."

"Dead now, Brucius." James dropped a highly classified report on top of the metal table. "Died in her sleep within a few days of being sworn in. Remarkable, isn't it?" The black man sat back and picked his teeth.

"With Bethany gone, then that . . ."

"Brings us to you. You're next in line. The line of succession is not disputable. The SecDef should have been the next president."

Brucius wet his lips. It was the last thing that he wanted, the last thing he had ever thought about.

"Whatever," James went on after a moment of silence. "It doesn't matter. What they've done is more than obvious, claiming you were dead and putting their own man in place."

Brucius grew intent. "Someone else is president?"

James nodded yes.

"Fuentes?"

241

"I'm afraid so."

"The guy's got the moral compass of a fish."

"That's an unfair comparison, don't you think?"

"I'll apologize to all the carp."

James almost smiled. "Anyway, they had to know we'd figure it out, but they don't care. This isn't a conspiracy any
longer, this is out-in-the-open war. And we've lost the first
battle, that's for sure. They saw their opportunity and they
took it. They knew if they could get their man in place before
we could react, it would be impossible for us to push him out
amid the chaos and confusion. Another thing they're banking
on—and I think they got this right—is that the American
people are consumed with only one thing: survival. Nothing
else. They don't give a flying bag of bones who's in charge so
long as someone steps forward to take care of them. They
would accept Stalin as their leader if he arranged to bring them
food. Hunger has a way of focusing the issue, and the protocol
of succession doesn't mean squat to the American people right
now." He fell silent, thinking, then concluded, "Brucius, we've
thought this out. The last thing the American people will suffer is a constitutional crisis over who's next in line, especially
with another guy already in place. He's getting ready to
address the nation. He'll say the right things, make all the right
moves, start getting the emergency supplies in place. They'll
look to him as their savior. It'll be hard to move him out."

Brucius shook his head. "Look, I want to be clear, I have
no more desire to be the president than I desire to have tooth-
picks driven under my nails. But there is principle. Precedent.
We can't just go wandering off into la-la land; we have to do
this right! If not now, then what about the next time? Who
gets to be the president then? If we don't have some kind of
order . . ."

"Believe me, Brucius, you're preaching to the choir."

"It's not about me. It's not about what I want or don't want. It's about the truth, the principle, doing this thing right!"

James shook his head and leaned forward angrily. "I'll tell you what it's about," he almost sneered. "In the long term, it's about defending the Constitution. You won't believe the things they plan to do. They will destroy the country. We'll be no better than any third world dictatorship with a worthless constitution of a power that barely moves along. In the short term, it's about not letting a group of thugs steal the presidency. It's about keeping the power with the people, not in a group of murderers' hands. That's what this whole thing is about. And that's why we have to act."

Brucius frowned. The smell of the food sitting on the table was making him sick. "Fuentes," he mumbled. "I can't believe that he's the acting president."

"He's not *acting*, Brucius, he is *the* president. It is done. We couldn't stop it."

Brucius shook his head and swore.

James went on, his voice dark. "It's too late, we know that. If you were to make a move on the presidency, the American people would perceive it as a greedy and pointless grab for power, especially if Fuentes is able to convince them that the measures he's proposing are necessary for their survival." James fumed, his breathing heavy, his eyes angry and alert. Brucius watched him, his head still bent, his eyes looking up through bushy brows; then he stood, moved toward the window, and stared out through the glass.

"They were coming for you, Brucius. Do you understand what that means? They were coming to your daughter's house to kill you."

The Secretary took a deep breath. "I had a meeting with a few of them a couple of days ago. They tried to persuade me to join them. They were adamant, although *adamant* is probably too soft a word to describe what they said. It was pretty convincing." He stopped, his voice trailing off.

James stood and walked toward his friend. "Let's be very clear about this, Brucius. Even if they are convincing, they *are not* right. They are traitors and deceivers. They thirst for power, nothing more. They know our country is on her knees now. She might not recover, we don't really know, but if these guys have their way, it won't matter anyway. We won't be a republic or democracy, we'll be a dictatorship and nothing more. Sure, we'll still call our "leader" Mr. President, but it won't mean a thing. Mr. President, Prime Minister, Party Chairman, King—call him what you want, he won't be working for the people, he'll be working for himself. Himself and his inner circle."

James started pacing nervously, then dropped down in his chair. "You were sleeping when I came into the room?"

Brucius shrugged and nodded.

"I hope you got some rest, because I'm going to lay it on the line. I'm going to tell you everything we know. And when I do, it'll be a while before you'll be able to rest again."

chapter thirty

OFFUTT AIR FORCE BASE
HEADQUARTERS, U.S. STRATEGIC COMMAND
EIGHT MILES SOUTH OF OMAHA, NEBRASKA

After leaving the confines of the interrogation room, Brucius Marino and James Davies turned right, walked down the hall, and climbed two flights of stairs. Down another long hallway, they walked to where the afternoon sunlight slanted through a set of glass doors. Two guards were positioned behind a thick pane of bullet-proof glass. James nodded as they walked toward them. The hallways and offices were busy with officers in uniform, none of whom paid any attention to the civilians in the hall.

Outside, they turned left and moved along the sidewalk that led to the base park. As the men walked, a black SUV followed them along the road. Occasionally, James glanced toward it, knowing his four man security team was inside. Otherwise he paid it little attention, concentrating on explaining the current political and military situation to the Secretary of Defense. Thirty minutes later, the two men stood atop a ten-foot dam that held back a small pond on the west side of the base, a result of extraordinarily heavy rains over the past couple of weeks. Brucius watched the waves move across the murky

245

water and wondered: drought in one area, massive downpours in another. Even Mother Earth was going crazy.

Turning, he looked toward the road. Funny how they seemed so out of place now, the military trucks and cars that filled the streets. Two weeks before, he wouldn't have noticed them any more than he would have noticed the air that he breathed, yet now, just a few days later, the working vehicles seemed amazing, almost magical, as they moved along the busy road.

Designed to continue military operations in the event of a catastrophic attack upon the United States, Offutt Air Force Base was staffed with military personnel from every branch of service. Well maintained, trained, and staffed, all the base facilities were hardened and prepared to continue operations in a time of war and, while the senior civilian leaders were gathering, organizing, and taking up residency in Raven Rock, Offutt was preparing to execute whatever orders they received from those leaders in the underground Command Center back in southern Pennsylvania.

The two men stood atop the earthen dam for a long time, the sun setting at their backs, the wind picking up, the brown waves slapping at the grassy shore. When he was finished, James nodded to a small bench near the water and the men sat, a flock of friendly ducks waddling along beside them, pulling feathers and fighting for position. The birds were hungry. With food in critical supply and a national calamity in the making, no one had stopped to hand out the chunks of bread and crackers they were used to receiving.

"Better watch yourselves," James mumbled to the fowl. "Kentucky Fried Chicken will be coming for you."

Brucius sat down, tugged at his pants, and stiffly crossed his legs. "Feels like winter's coming early," he said, his mood matching the coolness in the air.

James looked at the pale, gray sky. Seemed it was never clear or blue now, but washed out with plum-colored rain clouds and dust, though it was sometimes red, especially in the mornings when the night winds had blown. "We can't afford an early winter," he answered. "It's going to be hard enough as it is."

Brucius leaned forward and rubbed his eyes, his powerful fingers pushing onto the soft skin. "Can you imagine it?" he wondered. "Can you even imagine what it's going to be like? We're not prepared. No one's prepared. We thought we'd planned for everything. We've got backups to our backups, redundant military systems all over the place. We've got counterterrorist operations, military operations, intelligence operations, offensive capabilities, and defensive counter-measures. We've got a triad of nuclear deterrence. Allies. NATO. The list goes on. The only thing we don't have is . . ."

"Food." James finished his thought for him.

Brucius shook his head in despair. "I don't know; I just don't know."

James kicked at a duck that was pulling on his shoe. "Get some rest, Brucius. Get something to eat. Sleep on it. Things won't seem quite so bad in the morning."

Brucius hunched his shoulders and frowned as he kicked another duck.

"Do you have any final questions?" James asked.

Brucius shook his head.

"Okay then, here's the deal. As I told you, constitution-ally, Fuentes has no right to claim the presidency, not as long as you're alive, but I can't recommend you go after anything until we understand a little bit more about who's behind all this: who they really are, how they're organized, where they come from, what they intend to do. We don't know any of these things and it's critical—and apparently very dangerous—

that we find out as much as we can before we make a move. Yes, you could rise up and claim the presidency, we could fly you out to Raven Rock tonight, but it would do very little good. We could demand they relinquish power. Maybe they'd even do it, I really don't know. But even if they did, it wouldn't matter. As long as you're not willing to follow the path they have laid out, as long as you're unwilling to discard the Constitution and discontinue individual rights, as long as you insist upon defending our country, as long as you refuse to pull out of the Middle East or subject our military to the U.N. authority, they won't allow you to hold onto power. They will kill for this—they've proven that already."

The men fell silent, the evening breeze gusting stronger across the great Nebraska plains. A swirl of dead leaves blew before the wind, scattering brown and yellow across the grass.

"So," Brucius wondered, "what do you suggest?"

James had been waiting for the question and quickly leaned toward him. "We've got to keep you here. Keep you safe. Keep you in hiding. No one's going to know you're out here, at least not for a while. As long as they don't know about you, they won't know about the threat. And as long as they don't feel threatened, they won't come for us. More, a false sense of security will bring them out. That will give us time and opportunity to shadow the government and see what they really intend to do. We'll watch, see how far they'll go, try to figure out who is pushing this conspiracy and what they really want. Then, once we understand them, once we *really* know who they are, we can bring you out of hiding and let you stake your claim. For good or bad, whether you want this thing or not, you *are* the constitutionally mandated president of the United States. But they have the powerful advantage of operating in secret from inside the government."

As James talked, two of his security men climbed out of

the backseat of the black SUV and leaned against the doors, a signal that he had to go. James caught the lead agent's eye, nodded almost imperceptibly, then turned back to Brucius.

"To defend our nation against all enemies, whether foreign or domestic," he said. "That's the oath we both have taken. Our fathers were wise, Brucius, wise enough to see the possibility of this day. But we can't defend against domestic enemies until we know for certain who they are. So we let them move, let them act, watch them while they work. When we understand them, we bring you forward and put you in your place."

Brucius bit his lip. Another duck snapped at his feet. He closed his eyes to the dying light and let his head fall upon his chest. He was hungry and frustrated and weary to the bone. He needed food and rest. He'd been running on only fumes. Fumes and fear.

How long he sat there, deep in thought, he really didn't know. Time passed and his breathing settled into deep and measured sounds. But though his eyes were closed, his mind was racing. And as he thought, it seemed a deep darkness settled over him. He felt his body becoming heavy, as if he was being crushed by the very air above his head. He swallowed and tried to hide it, but the fear rolled up inside. Opening his eyes, he slowly turned to James, his face tight with dread. "Are you one of the enemy, James?" he wondered. "Are you with them in this accord? Are you really who you say you are, or did they send you here to me to kill me or to keep me out of sight?"

James didn't move, his dark eyes unfeeling as he stared straight ahead. "I've wondered the same thing about you, Brucius. I've wondered every day. Will you betray me? Can I trust you with my life? Because it's going to come down to that one day. If I can't trust you, is there anyone? Who am I to turn to? How deep does this go?"

Silence. The blowing wind. A car slowly passing by. A jay-bird flying overhead. Then Brucius finally answered, turning slightly on the bench. "I guess all we can do is trust our friends."

James slowly shook his head. "All of those who are dead now made that old mistake."

Brucius didn't answer as he wet his lips against the drying wind.

"... for by [their] sorceries were all nations deceived."
—REVELATION 18:23

"And it came to pass that there were sorceries, and witch-
crafts, and magics; and the power of the evil one was
wrought upon all the face of the land."
—MORMON 1:19

"And he shall send his angels with a great sound of a
trumpet, and they shall gather together his elect from the
four winds, from one end of heaven to the other."
—MATTHEW 24:31

chapter thirty-one

I saw an angel last night, Mommy."

Caelyn looked toward her daughter and listened carefully. "Really, baby. What did she look like?"

"It wasn't a she, it was a he-angel, Mom."

Caelyn's heart skipped a beat and she put her work down, resting the raw potatoes on the plate that was balanced on her knees. "A he-angel? Really. Like what, a little angel, a little boy or something?"

Ellie turned from her mother and looked off, her face crunching as if she were trying to remember. "Not really. He was older. Like a man."

Caelyn sensed her hands begin to tremble. *Don't do that!* she scolded herself. *It's just a little girl's dream. Don't read so much into everything.*

Still, a strange thought, cold and terrifying, slipped into her mind. "It wasn't . . . you know, it wasn't Daddy, was it, Ellie?" she asked in a breathless voice.

The blonde-haired girl shook her head. "No, it wasn't Daddy." She seemed puzzled by the question. "Daddy's not an angel, Mom."

The two were quiet for a moment. Ellie eyed her mother keenly, as if she knew something so obvious that it confused her how her mother couldn't know it too. "Daddy's not an angel, Mom," she said again.

Caelyn sighed with relief. "Did DoxMax see the angel?" she asked, referring to Ellie's imaginary friend. Caelyn didn't know a lot about DoxMax, how old she was, what she was like, how she had gotten her name—all she knew was Ellie spent hours talking to her, sharing tea parties, playing in the tree swing, hiding under the porch. And it seemed Ellie spent more and more time lately with her invisible friend, which worried Caelyn just a little.

Ellie turned and frowned. "Of course not, Mom." She shook her head in disbelief. "DoxMax was asleep. You know she has to be in bed by eight."

Caelyn made a face. "Silly me." She turned back to her work, cutting the potatoes into cubes for the soup.

Ellie thought while looking off again. "He was a pretty angel." She turned back to her mom. "And very nice."

"It was a good dream, then?"

"Was it a dream, Mom?"

"I think so, honey. It must have been."

Ellie nodded, accepting.

Caelyn watched her again. "Did he talk to you, baby?" Her voice remained tight.

Ellie tried to remember. "No, I don't think so. But it felt good to have him close. I like him a lot. I hope I see him again tonight."

Caelyn hesitated. "You mean in your dreams?" she prodded.

The little girl didn't answer as she reached for a small cube of potato that had fallen onto the ground. She tried to toss the dirt-covered bit into the metal bowl, but Caelyn caught it. She used a dish towel to brush it off, then dropped it into the bowl with the other pieces of cut potatoes. One didn't throw food away anymore just because of a little dirt.

Ellie frowned, then nodded at the barrel beside the porch that they used for a garbage can now. "It smells bad." She held her nose.

"It's some of the fat trimmings from the meat that we were smoking," Caelyn explained, though she knew her daughter wouldn't understand.

"Ugh!" Ellie held her nose again and turned away.

Caelyn watched the back of her head, the blonde curls just above her shoulders. The thought of Ellie talking to an angel lingered in her mind. "Did he have wings, Ellie?" she tested. For some inexplicable reason, she desperately wanted to know more.

Ellie fell onto the grass, sitting on her legs. "Angels don't have wings, Mom." She shook her head, evidently tired of the conversation.

Caelyn turned back to the potatoes. Three medium-size russets lay cut up in the bowl. A couple of cucumbers were still left in the garden. The family wouldn't go hungry, but none of them would be overly full after dinner tonight.

Caelyn and her daughter were sitting on the sunny side of the house. It was early afternoon and the sun had passed its peak. Ellie had on a jacket, Caelyn a sweater. The wind had shifted out of the north, bringing a cold chill. Caelyn heard the back door open and looked over her shoulder to see her mom leaning against one of the white pillars that supported the porch roof. She was staring past the line of trees that formed the windbreak fifty yards from the house. After a long moment Gretta called out, "Miller!" She whistled, her fingers in her mouth, looking for the old dog.

Caelyn turned to the empty fields. She didn't hear

anything, but she could tell her mother did. She followed the older woman's eyes.

Her mother whistled again, this time more loudly.

Far off in the distance, she heard the dog bark.

Gretta called again, "Miller! Miller, come on!"

Caelyn stood, peering toward the trees. There, in the wind, she heard it, barking and snapping. The dog was out there, past the tree line, beyond the pasture, down toward the hayfields where they had moved the cows.

Her mother cocked her head. "Someone's down there!" she said in fear. "Someone's in the herd."

Caelyn stood up. "Are you sure, Mom?"

Gretta nodded toward the highway. "I saw some trucks go past the house, heading north."

"What kind of trucks? How would they be working?"

"Big farm trucks. All of them were really old."

Caelyn stood and moved toward her mother, keeping her eyes on the fields beyond the row of poplar and cottonwood trees. The sound of the barking dog carried toward them on the wind, clearer now, more vicious, more constant.

Then she heard a sudden *pop*. Short. Loud. The sound echoed against the house.

Her mother's hand shot to her mouth, her eyes wide, her hands trembling with fear and anger.

Gunshot? Caelyn wondered, cold fear settling over her heart.

Another *pop*.

And then silence.

Gretta started to run.

chapter thirty-two

EAST SIDE, CHICAGO, ILLINOIS

Sam stood in the apartment courtyard, taking in the growing twilight. The sun was on his right shoulder and his outline cast a long shadow to the east. Luke was well enough to travel, so they had gathered up all of their available supplies. Tonight they were going to leave the city, and he was anxious to get on with it.

It was cold and getting colder with every passing moment. He watched his shadow grow, marking the passing of time. Funny, he thought, how it was all so distorted now. The shortening of days. The shortening of time. Everything seemed to crash together.

Sara watched, then moved to his side. "What is it, Sam?" she asked him, sensing his mood.

He acted as if he didn't hear her, keeping his eyes on the littered street that ran south. It reminded him of something from medieval London during the height of the plague: garbage and human waste and dead bodies in the street. He shivered, staring down the crowded avenue. Worthless cars and buses, a pile of old clothes—where had that come from?— broken sacks of garbage trampled by angry people.

The sky was clear of rain now, the heavy clouds having moved off to the east, and a faint red tint began to glow in the west as the sun moved toward the building-lined horizon. He sniffed, smelling the fires. He couldn't see them, but he knew that half a dozen flaming towers were consuming downtown one high-rise building at a time. The smoke filled the sky with an inky cloak of gray that seemed to drip like hazy fingers toward the ground. An army of people filled the streets, some of them fleeing the fires, some heading toward the ugly smoke, hoping to be entertained. Nothing was quite as exciting as the end of the world, Sam had learned, and the anarchists gathered to watch the destruction with drunken glee. The streets were full of them: drunk, jacked up, an orgy of narcissism, as if it hadn't yet occurred to them that they were going to die too. *"What! I've always been against the war. I invented anti-globalization. What do you mean, there isn't any food?"*

He looked carefully at the fools around him, which, he had decided, included pretty much everyone. There were so many now it scared him. How could he not have realized? How could he have been so blind as to what so many of his fellow-men believed in, what they really were inside? Even in his worst expectation, he was completely unaware, but there they were, laughing and cursing and dancing as they waited for death out on the street. *"Okay, I'm going to die, but so are you. So come on, dig the show. Pass the peace pipe, eat your last meal, then come on out and take off all your clothes."*

His hand moved toward the canvas holster at his side. When he felt the cool metal of his handgun, his mind flashed back to the evening he'd said good-bye to Bono back at Langley Air Force Base. He thought about him all the time now, wondering if he was okay, his wife and little girl, hardly able to force them from his mind.

Sara watched her son, then reached out and placed her

hand on his arm, gripping his bicep gently. "Sam, are you okay?"

He stared without replying.

"Sam . . ." his mother pressed.

He stood another moment, then shook his head and turned toward her. "I was . . . I don't know . . . I was thinking about Bono."

Something in his face worried her and she squeezed again. "Bono?"

"My friend from— "

"I know who you mean. Do you think he's in trouble?"

"I don't know. I see his face all the time now. I see his wife and little girl. Seems I can't get them out of my mind."

Sara hesitated, brushing a strand of fine hair from her eyes. "You should pray for them," she told him.

He kept on staring, watching the smoke drifting closer to the ground.

"Pray for them," Sara repeated, pulling on his arm. "Sometimes that's all you can do—but sometimes it's enough."

chapter thirty-three

The two women crawled through the high grass and weeds along the ditch that ran behind the trees. A barbwire fence stretched before them on the other side of the trees. Beyond that lay a large field of hay, grazed down to the nubs, another fence, then a field of brown grass. Caelyn lifted her head above the weeds and peered out. A gravel road ran north and south between the two fields. Three old farm trucks were parked along the road. Beyond the strip of reddish-brown, their herd of mother cows moved about, watching the trucks suspiciously. A dozen men moved around the trucks, maybe sixty yards away. She watched them carefully. Most of them were armed. Shotguns. Short-barrel rifles. A few pistols sticking out from jacket pockets. Two young women waited inside the nearest truck. Their dark hair was tightly braided and they stared ahead, seemingly paying no attention to anything going on outside the trucks. The men were dark-skinned and bushy-haired, but there was something else about them, something unfamiliar, something out of place. Caelyn thought a long moment as she watched from the cover of the grass; then her heart began to race. It was clear now: the

cowboy boots and heavy clothing, the checkered shirts, drooping mustaches, and long black hair. She glanced at the farm
trucks—models she'd never seen before. Old. Rusted. Huge,
rounded fenders. Like something from a foreign movie. She
picked up some of what they were saying, the sound drifting
across the open fields, and cocked her head to listen. What she
heard wasn't the Spanish of the border or the Spanglish she
had picked up out in California. No, these men came from farther south. Mexico City. The mountains of central Mexico.
Someplace far away.

Her mother moved a little closer to her, and Caelyn
dropped her head again.

"Do you recognize them?" her mother whispered.

Caelyn shook her head. Her mother's eyes were not as
good as they used to be.

"It's not that group from out near Baylor—"

Caelyn raised a hand to cut her off.

"Can you see them? Do I know them?"

"No, Mom, you don't know them." Caelyn pushed a
clump of brush away, hoping to see a little better. "They're not
from around here." She swallowed a knot of fear and lifted her
head above the grass again.

There were a couple of old men among the group, with
graying hair and fat bellies, but most of them were young. All
of them had the same look, dark and tough and mean. Hard
lives. Hard men. Men who didn't care. As she watched, the
oldest of the men moved toward their hiding place. Stopping,
he looked directly over their heads, staring at the country
house behind them. Caelyn's heart skipped. Ellie was back
there, playing in the yard! Had she seen them run? Would she
follow her mother across the fields? She gulped again in fear.

The stranger lifted a hand and motioned toward the

house. Another man came and stood beside him and they both laughed.

Beside the old trucks, one of the men snapped the bolt on his rifle, pointed toward the herd, settled on a target, and raised the gun. A loud *shot* thundered toward the women, far more powerful than the first sound they had heard. The thunder echoed across the open field, seeming to carry on for miles. The nearest heifer fell to her front knees, bellowed once, her back legs stiff and straight, then wobbled and fell over, her head thrashing blood and spit. Caelyn stifled a sudden scream. Another shot rang across the open fields. The young cow jerked once more from the impact, then didn't move again.

Caelyn lowered her head, her mother trembling at her side.

Another shot burst across the open air. Caelyn lifted her head above the grass. Another cow was down, the animal bellowing as it jerked its neck from side to side. The two women in the front seat climbed out of the ancient truck. Caelyn stared at their clothes, outfits from a different world: thick, multicolored dresses hanging to their boots; suede jackets with long sleeves rolled up past their elbows; floppy hats against the breeze. The women walked toward the downed animals, long knives in hand. The larger of the women stood over the first cow, pushed its head back with her boot, leaned over, and slit its throat with one long stroke. The ground turned dark red, almost black, from the spilling blood. The second cow let out a final dying bellow, thrashing its legs in pain, bloody-red froth spitting from its mouth. The other woman walked toward it, knelt across its head to hold it down, and expertly split its throat as well. Near the old green truck, the shooter dropped his rifle to his side, satisfied. Two of the younger men immediately started fighting for his gun. Caelyn could hear their shouting voices, which at first were merely angry but rapidly grew more full of rage. The larger of the young men prevailed, pushing the smaller boy back. Turning, he hoisted the rifle and raised it toward the herd. Aiming quickly, he shot, but he missed, and his father yelled at him, words Caelyn couldn't understand. The young man aimed again and fired, bringing down another cow. Another shot. Another cow down. Caelyn hid her head.

"They're going to kill them all!" she whispered in anguish. *"It makes no sense!"* Her heart sank into despair, a thick blackness all around.

Amid the blackness, Caelyn felt a stab of anger. "Heavenly Father, is this really the way you want it?" she prayed desperately. "If they kill our animals, we will starve to death! Are you going to beat me down until I have to fail? Is this supposed to keep me humble? Believe me, Lord, you've got me on my knees. Why have you left me here alone, without my husband, having to take care of my parents and my little girl!"

The thoughts came crashing even faster, a rush of hopelessness.

"Can you hear me, Heavenly Father? Are you there? This is more than I can handle. I want to crawl into a hole.

"I have always believed, even from the time I was a little girl, that you were out there and that you loved me, but I don't know if I believe that anymore. How else am I to read this? You don't love me. You don't love Ellie. You don't care about us anymore." Rolling to her back, she brushed away tears and frustration. "Heavenly Father," she whispered finally, "are you really there?"

The doubts gathered deep inside her and she stopped praying, falling into silence. Her mother watched her, reaching for her hand.

Caelyn thought the doubt and desperation that tumbled from her were coming from her soul, but the seeds were something different, something much more dangerous, more severe.

And though she felt him, she didn't recognize the blackness that was near.

"Heavenly Father," she repeated slowly, "tell me, are you there?"

chapter thirty-four

N*o, he's not there!" the Great Deceiver sneered as he paced behind Caelyn, taking delight in her despair. "Don't you know that you're alone here? He's not going to save you. Miracles are only for other people. He's not going to help you now!"*

Lucifer smiled as he spoke. This was when he was at his best. Get them scared. Get them to take fear in the future. Weaken their faith, and it was an easy step to convince them that God didn't love them anymore. So he kept his focus on her, twisting her natural apprehension into faithless fear.

Beside him, Balaam watched, a tiny turn of his thin lips toward his eyes. Other dark angels danced behind them, lesser servants of the Great One, not as talented, less determined, but still willing to participate in any scene of despair. And their delight was usually full now. So many scenes of horror filled the world.

To Balaam's right, a group of female spirits leaned toward the two women who were working over the cows. These evil spirits, Balaam trusted, for he had heard their cunning lies. The male servants of the Great One were far too clumsy, too abrupt and demanding to entrap the women in their deceptions. But his dark sisters were much more patient and subtle in their words. He shivered as he imagined the deceits that were coming through their lips. "No one loves you. You have nothing. Do what your man tells you and don't ever say a word. Don't complain. Don't stand up. You are lucky, you ugly fool. What other man would even have you?" Balaam smiled maliciously as he thought of their lies. "You are worthless. You are different. You're not worthy of anything but indifference and disdain."

Such were the lies the fallen women were whispering to the mortals, so effective over time. And the evil sisters knew them well, for they were the same words the Great Deceiver spoke to them every day.

Balaam watched his wretched sisters, closed his eyes, and shivered.

The Master focused his attention on Caelyn, his dark whispers so overpowering they bled despair into her heart.

Behind him, the lesser angels continued crying and shouting as they danced around the dying animals. Their lust for blood was nearly overpowering. Blood. Flesh. The human touch. All things of the body. The ache for such things they would never know or experience was all-consuming in their dark and bitter world, and there was constant glee in the killing of the gift they'd never have.

Balaam watched, disgusted at their ignorance. There was no reason for their shouting. He hissed, a snakelike sound emitting from his throat. Walking toward the other angels, he brushed them away with a violent motion of his hand, then, turning to the mortal men, he started speaking in their minds. "Kill the entire herd," he prompted in a whisper. "If you let the animals live, the Anglos will butcher them, providing food for the long winter. But if you kill their cattle now, they will starve to death. So kill the entire herd. Leave them nothing but rotting flesh. After what the Anglos have done to your people, they all deserve to die."

chapter thirty-five

Caelyn's stomach turned, the muscles in her chest growing tighter with every breath. Her mother grabbed her arm, her eyes red with fear and sadness. "Can you see Miller?" she whispered. "Your dad will die without him. Can you see him? Is he there?"

Caelyn shook her head. "No, Mom, I didn't see him."

"But did you look?"

"I didn't see him, Mom."

"My eyes aren't good enough to see anymore, especially in this dying light."

Gretta glanced fearfully toward the darkening sky. Where had all the light gone? What had happened to the sun? The afternoon had grown so dark so quickly, she didn't understand. But even she, an unbeliever, felt the evil of the black soul standing near. She didn't have a name for it, a name for *him,* but she felt the cold chill of his soul and shivered. She looked at Caelyn now, scared and uncertain at the sudden dying light. Reaching out, she touched her daughter's arm. "Will you *please* see if you can see him? Your dad will have to know."

Caelyn waited, then carefully lifted her head and looked out, her eyes scanning the ground around the men. Looking closer, she saw the dog, halfway between the trucks and the grass where they were hiding, a mound of brown fur stretched out in the dirt. She stared, then started crying, warm tears falling down her cheeks. "I'm so, so sorry, Mom."

Her mother clenched her arm, her fingers digging painfully into the soft skin, then raised her head and peered through the cattails that were rustling in the wind. "They *didn't* have to do that," she whispered angrily. "They didn't have to kill him."

Another shot rang out across the darkening sky. Another cow bellowed out in pain. The herd startled at the gunshot but still they didn't move—too dumb and domesticated to understand their own fear.

Caelyn almost retched in pain and fear. *"Please don't kill them all!"* she prayed again.

One of the fat men who'd been leaning against the old truck yelled and darted forward to pull the rifle from the shooter's hands, swearing and cursing all the time. Peering over the tall grass, Caelyn watched as he slapped the younger man upside the head. He was the leader of the gang, she could see that, his chest puffed with pride. Even from a distance, she could see that his arms were darkened with homemade tattoos. His hair was a wild mat, his Wranglers tight around his thighs, his gut spilling over the front of his jeans, a huge silver buckle flashing on his leather belt. Swearing again, he pushed the butt of the rifle against the younger man's chest. The kid wobbled—was he drunk?—swept his hands in a wide arc, gesturing toward the herd, and stepped back. The leader frowned, spoke as if he needed to instruct him, raised the rifle, and shot again, downing another cow.

Hearing the shot, Caelyn bowed her head again.

Two more shots. Two more cows down. She stifled the urge to scream. *"Please, Heavenly Father, please don't let them kill them all! Please, you've got to help us! The meat will rot! It will be wasted. Please, don't let them kill them all!"*

A flock of birds suddenly cried and lifted from the line of trees along the road. The afternoon grew even darker, the sun falling behind a bank of low clouds. She fell back against the grass, unable to watch the killing anymore.

What could they be thinking!

Then she realized.

They weren't thinking. They were killing. And now that it had started, it wouldn't end. The bloodlust, stupid and unexplainable, would drive them in a fury until the herd was dead. This wasn't about food. This wasn't about survival. This was about killing and destruction and that was all it was.

Across the field, the young women worked desperately to butcher the cows, paying no attention to the men. Caelyn felt the sense of blackness falling deeper.

Killing and destruction.

The spirit of the Dark One settled over her.

Killing and destruction.

She almost heard him laugh.

Then a cold and deadly chill ran through her, the hairs on her neck standing on end. A knot of new fear rose up inside her. Something different, something vital. What was it that made her panic? Something urgent . . . something worse than any fear she'd ever had . . .

"Ellie! Ellie!" a voice seemed to shout inside her head.

She turned instantly, looking toward the house. Ellie was walking across the open field, her light hair blowing in the stiffening breeze. Caelyn's heart shot up to her throat, her blood turning cold.

"Mom? Grandma?" Ellie called against the wind.

chapter thirty-six

S ara Brighton pulled again on Sam's arm. "I don't think it's such a bad idea to pray for them," she said.

Sam shook his head. "I've used up all my prayers, Mom." He smiled just a little. "You and my brothers forced me to cash in pretty much every prayer chip I ever had."

"God doesn't keep track of any prayer chips," Sara smiled back at him.

Sam turned away, looking down the crowded street again. "I think I'm being stupid anyway. There's no way the dude needs me. Believe me, Mom, if there's anyone in the world who can take care of himself and his family, it's Bono. He's probably sitting on his country porch right now, sipping a little hot chocolate, cleaning his gun, looking over a field of grain and counting the fat cows tied up in the barn. Maybe he's the one who should be praying for us here, you know? I'm sure he's doing just fine."

"I kind of doubt your friend is lounging around the old farm enjoying his two-week vacation."

Sam squinted against the falling sun. "Probably not."

"And you keep thinking of him?"

"All the time."

Sara let her eyes drift toward the ground. "Your prayers can make a difference. If there's one thing I have learned, I now know that's true. I have felt the power of others praying for me and my family—the Spirit has told me the exact moment when they have knelt in prayer. It can make a real difference just knowing others care enough to pray."

Sam turned and looked at her. "Do you really think so?"

"Yes. I really do. And there's more, Sam. Maybe lots more reasons than that. Why do we put our names on temple prayer rolls? Why do we fast and pray, sometimes as a family or congregation? We may not know, we may not see the miracles that take place on the other side of the veil, but they happen. There is a battle going on, and I know it can be influenced by what we do. We may not understand the help that is mustered there as a result of our humble prayers."

Sam hesitated, then turned toward her. "Help me, Mom," he said.

chapter thirty-seven

Balaam looked across the open field, sneering at the two mothers who were hiding in the grass. The young one he wanted with a particular gnawing rage.

He was the one who had convinced the foreign gang to cross the border. He was the one who had led them to this place. He was the one who had identified the young woman and her soldier-husband from the previous world, the one who'd realized what powerful enemies they had become. He couldn't remember every detail—much of the memory from the premortal world had been taken from them when they'd been cast out from the light—but there were enough fragments for him to know that Caelyn and her husband were two mortals he wanted to destroy. Worse, he sensed the coming battle and the part that they both would play. So he gloried in the killing of the animals, knowing it would bring suffering to the humans in the end.

Across the field, the Master turned away from Caelyn, stopping suddenly to turn. "Look! Look there!" the Liar cried out as he pointed toward the farmhouse. He ran toward his mortal servants who were busy shooting cows. "LOOK THERE, FOOLS!" he screamed.

272

It took a little while, but the mortals finally stopped their killing spree. For a moment they looked at each other, wondering what they should do now.

"TURN AND LOOK!" Satan cried to them, frustrated at their inability to hear his voice.

A small sound carried across the open field and the mortals turned at last. A small, blonde-haired girl was walking toward them. Drawing closer, she stopped, her eyes growing wide.

"GO!" Satan hissed. "Go now. Kill the girl!"

*   *   *

Coming closer to the strangers, Ellie finally stopped, looking from one man to another. She saw the dead cows, the pools of dark blood against the ground, and though she didn't understand what was happening, an instinctive look of terror flashed across her face.

Caelyn watched in horror for half a second, then, standing, she rushed toward her child. Gretta started to chase after her, then stopped and turned toward the men. Frozen there, she hesitated. Her face was long now, tight and stern. She wasn't frightened any longer, she was full of rage. Swearing, she tightened her fists and marched across the field toward the drunken men. "HEY THERE!" she cried, her voice shrill. "YOU KILLED MY DOG! YOU KILLED MY COWS. WHAT ARE YOU THINKING, YOU STUPID MEN!"

Running to her daughter, Caelyn grabbed Ellie and pulled her close, placing her hands over her eyes to protect her from the horror that lay before them. Gretta turned and shot a frantic look toward her. "*Run,*" she mouthed in desperation, "run, baby, run!" Turning back, she faced the strangers. "WHAT ARE YOU DOING HERE!" she screamed again.

The men stared at her as she approached. They didn't talk, they didn't lift their guns to protect themselves, they didn't

273

react at all. It was as if they were watching a stray cat move across the field.

Gretta glanced down at Miller as she passed. The blood-hound was stretched across the closely cut hay, his front legs reaching toward the house, as if he had tried to paw his way home before he died.

A couple of the strangers finally raised their guns. Gretta glared at them and kept on walking, coming to a stop in front of the gang leader. "What do you think you're doing!" she screamed in his face.

He could feel her breath and tiny dots of spit across his cheeks. If he understood her words, he didn't show it; his expression didn't change. She lifted her hand, jerking her thumb toward her dead cows. His eyes followed lazily to where she was pointing, then turned back, lids half closed. She pointed over her shoulder and he tracked her gesture toward the dead dog.

Behind her, Caelyn and Ellie were running toward the house. The men pointed at them and started shouting. "*ALTO! ALTO!*" they screamed angrily across the open field.

Caelyn cried, her legs beating across the dry ground. The dark clouds piled deeper, seeming to blacken out the entire sky. It came so fast, all jumbled together now, everything a blur of fear and dread. Caelyn running, Ellie against her chest. Short gasps of breath. Ellie crying. Caelyn's feet kicking the loose dirt. A shot across the open field. A burst of dirt spouting up beside her. The over-pressure from another bullet. A high-pitched vibration that stung her legs.

Caelyn hesitated, almost stopping. Another shot, this one closer. Her eyes opened wide in horror as she took a final step. Another buzz, this one right beside her, the bullet whipping past her ear.

She froze. She was holding Ellie so tight that it was hard

to breathe. If she ran again, they were going to kill her. She put her daughter down and slowly turned around, shielding the little girl with her body.

Three of the men were running toward her now. Back at the trucks, another had her mother wrapped up, his hairy arms around her neck. Caelyn started to scream, then held it. Kneeling, she turned to Ellie and pushed her. "Run," she whispered. But Ellie didn't move, clinging desperately to her mom.

Five seconds later, it was over. The three men had gathered around them. Two of them had her by the arms. The last one picked up Ellie. Working together, they pulled them back toward the other members of the gang.

＊　　＊　　＊

Lucifer knew he didn't have much time. If he gave the mortals a chance to think, they wouldn't do it. As evil as these men were, even they would need a reason before they'd kill human beings, and since there was no reason, he had to push them to act before they had time to think.

"Kill them!" he sneered inside the leader's ear. "Do it. Get it over with. Go on, you coward, raise your gun!"

＊　　＊　　＊

Huddled beside her mother, Caelyn felt the wind begin to blow, a cold blast against her face. She shivered visibly. The afternoon was dark, the thick clouds blocking the setting sun. The hair on her neck stood on end and a feeling of foreboding, deep and penetrating, settled over her. A warning. She knew it. She'd felt the feeling too many times before. She glanced in terror at the men around her and pulled Ellie close. She shot a look toward the Mexican women who stood among the dead cows. They were so young. Fifteen. Maybe sixteen.

The closest girl looked at her but didn't move. The smaller one—her little sister?—turned away. She knew what was going to happen and didn't want to watch.

*   *   *

"Kill them!" the Master screamed again into the mortal's ear. He had his arms around him, holding him in a cold and deadly grip. "Kill them now. Kill them all!" He cried with rage and fury.

The mortal hesitated.

"DO IT!" Satan commanded.

*   *   *

Caelyn dropped suddenly to her knees, driven to the earth by the sheer force of the Evil Master's will. It was so oppressive, so dark, so evil, so deadly to her soul. She felt as if the oxygen was being pulled from her chest, as if the core of life inside her was being sucked into a black and swirling hole. Her mind went blank and then black, and she had to close her eyes. She drew her hands up to cover her head, cried out, then rolled over, her hands reaching to the sky above. Darkness. A shrill voice. Laughing and cursing in her mind. Hate and rage and blackness. She felt her blood run chill. Her heart raced and then slowed, and for a moment she thought that she would die. It was so powerful, so evil. She didn't know if she could fight it. She didn't know if she had the will.

*   *   *

Lucifer turned the full force of his burning rage upon her. "I WILL KILL YOU!" he screamed, his voice powerful and shrill. "I WILL DESTROY YOU. I WILL KILL YOUR MOTHER AND YOUR CHILD. I WILL PULL YOU ALL TO HELL."

Then the Dark One, lord of all the darkness, master of every secret, king of every evil, creator of every pain, rose up in even greater rage and power, his back straight, his arms rising, his eyes on fire, his lips curled back to show his teeth.

Turning away from Caelyn, he rushed toward the mortal. "KILL HER NOW!" he screamed.

* * *

The gang leader faltered, a burning in his chest. He was taken in the moment, his brain turned completely off. Yes, he *had* to kill them. If he didn't they would . . . he didn't know, it didn't matter, he couldn't take the chance. He had to kill them and he had to do it now.

But he didn't. He hesitated.

"Why should I kill them?" the tiny fragment of good still left inside him seemed to say. "Why do I need to kill them? I have never killed a man."

The little girl was curled up on the ground, completely terrified. Her mother knelt beside her, looking up at him in fear. They were related, he could see that, a mother and her child. The mother was young and beautiful. How much was she worth on the trading block along the border? An awful lot, he knew.

Kill her? No. He wouldn't kill her. But he might do something worse.

Reaching down, he touched her blonde hair and she jerked away in fear.

* * *

Lucifer leaned so far toward the mortal leader that their two spirits almost met. The mortal didn't fight him, inviting him inside. "I will do it then," the Dark One whispered to him, exerting himself to take complete control of the man.

Lucifer felt the warmness of the body, the flesh and tissue, the blood and bone. He almost cried, partly from joy of taking control of the mortal's body, but mostly from the deep frustration of knowing that such a sacred temple would never really be his.

Slipping further into the man, he sensed the control he was gaining. He almost had him. He cried with passion. He was going to kill the woman with this man's hand.

Then he felt the unexpected power and suddenly he stopped. An angry groan welled up inside him. Screaming in fury, he departed from the man. The other dark angels stopped their dancing. They felt the power too.

Three angels of the Savior approached them from the line of trees.

Looking at them coming, the dark angels pulled back as if withdrawing from a flame. Too painful now to face them, too painful to hear their words.

Balaam turned and pulled a dry breath. It wasn't fear that leapt inside him. They had already hurt him beyond measure, leaving no reason now to fear. The only emotion he felt toward the angels now was hate. Raw and cruel, it cut him to the core and set his guts on fire.

Lucifer turned to face the angels of light, his lips pulled back, exposing yellow teeth.

He held his ground, his back straight, his eyes dark flames, his arms across his chest. Balaam saw a moment's hesitation and he quivered inside.

Yes, Mayhem was the master of this world, but in the presence of the Light Ones he was nothing but a slave.

chapter thirty-eight

Teancum moved out from the trees, two other angels of light at his side. As they emerged from the shadows, it seemed that time stood still. The mortals froze around them, the words that they were speaking left hanging in the air. They didn't move. They didn't breathe. It seemed as if their mortal hearts almost froze inside their chests.

Teancum approached them, paused, glanced toward the house, then moved toward the women and little girl. As he drew closer, he saw the anguish in Caelyn's face and groaned, hating to see her in such pain. He viewed her almost as a child—so vulnerable, so young, wanting to be strong but falling short, then feeling guilt and disappointment at her weakness and her fear. "It's not true, Caelyn," he thought. "You've done everything we could expect of you. You've done your best. That's all we ask. And you have always been strong." He reached out, hoping she would know somehow that friends were near. Then he turned toward the Dark One who was standing to his right.

The lesser spirits cowered but Lucifer stood his ground, defiant fury in his eyes. Moving slowly, he positioned himself between his mortal servants and the Savior's angels. "This isn't your

279

battle." He nodded to the women. "They aren't your family. These aren't your children."

Teancum thought before he answered, "We all are family, Master Mayhem. Have you forgotten that?"

Lucifer only scowled.

Balaam watched, then took a quick step forward. "What have you to do with us?" he sniffed.

"Silence!" Lucifer hissed to Balaam, shooting a deadly glare in his direction. The other dark angels fell behind their master, seeming to hide behind his presence.

Teancum looked around again, taking in the scene of death, then turned back to face the Dark One. "It is not your time," he said.

The Dark One nodded to the mortals. "Maybe not. But it is theirs."

"Their missions are not over. There are great things yet for them to do."

Lucifer sneered, his voice dripping with sarcasm. "It doesn't matter. Today. Tomorrow. I am patient. Either way, they are going to die." He swept his arms around him, taking in the darkened world. "There's not a soul left here worth saving. You are wasting your time."

Teancum shook his head. They both knew that wasn't true. He nodded toward the women. "It's worth saving them," he said.

Lucifer almost grunted, piglike and mean. "Go ahead. It doesn't matter. I'll still get them in the end. Soon there will be no one left upon this miserable earth except for the mortals I have captured and the spirits who have always been on my side. You not only lost this battle, you have lost the war." He started laughing, an ugly roll from deep inside his chest. "How many years now have you fought me, all to be defeated in the end? You thought it couldn't happen, but we both know that you have lost."

His wicked servants gathered closer, seeking power from his

rage. Lucifer stood before them. Tall. Prideful. Withered with blackness but always deep and strong.

Balaam was the only one who fell back. He knew the Master was lying. He knew they couldn't win.

Lucifer shot another angry look toward Balaam as if he had read his thoughts, then turned to face his enemy. "You cannot hurt me now," he whispered, feeling strength from those around him. "Not with just the three of you. My forces outnumber you at least fifty to one. And I alone am powerful enough to stop you. You are weaker than you once were."

Teancum almost smiled. "My authority is enough to stop you, Master Mayhem."

Lucifer smirked, then turned. Lifting his arms, he beckoned to his hidden slaves. Another host of dark angels appeared, moving forward to his side. They seemed to slip out from the shadows like mist rising from a swamp on a cold and bitter morning. Hundreds of them. Maybe more. They were angry. Lustful. Jealous and full of rage. Lucifer laughed at the presence of his followers, then turned to face the angels. "I don't think you can control me. Not here and not now—especially, Teancum, with so many of my dark ones willing to stand here at my side."

Teancum took in all the enemy's servants. "They that be with us are more than you might think," he said. He raised his hand and gestured. Behind him, along the tree line, angels of light started emerging from the dark. From the very end of heaven they came. Then, walking together, they came forward: ten, twenty, then a hundred, then more than they could count. Lucifer stared at them in horror, cowering at their light. They were so great. They were so terrible. It cut him to the core to see them, to feel them, to sense their glowing power. They were everything he would never be, full of mercy, peace, and power. He shrank, lifting his hands against his eyes to protect them from their light.

"You must go now," Teancum commanded as the crowd of heavenly angels gathered at his side.

Lucifer hissed, then nodded to his mortal servants, who were huddled around the women, lust and killing in their eyes. "Even if I go, it doesn't matter. They will kill them anyway."

Teancum ignored the comment. "You must go now," he said again.

Lucifer tried to hold his ground but it was pointless and he screamed in futile fury. He glared at the other angels a final time. So bright. So powerful. So full of grace and truth. Sneering, he cursed them, then slowly, painfully, hunched in fear and shame, the Master of All Darkness slunk away.

His other angels followed, crying and complaining and cringing from the light.

chapter thirty-nine

The violent gang of men seemed to pause. They couldn't hear, they couldn't see, they couldn't understand the battle that had taken place on the other side of the veil, but they knew somehow, deep inside them, that something had changed. They sensed the sudden loss of power, the loss of authority that had slipped into the dark. Worse, they sensed the unseen presence of the light now. To the west, the clouds had parted and a narrow beam of sun was shooting through.

The leader of the men turned toward the women. He was going to take them along. "Come," he shouted to his men. "It's time for us to go. Load the meat up, fill the trucks, and let's get out of here."

The gang hesitated and he glared at them, disgusted. The truth was that they were cowards and he was ashamed to lead these men. "COME ON!" he screamed, his fat gut pulling tight. "Get the meat. Leave the dead cattle. Grab the women and the little one and let's get out of here!" He was scared now. His courage had left him. He felt exposed and alone.

His men stared another moment, then sprang into action.

Working together, it took them only half an hour to quarter up the two cows, wrap the meat in black tarps, and throw it in the back of their ancient trucks. They moved like scurrying rats, anxious to move on.

Caelyn watched them work. She understood what the leader had in mind. They would take them. They would destroy them and then sell them. It would be far worse than death.

But she wasn't frightened any longer. The evil had evaporated as the darkness before the sun. She felt the power of the light around her and she stood, her face determined, her eyes bright.

＊　　＊　　＊

Teancum walked toward her, looking directly into her eyes. "I am with you," he whispered to her. "All of us are with you, Caelyn. If you could see us, you would know that. But still, you have the faith. You have the power. Everything will be all right."

＊　　＊　　＊

Holding Ellie tight, Caelyn leaned toward her mother. "They're going to try to force us to go with them," she whispered. Hearing her, one of the younger men ran toward her, thrusting his gun into her face. She cringed, twisting to place her body between him and Ellie. Gretta gritted her teeth and stepped toward him. "Are you kidding me?" she shouted. "If you think I'm going with you, you've got holes in your head. You're going to have to kill me and throw my body in the truck because that's the *only* way, little man, I'm going *anywhere* with you!" The Mexican stared, not understanding but shrinking at her rage. She raised a hand as if she would slap him and he took a quick step back.

The gang leader heard Gretta screaming and ran toward them, an ugly frown across his lips. He knew enough English to understand most of what she had said and he grabbed her arms and threw her down. "You true," he sneered at her in a rage. "You not going with us. You old. No good. You die here, *hermana.*"

He turned to the young man, gesturing for his gun. The kid, pock-faced and dark-eyed, hesitated, then extended the old 30.06 bolt action weapon. The man took it, checked the chamber, and turned to Gretta, who was lying on the ground. Looking up at him, she threw a handful of dirt in his direction, then stood and rushed toward him. Caelyn screamed as she tried to hold her back, but Gretta pulled out of her grasp. She beat upon the leader's chest and he pushed her to the ground again. Raising his weapon, he checked the safety . . .

Caelyn pushed Ellie toward the truck, then rushed forward, placing herself between her mother and the shooter. She stood there, her eyes burning, her hands clenched into tight fists at her side. And as she stood there, a sudden sense of power settled from the heavens, white and electric and more mighty than anything on earth. It seemed to lift her up and square her shoulders. She was taller. She was lighter. She almost glowed with righteous anger, and she lifted her hand toward the man. "You will go now!" she commanded, her voice as full and rolling as the thunder of a coming storm. "You will go now. You will leave us!" She gestured toward the other men. "All of you will leave us. You will leave us, every one!"

The man froze, his face contorted with pain and uncertainty and rage. He took a breath, shot a nervous look toward the others, then glared in rage and raised his gun again.

Caelyn's face was white and peaceful. There was an incredible power there. Commanding. Great and terrible, she stood her ground. Then she took a step toward him, filling him with terror from the power of her eyes. "I tell you now," she whispered, her voice softer now but sure. "If you raise that weapon again to hurt us, my God will strike you dead. He will take your life and puff it out as if it were a candle in the storm. He is my Master. He is my Father and He has sent His servants here. You know it. You can feel it. The darkness has left you. There is nothing here but light. You are alone now and you will die here if you threaten me again.

"Now you will leave us. And you will never come back here again."

The man dropped his head and mumbled.

"Go now or you will die."

He turned toward the others, his eyes low, always looking at the ground. Terrified to even look at her, he gestured to his men. The others felt it and they too cowered before her presence.

One by one, in utter silence, they gathered their things and climbed into their trucks. The engines spouted to life, belching smoke and oil.

The two women in the field didn't move. They didn't want to go. A couple of the men cursed at them. Still they didn't move. None of the men dared to get out of their trucks, but finally, their eyes avoiding Caelyn, three of them climbed out of the vehicles, ran toward the women, grabbed them by the hair, and jerked them toward the trucks, throwing them into the back.

Spewing smoke and noise, their gearboxes grinding, the ancient vehicles bounced away, leaving the two women and the little girl standing in the middle of the field.

Caelyn watched them go, then fell down, her shoulders slumping, her hands trembling at her side. Turning, she motioned toward Ellie, who cried out as she scrambled to her mother and fell into her arms. Caelyn held her, brushed her hair back, then burst into sudden tears, her body shaking, her shoulders heaving, her breathing coming in sobbing gasps.

Gretta stood back, her mouth open, her eyes wide in wonder. "Oh, Caelyn, oh, Caelyn," she repeated again and again. "Oh, Caelyn, how did you do that? I saw it, I felt it, but baby, I just don't understand."

Caelyn and her daughter held onto each other as they sat crying in the open field. Caelyn kept her eyes closed. It was just too much to bear. Holding Ellie, she rocked her back and forth, her vision blurred by salty tears.

Then she heard his voice.

She almost ignored it. She didn't think it could be real.

He called out again, his voice drifting with the wind across the dry ground. "Caelyn! Caelyn, can you hear me? Ellie, it's your daddy."

Caelyn's heart burst inside her chest. She stood and stared, tears burning her eyes and cheeks.

He called her name again. She whispered something, then wiped her hand across her face. Letting go of Ellie's hand, she ran across the open field and fell into her husband's arms.

*"O that we had repented in the day that the
word of the Lord came unto us; for behold the land is
cursed. . . . Behold, we are surrounded by demons, yea, we
are encircled about by the angels of him who hath
sought to destroy our souls . . ."*

—Helaman 13:36–37

chapter forty

It was time to go.

The apartment was dark now. A single candle burned in the living room, casting a dance of shadows across the floor and the walls. It was also cold, a hint of frost building on the corners of the windows. Sam stood at the kitchen window looking down. The others worked around him, gathering what they could. They were going to have to walk and they had to travel light, but there was little inside the small apartment that was going to help them on their journey anyway. Still, they packed up everything that made sense, working quickly now that it was time to go.

Sam didn't pay any attention to the others as they collected what little food was left, a bundle of children's clothes, a couple of tools, a few dollars cash. Ammon was stuffing an extra blanket inside a threadbare child's sleeping bag when he looked up at Sam. His older brother had climbed onto the cracked kitchen counter and was kneeling at the window, looking straight down. His face was tense, his eyes moving, and Ammon immediately knew that something was wrong. He dropped the sleeping bag onto the sofa and walked toward him. "What's up?" he asked, his heart skipping. Something inside him seemed to tighten up.

"It's going to be a problem."

Ammon almost laughed. "Pretty much everything's a problem right now, man."

The young lieutenant shook his head and motioned for Ammon to climb up. He easily pulled himself onto the counter and looked down. Most of his vision was taken up by the dirty brick wall of the nearest building, but by looking down and to the left, he could see the street below. It was getting dark and the shadows had already grown deep and full. He looked south. Dead cars. Lots of people. A couple of smoky fires on the street corner. The crowd seemed to cluster around in gangs now. It was cold. Most were wearing heavy clothing. Hooded faces. Tight circles of people around the fires, their shoulders touching. Lots of guns. Some were holstered, some were brandished. It seemed that everyone was armed.

Ammon shook his head in dismay. "Dude, looks like the Wild West down there." He watched another moment, sucking his lip, then glanced at Sam. His brother was so comfortable with the army-issue handgun hanging at his side that he seemed to notice it little more than the belt around his waist. Ammon arched his back, the handgun they'd brought from Washington tucked uncomfortably beneath his jacket. Reaching to his side, he pulled it from its leather holster. It felt so heavy in his hand. "Sam, I'm not . . . you know . . . I'm not a soldier, like you, bro. I'm not all that experienced with a gun."

"Not all *that* experienced? Dude, are you kidding me! Have you *ever* shot that thing?"

Ammon's face burned. He knew that he was blushing.

Sam was smiling at him, the shadows playing with the lines around his mouth and his eyes. "Let's not kid ourselves. When it comes to handling a weapon, you're like a child."

"Hey, Dad taught me a thing or two." Ammon was only half defensive.

"Dad taught you not to shoot your brothers or stuff a loaded weapon inside your pants. I suspect that's about all he had the time to teach."

Ammon tossed the weapon to his other hand in a gesture of confidence. "I can handle this."

Sam shook his head, his smile growing wider. "Sure you can, dude. You're a regular Pistol Pete."

"Pistol Pete was a basketball player, you conehead." Every conversation between the brothers eventually degenerated into "dudes" and insults.

Sam turned more serious, watching Ammon with the gun. "It's going to be okay," he said.

"I know it will. I'm just saying, you know, if things get kind of ugly, I'm not so sure that you'll want me on the front lines with this thing. I haven't shot anyone for, you know, a long time now. I'm not sure that I'd know what to do."

Sam leaned toward him, his face soft, his voice low. "Don't worry about it, man. I'll be there. Follow my lead. Take your cues from me."

Ammon looked into his brother's eyes, then turned back to the window and nodded toward the street corner. A group of dirty men had circled around two young women. Tall and slender, they looked familiar with the streets: tightly braided hair, short shirts, spike heels, and gaudy handbags. What could they be thinking? Ammon wondered in disbelief. He shook his head as the thugs closed around them, animals circling for the kill. Shaking with frustration, he clenched his jaw. Both of the women were on the ground now. "It's a war out there," he said.

Sam watched, feeling sick, then looked away. What he saw would have been impossible to even conceive of just a week before. "It's going to be a little tough."

"So what's the plan, dude? We go out shooting? Butch Cassidy and the Sundance Kid?"

Sam didn't answer. He'd never seen the show.

"It's getting worse every day," Ammon said. "Every hour. It's worse now than it was this morning. Lots worse than when we got here. I think they've finally figured out the police aren't coming. No Red Cross. No National Guard. No firemen or army guys to save the day."

"It didn't take long for things to completely fall apart."

Ammon watched through the window. For some inexplicable reason the thugs had let one of the women go. She stood, watched for a moment, seemingly offended, then turned and huffed away. A thick-armed man moved forward, gripped the second girl by the back of the neck, and pulled her caveman-like into a narrow alley, followed by his friends. Through the thin window, they could hear her screams, then lustful cheers.

"It won't be like this everywhere," Sam said, as if trying to convince himself. "It *can't* be like this everywhere. Somewhere there is sanity."

"Yeah, I think you're right," Ammon forced a hopeful voice. "This place was like a war zone even when things were normal. But if we can get out of the city, get to where we're going," he thought of the stake they had selected on the outskirts of Chicago, "I think we'll be okay."

"One thing we know for certain. It won't be worse."

Azadeh came into the kitchen, grabbed a couple of cans out of the cupboard, leaving it completely empty, then disappeared into the back bedroom again. Sam and Ammon noted her long hair falling down her back, her trim waist underneath a skirt and black belt. "You know, I just don't see us walking out of here without some issues," Ammon whispered after they had watched her go. He nodded toward the back bedroom. "It's going to be a problem. A problem for so many reasons."

Sam scratched his head. "All the women will be targets."

"We'll all be targets. Some will just be a little easier to hit," Ammon said. "There's you. Me. A couple guns. Luke will be okay, but it's going to be a while before he'll be strong enough to help us in a fight. And that's about it. Compared with . . . well, just look down there."

Sam stared a long moment, nodded, then climbed down from the counter. "I've seen worse," he said. "Fallujah. Tora Bora. I think both of them were worse."

Ammon looked at him and laughed. "Really!" he exclaimed. "Because I've got to tell you, dude, from the look on your face, I find that a little hard to believe."

Sam moved toward the front living room, then looked back. "Fallujah was worse. Certainly more deadly. But not as ugly. In that, you are right."

Ammon sadly shook his head. "It's hard to see it in our country."

"Never thought it'd be like this over here."

*　　*　　*

They waited, hoping the crowds on the streets would break up. They never did. So, finally, late at night, they just left.

They walked silently down the stairs, Sam in the lead, Ammon at the back. Luke followed Sam, moving on his own but walking slowly, putting each foot down tenderly and grasping onto the worn stair rail. Mary followed Sam, holding Kelly Beth's hand so tight she squeezed her little fingers together; then came Azadeh and Sara, who were walking side by side.

It was very dark, almost cavelike, the stairs illuminated only by the faint hint of starlight that shone through the tiny stairwell windows. But all of their eyes had adjusted to the darkness and they moved carefully but surely down the stairs.

Pausing at the ground-floor landing, Sam held up his hand and listened, then turned to face the group.

The men had heavy backpacks. Sara had a smaller one, which she had tried to hide under a heavy jacket. All of the women were dressed in men's clothes. Azadeh looked particularly ridiculous. Her hair was pulled back and hidden beneath an oversized baseball cap, Mary's work jeans drowned her, and the baggy shirt hung down almost to her knees. The clothing helped, but just a little, for it was hard to hide her beauty, no matter what they did. Sara had tied her own hair up as well, and she had on comfortable jeans and hiking boots. Mary kept Kelly by her side, pulling on her shoulder to keep her close. The little girl was weak—it would take weeks to put back on the weight the cancer had stolen from her—but she moved with enthusiasm, her feet light. She didn't understand what was going on, so, though she sensed the danger, she didn't seem scared. Sam knew, because Mary had told him, how happy Kelly was with her mother's new friends. Still, she tended to hang out near Ammon or Luke, sometimes reaching for their hands, sometimes crawling into their arms. Sam, on the other hand, seemed to scare her. He didn't know why—his uniform, he suspected— but he could see the hint of suspicion in her eyes.

Sam checked the group a final time. "Okay," he gave his last instructions, "remember to keep moving. Don't stop regardless of what happens. Keep it two abreast. Stay close together, but not too close. Try not to bunch up too much— a group will draw more attention than two or three people traveling together. And don't *look* at anyone. Anyone talks to you, ignore them and keep on moving, no matter what they say. Anyone gives us any trouble, let me do the talking." He glanced at Ammon. "You've got Kelly, right?"

Ammon reached out for her hand. "Got her." He smiled down.

"Luke, you stay with me. Mom, you stay with Mary. Azadeh . . ." Sam hesitated just a moment, a flicker of uncertainty in his eyes. "Azadeh, you understand the problem?"

She looked at him and nodded.

"Try not to let them see your eyes. Keep your head low. Keep your hair tucked up and don't speak—that's the last thing you want to do. If they recognize the accent, it will set them off. Stay by me. If I get distracted or have to deal with someone, then hang onto Luke." He took a step toward them. "Keep on walking. Stay close. We're going to be okay."

The group looked at him and nodded. He was obviously their leader, and they were prepared to do anything he said.

Mary gestured toward the street that lay beyond the metal door. "Some of them have guns."

Sam nodded. "Yeah, they do."

"If there's any problems . . . ?"

"Don't worry about it, Miss Dupree. I can take care of them."

"Not all of them, Lieutenant Brighton."

Luke put his hand on Mary's arm and laughed. "Hey, look, I've got a plan. If anyone starts shooting, everyone jump behind me. I seem to be impervious to bullets. All of you hide behind me and I'll take 'em for the team."

Sara frowned. Sam laughed. Mary didn't understand. Ammon slapped him on the back. "Good plan. I like it. You stay in front of me."

Sam pulled the drinking tube on his CamelBak, took a sip, and gestured to the others. "The last thing we want to do is advertise the fact that we've got food and water, so tank up now," he said. Everyone drank except for Mary and Sara, who insisted they weren't thirsty, then tucked the drinking tubes away, hiding them beneath their clothes. Sam looked at them a final time. "Ready?" he asked.

"Go for it, baby," Luke answered.

Sam turned and pulled back the metal door.

* * *

The streets were dark and smoky, both from the small fires on every corner and from the huge, high-rise fires that were burning downtown. The wind had shifted from the west, blowing cold air and smoke across the city. Exiting the apartment building, with its soot-covered brick and filthy hallways, Sam moved across the parking lot toward the street. The others followed in pairs, ten or fifteen feet between them. After crossing the cluttered parking lot, Mary looked back. This had been her home for almost thirty years. *Will I ever come back here?* she wondered. Something told her that she wouldn't, and she sighed, half from nostalgia, half from relief.

Reaching the street, Sam turned south, the shortest distance out of the city. All around them, crowds huddled together: men and women, young and old. *Where are all the children?* Sam wondered with a chill. Some of the men stared at them as they passed. Sam had on his uniform, which seemed to help. Unlike back in D.C., when everyone had been asking him for help or information, here they seemed anxious to ignore him, letting him pass. Moving from the shadows of the buildings, the family walked across the street. An old man, his face lost in the utter blackness, stepped suddenly toward them, almost running across the street. Stopping in front of Sam, he turned, cursed and shouted, then turned and ran again. Sam didn't slow but kept on walking. Stopping at the street corner, he looked up and tried to read the street signs, but it was too dark. Catcalls emerged now from the darkness. "Hey, there!" men called to Azadeh. "Come on over here, little girl. Got plenty more of this!" Azadeh kept her head low, barely looking up. Luke pulled her close, putting his arm around her.

"Little man gots himself a woman." Bitter laughing from the dark. "Git over here, man-child. I'll give you something you can show her later on!"

A group of young men drew near. Sam stepped closer to his mother. Someone spat. He felt the light spray on his face, warm and wet. A shot rang out farther north. The whites of half a dozen eyes moved in that direction. Mary moved up beside Sam and nodded quickly to show the way.

"What you doing with this soldier?" one of the young men sneered at her. "You go on. Get out of here."

The little group turned and ran. Kennedy Avenue. Columbus Street. East Chicago Avenue. Sam could smell the city all around him: Ispat Island, the fuel tank farms, the railheads, U.S. steel—all were shut down now, but the smell of diesel and coal and filth still lingered in the air. Lake Michigan was behind them now. They came upon another corner. Another crowd was huddled in the middle of the street, chaotic, mean, and noisy, blocking their way. People turned toward them and started cursing. Sam felt a sick feeling roll inside him, his eyes moving desperately. Ammon jogged up and stopped beside him. "Take the alleyway," he said. Sam thought, then nodded and turned into the alley. A couple of the strangers watched them disappear, then cut away from the group and followed. Moving into the deeper darkness, Sam pulled suddenly to the side and pushed against the wall, allowing the others to pass. "Keep moving," he whispered to them.

Silence. Then heavy footsteps. Four men emerged from the darkness and stared at his family as they walked down the narrow alley. Sam watched them from his hiding place between two brick walls, the starlight just enough to illuminate their features. Dirty faces. Filthy clothes. They smelled of smoke and urine. "You see that white woman?" one of the older men sneered. "She don't belong here. Gonna show her she shouldn't be here."

Sam stepped quietly out behind the man and pressed his gun against the back of his neck, the cold metal pushing against the thin skin that stretched over his hairy skull.

"You're talking about my mother!" His voice was cold and deadly. The man put his hands out, choking on his laugh. There was no doubt in anyone's mind that Sam would pull the trigger. The four men slowly turned around. Sam moved the weapon back and forth to cover them all. "On the ground!" he commanded. He was quick. He was efficient. He knew what he was doing, it was clear. "Down. Get your hands back. You boys know the drill."

The four men dropped facedown on the sidewalk. Sam patted down them quickly, extracting two short-barrel handguns, a couple of empty plastic bags, a crack pipe, a well-made switchblade, and a wad of cash. He held the cheap guns, feeling the light weight, short-hair triggers, and poorly balanced grips. Saturday Night Specials. He dropped one gun and shot it with the other, sending shattered pieces of metal scattering across the ground. Then he shoved the second gun in his pocket and kicked the nearest man. "Stand up," he ordered. They all stood and he motioned to them. "Get out of here," he said. They turned away and started walking slowly down the street. "RUN!" Sam screamed at them. They broke into a halfhearted jog.

Turning, Sam walked quickly down the narrow alley. His group was waiting, just beyond where he could see. Ammon's gun was in his hand. "I had you covered," he said.

Sam smiled and slapped his shoulder. "Come on," he said, hurrying past.

Out of the alley. Another corner. He studied the street signs, then turned left. A huge Norfolk Southern rail center lay two miles straight ahead. They planned to make their way to the rail yard, then follow one of the railroad lines heading south, hoping to avoid the crowds on the streets.

Moving quickly, Sam felt a sudden shudder. He was growing anxious, the hair on his neck rising on end. The night was dark. Every street was crowded. He looked at his watch, its luminescent dial barely visible in the dark. 0234. Didn't these people sleep? Why did they love the darkness?

His hair prickled once again.

Something deep inside of him knew.

* * *

Balaam could have chosen any of a hundred. So many evil men around him, he could have chosen any one—they were so ready, so anxious, their dead eyes waiting, their empty souls ready to step into the dark. Still, he took his time deciding. He wanted to select the perfect one.

Moving through the crowded, filthy streets, he watched and listened, evaluating the darkness that emitted from their souls. Observing the empty mortals, he couldn't help but smile. So many had already forfeited their sacred agency by violating their bodies with sludge and filth. Alcohol. Drugs and needles. Pain and deep despair. The addictions they had assembled were wide and varied: Sex. Violence. Pornography. Malignant and deadly thoughts. Hatred for a brother. Hatred for all men. It had taken a long time—the truth was, Balaam and his angels had been working on these mortals for generations now—but their work was paying off. This neighborhood was a cesspool of breeding evil, strong enough to steal the light from even the most innocent of the children who were born to them now.

Moving among the mortals, he considered and then selected.

He was a small man, thin, long fingers, a wispy beard. Dark eyes and angry mouth. A man who'd killed before.

Yes, he was the right man. "Come to me!" Balaam hissed.

301

The man was filthy and just coming down from the last trip of opium he would experience in this world. Better, he was full of a raging hatred that he couldn't even begin to understand. Balaam looked at him, studying the deadness of his eyes. Yes, he would do what he was told.

"Come with me!" he said again.

The man started walking toward the darkness.

"Bring your others!" Balaam commanded.

The man stopped and turned toward his friends.

* * *

GO, GO, GO! the Spirit told him. Sam looked back at the others. They all felt it too, and, as if at some unheard command, they all broke into a run. Down the middle of the street they ran now, heading west, toward a growing crowd. Ammon kept his arm around Azadeh; Luke held onto Sara and Sam, supporting himself against their shoulders, sometimes stumbling as he ran. Mary led the way now. She knew where she was going, and the others followed through the night. They passed through a wide intersection littered with cars, taxis, and city buses: East 169th and . . . something else, Sam couldn't read the street sign as he passed. They ran for blocks, their breathing heavy, the adrenaline surging through them, giving lightness to their feet. As they crossed a wide T-intersection, a huge building loomed before them and Mary drew up to a stop. "This is it," she muttered through gasping breaths.

The building was tall and long, stretching almost the entire city block. A twelve-foot, razor-wire fence extended from the corners of the building on both sides. The enormous railroad yard was on the other side of the dirty building.

Sam hesitated, then ran up the cement stairs that led to the front door. He pulled on it. Locked. He returned to the group, his eyes darting back across the road.

They all looked behind them.

Something was out there in the dark.

RUN! They sensed the warning.

"This way!" Ammon cried. He led the group south. The razor-topped fence met the corner of the building. The dirt on the other side of the fence was black: old coal, blackened gravel, broken asphalt, and spilled oil, a hundred years of railroading spread across the enormous yard. A series of railroad tracks, it looked like there were dozens, glinted in the starlight, their shiny tops melting into the darkness as they extended left and right. Abandoned railcars and locomotives stood silent in the night. No one was around.

Ammon pushed against the fence. The chain links were high and tight. Sam moved beside him, pulled out a military Handyman, extracted a set of wire cutters, and started hacking, cutting low, near the ground. The others gathered around him. The fear was rising, cold and real. A sudden sense of electricity sprung through the air, tart and tangy. Sam's hand slipped and he cut himself against a strand of wire, the blood oozing around the back of his thumb and dripping from his palm. Ammon saw the blood and pulled back. He thought that he could smell it, coppery and wet. Another chill ran through him. Shaking his head, he grabbed the wire as Sam cut another section of the fence, holding the cut links back. The work went more quickly and a couple of strands of metal snapped from the building tension as Sam cut. When he guessed he had enough, Sam moved to the side, pulled the cut-out section, and motioned to Sara. "Go, Mom, go!" he whispered fearfully. His eyes were always moving, searching the darkness that seemed to swallow up the moonlight. Sara dropped to her knees. She'd already taken off her backpack and she pushed it ahead of her, then quickly crawled through the hole in the fence.

Ammon motioned to the others.

Sam held his gun tightly at his side, his back against the fence, his eyes glinting in the night.

Something was out. Something he'd never felt before. Something evil. Something near.

* * *

Sam finally saw him. He walked low, almost like an animal, his knees bent, his head down, as if he were sniffing the ground. A shudder of fear ran through him. He pulled back the fence again. "Go, Mary. NOW!"

She bent, her arthritic knees slow to move. Ammon stepped beside her, helping her through the fence. Kelly held desperately to her hand, tears now in her eyes. She didn't understand the urgency, all she knew was that a sense of darkness had taken hold of her. "Mama," she pleaded in a whisper as Mary knelt down by the fence.

"Come on, baby," Mary said as she reached out for her child. She motioned in the darkness. "Come on, baby, come with me." Her voice was calm and soothing and Kelly quit her crying. Crawling on their bellies, Mary and Kelly moved through the small hole in the fence.

Luke was standing next to Sam now, looking back across the street. Abandoned cars and semis filled the deep shadows. He saw it again, lurking behind one of the cars. White eyes. Yellow teeth. A tight and wicked smile. The wind gusted and he smelled it, a dank and burlap kind of smell. Wet dog. City garbage. He shivered as he stared.

The man lurched from the shadows, moving closer, running toward another car. Just before he got to it, he seemed to drop down to all fours.

Sam sucked in a sudden breath, an unspeakable fear welling up inside him, fierce and bone-chilling. The evil fell upon him, sucking the breath out of his chest. Then he heard the garbled gutter of the chant that was emitting from the dark. His heart froze. He didn't move. His blood turned icy cold.

Kill them for the Master.
Kill them for the King.
Kill them for the Master.
Kill them for the King.

The stranger chanted from the darkness. The night grew darker. A suffocating sense of evil sucked up the dim starlight.

Then he saw the others.

A dozen strangers on the street.

Half of them were women.

All of them were moving toward them now.

＊　　＊　　＊

They scrambled through the hole in the fence, Sam the last one through, then stood together on the other side, unsure of what to do. Looking back across the cluttered street, they saw them coming, bent men and hissing women, animals filled with hate and lust and burning evil. Sam shivered. For the first time in his life, he was utterly terrified. He didn't know this enemy, and it scared him to the core.

Turning, he started running toward the railroad tracks, moving into the open rail yard, black gravel slipping under his feet. He stopped suddenly. It wouldn't do. There was no place in the open yard where they could hide. The others bunched up behind him. "Come on, Sammy!" Ammon whispered, lifting his handgun awkwardly. "Come on, baby, we gotta go!"

Sam hesitated, then turned toward the building. "Follow me," he said.

He ran toward the side of the rail building. It was dark and tall, four stories high, dirty brick, flat roof, white cement arches over a set of eight-foot windows, an old administration building that was used for storage now. A row of narrow steps ran

305

up to a tall, metal door. Sam ran toward it but stopped, knowing that it was locked. He turned and ran instead toward the
nearest window. "Ammon!" he called as he ran. Ammon followed. Sam bent and picked up a rusted piece of rebar, holding it in his hand.

A sudden *clang* sounded from behind them. A stranger
pressed against the fence, his dark eyes peering at them desperately, his fingers stretched between the metal links. "*Kill
them for the Master!*" he chanted as he stared. His voice was
thin, sarcastic and hysterical. His dark eyes wandered to the
women. "*Kill them all,*" he sneered.

Another man ran up behind him and pressed his face
against the fence.

Sam turned to the window. "Help me up!" he shouted.
Ammon bent and grabbed his foot, bracing Sam against his knee.
Luke broke away from the women and helped Ammon lift. Sam
held the rebar over his head and broke the window. Large pieces
of old-fashioned glass fell in huge sheets at his side, shattering
across the ground. Sam used the rebar to break away the shards
of broken glass from off the window frame; then he reached up,
found a handgrip, and pulled himself into the building.

Falling onto the dusty floor, he rolled over and looked
around. The room was almost completely black and empty. He
quickly turned and reached back through the window. Starlight
filled the rail yard. The others were waiting, six feet below.

More chanting from the dark streets. A group had formed
along the chain-link fence. They pressed and felt their way,
looking for the hole they knew was there. Sam reached down,
bending through the window. "Come on, Mom!" he cried.
Sara reached up and Sam almost jerked her from her feet. She
scrambled and fell into the building. "Mary!" Sam said, reaching down again.

A terrible scream emitted from the street. It echoed

between the buildings, a painful sound that cut through the darkness of the night. Piercing. Angry. Animal-like in fury, it rolled through the broken window and bounced off the bare back wall. Sam cringed and looked toward the streets as the scream faded slowly. The crowd was growing larger. Some had come to watch. Others had come to kill. The thin man pressed against the fence, probing with his fingers, searching for the cut-out section. Ammon had lifted Kelly below the broken window. "Got her?" he cried to Sam as he lifted the little girl.

Kelly held up her arms toward the soldier. "Sam, you got me. Please don't drop me." Her voice was nothing but a whisper in the dark.

"HERE! HERE!" an old man screamed out to the others, finding the hole cut in the fence. He leaned down and started crawling. A gunshot rang out from the darkness. The brick beside Luke's face seemed to shatter, sending broken pieces of baked clay into the soft skin beneath his eyes. He turned, his own gun raised, and fired toward the growing crowd, aiming low, a quick shot of white-hot sparks erupting at the crowd's feet as the bullet ricocheted away.

"COME ON, COME ON, COME ON!" Sam cried from the broken window. He was reaching down for Azadeh now, bending so far through the window that it looked like he might fall. She jumped, grabbed his hands, and quickly pulled herself up, her feet scrabbling against the brick.

Behind them, the first man crawled through the cut-out section of the fence. He didn't wait for the others but ran toward the building. Sam reached through the broken window. "LUKE!" he cried. Luke jumped, gritting his teeth in pain. Ammon pushed his brother's hips, then his feet toward the window, feeling his weight until his wounded brother finally fell onto the other side. Another gunshot from the darkness. Another explosion of shattered brick against the wall.

Ammon felt the sting of fractured clay and squinted as a stream of blood began to dribble into his eyes.

Ammon was alone now. The killer was getting closer. Other men were crawling through the fence. Ammon could hear the first man panting as he ran. He glanced over his shoulder to see him coming. He cried, half in fear, half in fury, and looked up at the window. Sam had disappeared, having fallen with Luke onto the floor. Footsteps now behind him, just a few feet away. He raised the gun to fire, but it was too late. The man was too close. Too fast. He screamed as he ran, then lowered his head, making himself into a running ball of bone and speed. Ammon braced. The stranger smashed into him, hurling his weight against his chest. He fell back. The brick caught him and his neck shot back, slamming his head into the wall. With a violent *ooofff* the air escaped him. His head spun. His chest burned. He thought he heard the cracking of his ribs. He fell down. The man was on him. Somewhere above him, his mother cried. The stranger joined her, almost screaming in his ear. Pounding with rage and fury, he beat Ammon in the face. But he was weak and lifeless and there was no power in his fists. Ammon lifted his arms to protect his face, then rolled and kicked his leg up, slamming the tip of his boot into the back of the stranger's head. The man cried in pain and anger, completely out of control. Ammon twisted and threw him off, smashing him into the wall. There was a thud, and suddenly Sam was standing at his side. He reached down, picked the man up by the collar, and threw him into the wall, slamming his head into the brick. The man started sliding downward. Ammon kicked him in the jaw as he fell. The man's eyes rolled back and he groaned once before rolling lifelessly to the side.

"UP, UP, UP!" Sam commanded. Luke was standing at the window, reaching down to them. Behind them, other voices. Other footsteps. Sam recognized the sound of a

12-gage shotgun being cocked, and the blood turned even colder in his veins. Ammon jumped. Luke pulled. Ammon fell inside. Sam stepped back, ran three steps, and leaped. He reached the splintered window sill and pulled. Ammon and Luke each grabbed an arm and yanked him through. A powerful explosion shattered the brick wall behind them. They rolled across the floor. "Stay down. Stay away from the window!" Sam screamed as he rolled.

Another gunshot. Another explosion through the window. The sound of voices, all of them closing in now.

"He's got a shotgun!" Sam shouted. He rolled to his knees and halfway stood, keeping his head down; then he started running toward a dark outline of a shadow against the back wall. "Come on, come on!" he cried, motioning toward the door.

The others followed. An empty hallway. Layers of garbage across the floor. A stairway on their right side.

"This way," Sam cried.

✳   ✳   ✳

High ground. Cover. Line of fire . . . Sam's mind raced with the tactical considerations as he moved up the dank and smelly stairs. Everything was filthy and he wished he was wearing combat gloves. Running, he looked around desperately. Where to go? How to protect the others? What was the best way out? If he had been by himself, it would have been so easy to shoot his way out of this mess. But there were his mother, the other women, and Luke, who was still not even close to being well.

He heard the thud of heavy footsteps below them now, then the sound of angry voices and shrill laughter emitting from the hallway on the first floor. Breaking glass. A thunderous *BANG!* as the front door was shot off its hinges. More voices on the street. A building surge of panic. Who *were* these people? Where had they come from? *Why did they want to kill them!*

309

Nothing made any sense.

The evil all around him thickened. He could feel them. He could feel *him*. He felt like throwing up. The darkness was so real, so oppressive, it sucked the life right out of his soul. Depressing and despairing, the evil gathered nearer. He could almost hear the voices of the spirits that were watching them from the empty halls.

Sam shivered, stopping on the stairwell, unsure of what to do or where to go. His mother moved beside him, her eyes barely visible in the dark. She leaned into him and whispered in his ear, "Do you feel that, Sam?" He sensed the tears of fear that wet her eyes.

He tried to speak but couldn't answer, so he slowly moved his head. Then, despite the utter darkness, a scripture sprang into his head. He didn't know it, at least not really, but the words came with clarity to his mind. "*We wrestle not against flesh and blood, but against principalities, against powers, against the rulers of the darkness of this world.*"

He shivered once again.

This was his day of glory. His night of splendor. The last days of his pride.

The rulers of the darkness. Sam forced himself not to cry.

So that was what they were up against. But at least he finally knew.

Turning, he raised his fist and raged back at the darkness. "You do not own me or my family. We are your enemies. We are your weakness. And this is not our time. Do what you will with your mortal servants, but you will *not* move us from this place!"

He waited, half expecting to hear an answer, then turned suddenly toward his mother.

"Do you feel that?" she asked him. Ammon and Luke had gathered beside them on the creaking stairs.

Sam put his arm around her shoulders. "It's going to be

okay," he said. He didn't waver. He didn't hesitate. His voice was hard and firm. He felt cold despite the beads of sweat that ran down his face to sting his eyes. Looking at his younger brothers, he saw the courage and . . . what was it . . . the *light* that emitted from their faces. It was then it finally hit him, the confusion lifting as he stared into their eyes.

The battle was in motion. The same battle from long ago. The battle for the souls of men, for the soul of their country, for their own family. Eons of waiting and preparing. And now the final days were here.

But he was ready. They all were ready. Lucifer had not defeated them—and he wouldn't defeat them now.

Turning, he raced up three more flights of stairs to the final landing. Stopping at a locked door, he pulled out his pistol and shot the rusted lock. He pushed the door open and they ran onto the roof.

Ammon quickly looked around, then raced toward the low wall that ran around the rooftop. They were four stories above the streets. Huge fires were burning now below them and a raging crowd had gathered, filling the shadows of the night. "Well, at least we got the high ground," Ammon said as they moved across the tar-and-pebble roof.

Sam angrily shook his head. "This isn't Gettysburg," he answered. He looked around desperately. The nearest building was at least forty yards away, across the street. "We don't have an escape route." He ran to the west wall. The rail yard was empty. It was a long way down. "Why did I come up here! It was stupid. This is the last place we should be."

Ammon grabbed his shoulders. "Dude, it doesn't matter. We're not leaving this place anyway."

Mary was standing by the door. "They're coming up the stairs!" she cried. Ammon and Luke ran toward her. It sounded like an army on the other side of the door.

"Kind of wish we had that lock now," Ammon said as they pushed against the door.

"Doesn't matter. One blast with that shotgun is all it's going to take," Sam called back.

Ammon pulled out his weapon. "So we shoot them as they come through the door."

He heard his mother gasp. "You can't do that, Ammon!" she cried.

He turned to her. "Mom, what *are* we going to do, then?"

"I don't know. But you can't just shoot them. I don't care who or what they are. You can't shoot them, Ammon." She turned. "You hear me, Sam! That is not who we are."

"I'll tell you who we are, Mom," Sam cried in a deadly voice. "We're dead if we don't stop them. They are coming, they want to kill us, and they've got lots of guns."

"Sam, we can't—"

"No, Mom," Sam shot back. "We *will* protect ourselves." He turned to Ammon. "We can *not* let them on the rooftop. If they come through that door, we shoot them. You understand me, dude?"

Ammon's hands were shaking. Sara let out a cry. Mary moved to her and put her arm around her shoulders. "I've got my baby here," she whispered, hoping that Sara would under-stand. Azadeh hesitated, then moved forward. "Do they want me?" she wondered weakly. "If they do, then I'll go down there. I will talk to them—"

"No," Ammon told her. "This has nothing at all to do with you."

The noise was getting louder, swearing and cursing and shouting from the stairs behind the door. Someone threw a rock onto the rooftop. Another shotgun blast echoed from down below. The night was completely dark now, the stars hidden behind a wall of clouds. The cold wind seemed to gust with fury, as if it could blow them from the roof. Pounding on the stairwell. Heavy footsteps. The foulest cursing. Heavy fists upon the door. Words they didn't understand. A cold chill upon the air. Ammon fell back and aimed his weapon. Sam moved to his side and crouched. Luke pushed his mother and the other women toward the farthest corner of the roof. Kelly Beth was crying now, grasping at him, and he had to tear her from his arm. He huddled the women together. "Stay here," he commanded before he turned.

Then silence. Deadly silence.

Luke ran back toward his brothers.

"Stay away from the door!" Sam screamed to him. "Get into position . . ."

The shotgun blast shattered the wood frame around the door, sending splinters and dust and pieces of broken metal exploding through the air. Luke fell back and scrambled across the pebbled rooftop. Ammon raised his gun and fired.

"NO, NO, NO!" Sam screamed. "Don't waste your ammo, man!"

Another second of ugly silence.

Another shotgun blast.

The door twisted on its hinges, then fell back.

The thin man with the crooked smile was standing there. His eyes were yellow, his teeth exposed, his lips pulled back in wild fury. "It's time to shine!" he whispered in a dark voice that seemed to emit not from his mouth but from somewhere in his chest. He raised the shotgun and stepped forward. Ammon aimed at his chest and was about to fire when something caught his ear. Something in the wind. Loud. Powerful. A dull *whop* of spinning rotors.

The helicopter swooped in from the north, the sound of its turbine engines and massive rotors swallowed up in the wind. Getting closer, it turned on its spotlight and aimed it at the roof. The chopper was flying so fast it almost overshot the rooftop before coming to a hover at the corner where the women and little girl were crouching. The spotlight was blinding and Sam raised his hands to shield his eyes. The chopper was all black. Army markings. He almost cried in relief.

A loudspeaker under the nose of the helicopter shattered the dark night. "You there, with the shotgun. Drop your weapon and turn around!" Sam could see the door gunner now, his 50-caliber Gatlin gun moving on its floor-mounted hinges to turn his way. At 6,000 rounds a minute, the Gatlin could cut a man in two. "DO IT NOW!" the speaker sounded. "DROP YOUR WEAPON OR YOU DIE!"

The man with the shotgun backed up, waited, sneered, then raised his weapon and aimed it at the women who were huddled at the corner of the building. He didn't have time to fire. Sam's bullet hit him in the head, almost directly in the ear.

The chopper settled to a lower position. "GET IT!" the loudspeaker blared.

A group of shadows scurried from the doorway of the building. Two or three men ran through. A half-second burst of gunfire emitted from the Gatlin gun, fire spouting from the barrel, smoke and white-hot tracers shooting through the darkness. The doorway shattered into a million pieces. Almost three hundred bullets impacted within a few feet of the center of the door. Another burst of gunfire, this one longer. The men were cut in pieces, blood and bone scattering through the air.

Ammon stared, too amazed and sick to even move.

Sam shook his head, grabbed his brother's shoulder, and started running.

Two Army Rangers jumped out of the hovering helicopter and ran toward them.

*"He will swallow up death in victory; and the Lord
God will wipe away tears from off all faces. And it shall be
said in that day, Lo, this is our God; we have
waited for him, and he will save us."*

—Isaiah 25:8–9

chapter forty-one

Sara was terrified and angry. The metal door was locked, there were no windows, and she was cold. The room was dim and small and quiet, and although she could hear occasional footsteps in the hall, she felt so lonely, as if she were the last person in the world.

Sometime before, they had allowed her to eat and shower—clean! the most wonderful feeling she could imagine—then immediately brought her back and locked her in the room. Alone again, she'd thought back on the helicopter ride through the long and lightless night. Not a word had been spoken to them, not a hint of explanation or justification for what they'd done, no indication of who the rescuers were, how they knew about them, or what they intended to do with them now. Before the helicopter had landed at their destination, just as the sun was coming up, hoods had been placed briskly over all of their heads, their hands secured behind their backs, Sam's and Ammon's weapons taken. Touching down, the helicopter's turbine engines still screaming, they'd been pulled from the helicopter one person at a time, all of them resisting except Sam. Separated, they were driven away in

317

different cars. Now she didn't know where her family was, how long she'd been there, or even where she was.

She lay on the small bunk in the corner and stared up at the security camera that stared down at her. She blinked. It didn't. She rolled over on the bed. A dim light burned in the deeply recessed, wire-covered socket on the ceiling, but if there was a light switch to control it, she didn't know where it was. She was tired and cold and wanted to scream. Getting up, she paced until her feet hurt, then lay down once again. But she couldn't sleep and sat up on the bed. Was it day? Was it night? She didn't know what to think.

The door finally opened. A man she'd never seen before was standing there. Blue shirt, dark suit pants, gray tie. A military haircut. Stern. Not overtly threatening, but serious. "Mrs. Brighton," he said, "will you please come with me?"

Sara stared at him. "Who are you?" she asked in a fearful, angry voice.

He stepped into the room. "Please, ma'am." He held the door back.

"Who are you?" she demanded, not moving from the bed.

"Ma'am," his voice was firm.

"Show me some ID. I want to know who you are with."

The man held the door back a little further and she glanced into the hall, catching a glimpse of a passing military uniform. Her heart skipped, the familiar sight an uncertain comfort. It wasn't like she suddenly trusted the military more than any others—she didn't trust *anyone* right now—but it was enough to give a hint of where she was.

"You don't need to know who I am," the man said as he held the door ajar. "It doesn't matter and it doesn't help you anyway. But if you'll come with me, I think you'll have your questions answered."

"I doubt it," she answered suspiciously.

The stranger cleared his throat, growing impatient. *Let him,* Sara thought. *Let's see how he reacts; that'll tell me more than anything what he's really about.* "Where are the others?" she commanded, her voice rising. "Where are my sons, the black woman, the girls?"

He looked at her blankly. "Ma'am, I understand your fears and skepticism, but the truth is, I don't who or what you're talking about—and even if I did, I'm sure I couldn't tell you. Not right now. Not yet. I'm not the one you want to talk to. There are others who will explain."

She looked at him as if for the first time. He looked familiar. Yes, she was certain. She had seen him before. Sometime recently. "Did you know my husband?" she asked, the sudden hope in her voice betraying her utter weakness.

"Your husband?" he answered slowly, looking past her.

Sara saw the flicker of recognition in his eyes even though his face remained passionless, his thick arms hanging at his side. "You knew him. Were you with him when . . ."

He suddenly moved toward her. He was so much bigger than she was, at least a hundred pounds, and she quivered as he grew close. He reached out and she recoiled. Kneeling before her, he looked directly into her eyes. "Please, Mrs. Brighton, I understand a little of how you're feeling. Now please, ma'am, just come with me."

＊　　＊　　＊

Sara was led into a large conference room. It was midday and the large Venetian blinds on the three walls opposite the door were opened to the light. Beyond the heavily tinted glass stretched a complex of low, brown-brick office buildings, militarily efficient, attractive but simple. Lots of grass between them. A large parade ground. An old fighter aircraft on a pedestal in a roundabout down the road. Seeing the blue sky and open space, she immediately felt better, her spirits lifting at the warmth and feeling of the sun. A large wooden table, surrounded by deep burgundy chairs, took up the middle of the room.

Brucius Marino, the Secretary of Defense, sat at the head of the table.

She froze, staring at him. An old friend? A new enemy? She didn't know. Near the window, her oldest son was waiting, fresh and clean in a set of formal army greens, his chest decorated with a double row of military ribbons and medals. Sam looked at her and smiled and she ran to him, putting her arms around his shoulders. He seemed reserved, almost anxious, uncertain and tight. She stepped back and studied his face, then turned.

The Secretary waited. Sara was suspicious, her eyes darting. She'd known him for many years, but she hadn't seen him in several months even though the Secretary and her husband had worked together almost every day. He looked older now and tired, his dark eyes weary. She waited for him to initiate the conversation, but when he was quiet she turned back to Sam. He moved forward, taking her into his powerful arms again. She held him, standing on her tiptoes, her arms around his neck. "It's okay, Mom," he whispered quietly into her ear. So tender. So quiet. No way the other man could hear.

They held each other a few seconds, then pulled apart. Sara wiped her eyes, drawing her fingers quickly across her cheeks. "Where are Luke and Ammon?" she whispered.

"I just got through talking to them."

"They're okay?"

"Of course, Mom, they're fine. Azadeh and Miss Dupree. Kelly Beth. They're all okay."

"You've seen them?"

"I haven't seen the girls yet. Azadeh is with Kelly Beth

down at the infirmary. They wanted to get some liquid in her, they thought she was dehydrated and undernourished. Kind of hard to tell them that a few days ago she was dying of cancer and that's why she is so thin."

Sara's shoulders shuddered visibly. She lowered her voice and turned away from the table, her eyes on the floor. "Are you . . . okay?" She didn't know how to put it without just saying it out loud. Was he here because he wanted to be? Was he operating under any duress?

Sam read the worried look on her face. "It's okay, Mom," he repeated. "You're going to understand."

She took a deep breath and steeled herself, then turned toward the SecDef once again. "Hello, Bruce," was all she said.

He walked around the corner of the table, extending his hand. She looked at it before she took it. His shake was warm and firm. "Sara, it's good to see you." He sounded so sincere. "It is so good to know that you're okay."

She didn't answer, staring at him. She couldn't let him know how much she knew. She had to be careful. She had to use her judgment—and hope that he was on her side.

Marino nodded to the closest chair and she sat down, Sam pulling up a seat beside her. Marino returned to his chair at the corner of the table. "Sara, I don't know how to say this, so I'm just going to get it out. First, and most important, I want you to know how I felt about your husband, Neil."

Sara turned her head away.

"I was with him, Sara, right up to the last day. It was only by the grace of God that I wasn't killed with him. I should have been. They thought I would be. Sometimes I wish that I had been. But it didn't happen. I am here. He is not. There's nothing I can do to change that. There's nothing I can do to ease the pain for either of us now. You lost your husband. I lost my best friend, a man I trusted more than any other in this world. There isn't an hour that goes by that I don't think about him, not an hour that I don't think about what happened in D.C." His voice trailed off, suddenly caught up with emotion. His lower lip trembled and he blushed with embarrassment and looked away.

Watching him, Sara saw the naked grief that pulled the lines around his mouth. She immediately leaned toward him. "Bruce," she asked, "is Julia okay?"

The Secretary took a breath to catch himself, forcing his composure once again. He face was tight, the edge of his lips white with pressure.

Sara understood. Reaching out, she took his hands in hers. "I'm so sorry, Bruce, so, so sorry. I didn't know. I had no idea. The news said that you were killed in the explosion . . . there was just no way to know . . . I've thought about you both a thousand times . . . I've wondered about her . . ."

The two friends sat in long silence, both of them lost in pain. Marino cleared his throat, tried to speak, waited, cleared his throat again, and said, "She was downtown with my youngest daughter. Someone called her and told her . . ." He stopped and swallowed, his Adam's apple bobbing painfully in his throat. "Someone called her and told her to come downtown. They sent a driver for them, said I was going to meet them . . ."

Sara sobbed quietly for him, her cheeks tracked with rolling tears.

"They sent her downtown . . . they knew . . . I was supposed to meet them . . . they were going to kill us both." His voice grew hard and jagged as shattered glass. "They killed her. They killed my wife and daughter!" He fought to control himself, pain-driven rage burning in his eyes. He stood suddenly and walked around the chair, moving angrily toward the window. "I'm sorry," he muttered, staring out.

The room was silent. A large clock ticked a full minute on the wall. Sara stared down at her own hands. Marino stared out the window. Sam stared at the picture-covered wall, feeling like a voyeur. He shouldn't have been there. He shouldn't have witnessed such a personal and private scene. *This was the next president of the United States.* He almost shuddered. He couldn't have felt more out of place.

The two grievers waited another moment in silent pain.

"I'm sorry," Sara said again.

Marino turned around, his eyes red but clear and hard now. "I'm the one who should be saying that to you. Neil was the best man I have ever worked with. You know that I'm the one who chose him, the one who brought him to the White House? The president respected him as much as I did." He fell silent. "I wish that he was with us now."

Sara thought of all the people dead or missing. "I wish a lot of people were still with us."

"Of course." The Secretary returned to his chair, pulling out a white handkerchief and extending it to her. She took it and wiped her eyes, then grasped the white cloth in a tight fist.

"Sara, I have to ask you something now. I have to know. We've got to lay it on the table and get it out. So tell me. Do you trust me? Can I trust you?"

She shifted in her seat, her eyes boring into him. "You tell me," she answered with a question. "Fuentes? Is he your friend?"

Marino shook his head. "Sara, do you understand the line of succession of the presidency?"

"I understand."

"Do you realize that I should . . ."

" . . . be the president? Yes. I understand that."

"Fuentes is my enemy. *Our* enemy. But he isn't alone, Sara. He has many, many friends. And he isn't the ringleader, I can promise you that. I don't think Fuentes could lead a Scout troop across a parking lot if he had a map and GPS. No. He's not their leader. He was in the right place at the right time and willing to sell his soul. Maybe he sold himself for money. Maybe not. Maybe all he got in return was the opportunity to keep on breathing in this world." Marino hesitated, thinking of the shootout at his daughter's house, knowing they would have found Fuentes quivering under a blanket in the closet if they had come for him the same way. "The man has all the courage of a rabbit," he continued. "I don't know what he's thinking—none of us can know or judge him *yet*—but we know that we can't trust him. And he *shouldn't* be the president."

"Then stand up!" Sara shot back. "Stand up and claim the presidency. I have been waiting to hear your name in any of the news. They said you were dead. That had to be the only explanation, but now I find you hiding *here*. Do you realize, Bruce, how much they need you out there!" She jabbed her finger, pointing to the outside world. "It's slipping away, Bruce, do you understand that? We need you. We need you to make a stand. You don't have much time. You've got to take action. Why are you hesitating? I don't understand why you won't act! You are the president, not Fuentes. What are you waiting for!" Her voice was agitated, even angry. "Neil said that I could trust you. He said you'd do the right thing. He warned me about Fuentes, all the others. He warned me about . . ." She caught herself and stopped, her dead husband's words almost sounding in her ears. *Go slow. Be careful. Don't say anything until you are certain. Don't trust anyone. I don't trust anyone. Think before you talk!*

She fell silent. She'd said too much already. She almost bit her tongue.

Marino watched her, smiling. "It's good to have the old Sara back," he grinned.

She looked away and blushed. "I'm sorry, Bruce," she muttered awkwardly. "I have no right to talk to you that way. I'm embarrassed for myself."

Marino smiled again, then stood up. "It's all right. I hold no grudge."

"And I shouldn't call you by your first name. What should I call you? Mr. Secretary? Mr. President? You should be the president, and I should call you that."

He didn't disagree. She probably should. But it wasn't true, not yet, not formally, and the last thing he wanted was the perception of presumption. "There's so much you don't know yet," he went on. "So much you don't understand. I know Neil told you a little bit, but I'm certain he didn't tell you everything. For one thing, he didn't know. For another, he would have been very careful about what he told you, knowing it would only make things more dangerous and difficult."

Sara sighed. "I don't know how much more difficult it could possibly have been."

"Trust me, it could have been worse. You don't even want to know."

"All right," she straightened suddenly, "what have I to do with this?"

Marino hesitated. "Maybe more than you think."

She stared at him blankly.

"Surely you realize what an exceptional effort it took to find you."

Sara's mind shot back to the military spy outside her

325

window in Chicago, the night run through the city, being trapped atop the building. She shuddered as she thought.

Marino saw her shoulders tremble. "From what I hear, it's a good thing that we did," he added.

"But why? Why did you bring us here?"

"Because I need your help."

Sara caught Marino's anxious glance toward her son. Up to this point, Sam had been quiet. Intimidated by the Secretary—no, not just the Secretary, the *president of the United States*—he had hardly dared to speak. But he sat forward now, his back ramrod straight. "I'm a soldier, sir. You're the Secretary of Defense. I'll do anything that you tell me to."

"I know you will, lieutenant." Marino turned back to Sara and smiled again. "If your son is anything like his father, he'll soon be leading his own army. There's no question I can rely on him." He leaned toward the soldier's mother. "It's you that I'm worried about."

Sara hesitated. "I don't understand."

"I need you, Sara."

"Me! You need me? Come on, Bruce . . . Mr. Secretary, what could I possibly do for you? What could I possibly do with any of this?"

Before he could answer, the back door to the conference room slowly opened and they turned. Azadeh slipped inside, pulled the door closed behind her, then stood, her shoulders slumping, her eyes always on the floor. She seemed to melt into the wall, her face betraying her desire to be swallowed by the concrete floor. Following the instructions she'd been given, she waited without speaking by the door.

Turning back to Sara, the Secretary went on, his voice low but powerful, overflowing with emotion. "I *do* need you, Sara. The presidency needs you. Your country needs you. I need you more than you could know. The plan we've put together is going to scare you. It's going to be down in the trenches, filthy, gruesome work. And I can't promise you a favorable outcome. I can't promise you that we'll be successful or even that any of us are going to live."

The room fell into such deep silence that Sara could hear herself breathe. She thought, her mind racing, her hands growing damp with sweat.

"I need you all," Marino finished. "I need Azadeh. I need your son. I just can't do it by myself."

"You are the president!" she whispered to him. "You have all of the power of the United States behind you. If you'd just come out and claim the presidency . . ."

" . . . I'd be dead. If I do that, they will kill me, there's not a shred of doubt. Before I step foot off this base, I'll be dead. Now, I'm okay with that, the good Lord knows, and I don't mean that in a profane way, I mean He knows that I'm not afraid of death. But my passing would eliminate the last chance we have of putting a legitimate presidency in place. I can't do that. There is far too much at risk."

"Mr. Secretary, I simply can't believe that we have slipped that far. Do you really think that they will do . . ." she couldn't say it, "you know, do what you say?"

"Of course they will. Two of my predecessors have been killed already. I would be the third. But, as it is, they think I ran away, choosing to get out of the race. They think I cut and ran, willing to cede the presidency to them. As long as they think that I've gone into hiding, they'll keep their focus somewhere else. And that's the most powerful weapon we have against them, the ability to work behind the scenes. So we take advantage of the time they give us. We grow a few cells of patriots, a very select group of people we trust, people they won't be looking for."

Sara reached across the padded armchair for Sam's hand.

"Okay. I understand that much. But what I still don't understand is what you could possibly need from *us*."

The secretary opened a manila folder and dropped a picture on the table, tapping the dark face with his finger. "King Abdullah is the one who did this to us." He kept his eyes on Sara while motioning with his head toward Azadeh and Sam. "So your son is going to take a team and snatch him and bring him back here. Azadeh is going to help them."

Sara's face turned white, and her breathing became labored. She gripped the handkerchief as if it were a lifeline, keeping her from going under. The Secretary nodded solemnly. "They're going to go and get him, then we're going to put him on trial for the things he has done."

Sara opened her mouth but no sound came out. "You're a fool," she finally muttered. "You're talking about the king of Saudi Arabia, the most powerful, the wealthiest man in the world. He has entire armies that protect him. No one could even get close."

Marino shook his head. "Abdullah is about to do something very foolish. We think we can take him then."

Sara didn't believe it for a second—the look on her face made that clear.

The Secretary didn't give her time to think. Pulling out another picture, he dropped it on the table. Three men. Close together. Intense conversation. Their faces tight. The interior of a small café. Foreign cars out on the street. "These are the men behind Fuentes, the men who conspired and murdered to put him in place. Now, listen to me, this is important: Did these men help to plan or carry out the attack against our country? No, I don't think so. Did they know it was coming? You bet your life they did. Could they have stopped it? Maybe. Probably not. But did they see this as the opportunity they'd been waiting for to make their grab for power? There's no question that's the case. We need to find them. We need to stop them. And we don't have any time."

Sara reluctantly lowered her eyes to the table. Staring hopelessly at the second picture, she sucked a sudden breath, her face draining of color, her hands trembling on her lap. "No," she almost groaned. "No, no, please, not him." She lightly touched the middle man in the picture, then looked up, her eyes wet, her face exhausted. "He was our friend. We both loved him." She sounded like she might break down. "Neil and I would have trusted him with our lives."

"Exactly!" the Secretary answered, his face patient but still determined. "You trusted him. He'll *still* trust you! We can use that trust against him as long as he doesn't know."

Sara bent her head again and swallowed. It was simply too much to comprehend. Too much betrayal. Too much treachery. Too much disloyalty from those they'd loved. Her mind was on the edge, tilting toward the dark, and she was mute as she fell into despair.

The Secretary let a few seconds pass in silence, then leaned toward her. "It's a nasty thing we have to do. And heaven knows that I can't force you. If you can't do it, I'll understand. But there are so few people I can turn to, so few people I can trust, so few people who can really help me. Sara, you are one. Was it a coincidence that we were able to find you?" He tapped the second picture. "Was it a coincidence he is your friend?" He nodded to the dark-haired girl pressed against the wall. "Was it a coincidence your son was with you? A coincidence that you are with a young girl from Iran, which is where we have to go? Was any of this a coincidence? I don't know. You'll have to make that judgment for yourself. It seems to me unlikely. And if it wasn't some lucky happenstance, then you have to ask yourself, Why are we together now? And what does God want us to do?"

He stopped and took a breath, exhaling with a sigh. "Is this an ideal situation? Certainly not. But you go to war with the army you've got, not the army that you wish for. What I got is what I got. And if we're going to save this country, I'm going to need your help."

epilogue

Teancum walked, the mountain sloping up before him, the trees swaying two hundred feet over his head. It was a perfect morning. It had rained the night before, and the air was cool and damp and smelled of rain and wet grass and flowers in bloom. He reached a break in the trees and looked up. The morning sky was so deep and blue it felt like he was looking into space. As he worked his way across the clearing, his steps were strong and quick, and though he didn't fail to see the beauty of the morning, his thoughts were somewhere else.

He sensed it now. No, it was more than that, he knew it, what the future had in store.

Looking up the trail, he doubled his pace.

Would his good friend be there waiting? Had he the wisdom to sense it too?

The mossy trail wound up the back of the mountain, spongy and giving under his feet. Higher and higher he climbed, never growing weary, never slowing down. As he ascended, the trees grew smaller and then thinner, then completely disappeared, leaving a well-defined tree line as the

331

backside of the mountain opened up. There were more rocks along the trail now, less greenery and more low brush. An expansive meadow lay before him, the slope much more gentle. Granite peaks, snow-capped and steep, jutted out on both his left and right. The trail cut across the meadow and then stopped suddenly.

Teancum looked but didn't see him. He kept walking toward the cliff and was almost upon him before his old friend finally came into view, sitting below a large boulder. The man was looking out on the enormous valley. The low clouds hung over the shoreline where the rising sun cast a golden line across the water, a billion diamonds flashing from the cresting waves. The father looked up, then stood as Teancum drew closer.

"I knew I'd find you here," Teancum said.

The father gestured to the morning. "I've been waiting here a long time."

Teancum put his hand on his shoulder. "I knew you would."

The father looked at him as if awaiting his instructions, and Teancum broke into a smile. "Come, we've got to hurry."

Without another word, the father turned and started walking.

They were his children, and he loved them even more than he had loved them in the mortal world. He watched them. He shared their pain and joy. And he knew they needed him now.